Bay of Martyrs

Tony Black and Matt Neal

**FREIGHT
BOOKS**

First published 2017

Freight Books
49–53 Virginia Street
Glasgow, G1 1TS
www.freightbooks.co.uk

A CIP catalogue reference for this book is available from the British
Library.

ISBN 978-1-911332-36-7
eISBN 978-1-911332-37-4

Typeset by Freight in Plantin
Printed and bound by Bell and Bain, Glasgow

the publisher acknowledges investment from
Creative Scotland toward the publication of this book

Tony Black was born in NSW, Australia. He is the author of 13 novels. He has been nominated for seven CWA Daggers and was runner-up in the *Guardian's* Not the Booker prize for *The Last Tiger*.

He has written three crime series, a number of crime novellas and a collection of short stories. For more information, and the latest news visit his website at: www.tonyblack.net or his blog: www.pulppusher.blogspot.com

Matt Neal is an Australian journalist, musician and Rotten Tomatoes accredited film reviewer. He posts a song every few weeks on his blog Doc's Anthology. He lives in Warrnambool with his wife and son but will probably be run out of town when this is published. *Bay of Martyrs* is his first book.

Dedicated to Danni and Reggie – my two favourite people in the world. And thanks to Tony for making a lifelong dream come true.

Chapter 1

It was damned hot and only going to get hotter.

By 10.30 a.m. the mercury was already hovering close to thirty degrees. The sweat was seeping through Barry Morrison's faded Midnight Oil T-shirt, but he refused to take it off. The middle-aged spread, the hairy back, the office tan – these weren't things he felt comfortable showing off, even on a beach surrounded by those who were older, hairier, and fatter.

Barry wiped another trickle of sweat from his brow and watched his kids dig into the wet sand at the water's edge. From his position, propped on his elbows, lying on a frayed and faded beach towel, he could see Jack and Millie having a fine time. They'd grizzled and groaned for much of the drive from Melbourne to Peterborough, but to see them enjoying their first visit to the beach made it all worthwhile.

Simone, ever the sensible wife, had argued they should have taken the highway and made better time, but Barry was emphatic that they take the Great Ocean Road.

'How could you not want to see this?' The Twelve Apostles had loomed up like an approaching film set, all those craggy peaks pointing to travel-brochure skies. You just didn't get views like this in the city.

He'd chosen to stop in Peterborough, at a sheltered spot called the Bay of Martyrs, on a tip off from a friendly local.

'Head out the road a mile or so towards Warrnambool and there's the Bay of Martyrs,' said the old man behind the desk at the caravan park. 'It's where all the locals go. No one will trouble you there.'

The last bit had been punctuated by the old man tapping the side of his nose. Of course, when he got there Barry realised this place was no great secret and he probably would have bet that most of the people here were tourists. To be honest, it

1

didn't even look like a good place to swim. But it didn't matter. The Morrisons were at the beach and it was perfect, despite the burning heat.

Jack and Millie had moved on to decorating a heap of sand, which a generous person might have called a sandcastle. They dotted it with shells and rocks. Jack tugged at a pile of seaweed and a piece snapped off. He tumbled backwards onto the sand, laughing, and then crawled to the sandcastle, where he draped the kelp over it. Here was a new game. Millie joined in and the pair pulled at the large pile of seaweed, breaking it off in segments that sent them rolling across the sand, giggling.

'Leave that stuff – it smells,' said Simone, but the kids kept grabbing strands of kelp and yanking until it snapped. They combined their efforts, clasping hands on a giant rope of seaweed and pulling. This time the weed didn't break; instead it unravelled and the two kids ran up the beach trailing a lengthy piece of kelp behind them.

As they went Simone laughed; it was great to see the kids having such a good time, but then her laughter stopped abruptly.

'Barry.' Her tone drifted back to her husband like a warning siren.

'What's up?' He looked up from his beach towel, trying to take in his wife's dramatic change of tone.

'Get over here. Now,' she snapped.

Barry stumbled to his feet, keeping one eye on the kids, who were running zigzags along the beach with the seaweed trailing behind them. 'What's wrong, Simone?'

His wife's gaze shifted up the beach to the happy kids, then back to the shoreline, where the sea lapped the walls of kelp. Simone looked urgent, panicked; Barry started to jog.

His wife stood staring at the pile of seaweed. She was quiet, still. As Barry arrived at her side he could see there was something buried among the dark brown tendrils of kelp.

'Look at it…' said Simone.

'What the hell is that?'

Barry crouched down to get a better look. A large fleshy mound, greyish-pink in colour, stared back at him.

'Is it a dead shark?' he said.

Simone didn't say a word, she shook her head and started to circle the strange pile. Her eyes were moistening, her hands flapping in front of her face like she was shooing invisible flies. 'It's not a bloody shark!'

She was stifling a scream.

'What? *What?*' said Barry. He was missing something; the shapes were familiar, but not familiar enough to come together in his mind.

Simone pointed. 'There, look…'

He followed her finger. The sight swirled, perhaps swayed a little. Was it the heat? The smell? Something clicked inside Barry and the enormity of what he was taking in welled up.

'Jesus,' he yelled, leaning back, pushing his feet into the wet kelp.

Simone jumped aside as Barry slid backwards, rapidly forcing a mound of seaweed beneath his feet. The rolls of kelp applied enough pressure on the object for it to turn, revealing two rotting holes like eyes, and a darker cavity beneath, like a mouth.

Now she screamed.

'Did you see that?' said Barry. 'It's a face, somebody's face.'

'I know. I *saw* it.'

Down the beach, the kids stopped playing. They both turned to stare as their parents scrambled over the seaweed and ran towards them.

Chapter 2

Clayton Moloney hated all Sundays, but he simply loathed the one laid out in front of him.

The hot northerly at his back was a constant reminder that a long-sleeve business shirt and slacks was too much for the beach. It was just too bloody hot: Clay was dressed for the office and its air-conditioned serenity. He longed to return, to ditch this punishing sun and go nurse his bitching hangover in more sympathetic surroundings.

But here he was, on the western edge of Peterborough, one of the last unmodernised villages of the Great Ocean Road, standing in the car park at the Bay of Martyrs. The asphalt exuded as much heat as the stifling air. It was like standing in an oven.

A thin strand of blue and white chequered tape blocked the top of the wooden steps leading down to the beach. Clay couldn't see the beach from the car park. It was hidden from view, firstly by the scrub that covered every spare patch of land around this coastline, and secondly by the large crowd of tourists and locals gathered at the top of the stairs, wondering what was going on.

Clay edged his way through the crowd, notepad and pen in hand. Once he reached the police tape he offered a forced smile to the assembled crowd baking in the sun, and slipped under the plastic ribbon.

'What's happening down there?' Clay estimated the man to be in his early seventies. The old fella had spotted Clay's notepad, nodding his head and terry towel hat at it.

'I think a body washed up,' said Clay, buggered if he'd sugarcoat it for him.

The man scratched beneath his hat, unperturbed. 'Fair enough,' he said, before disappearing into the crowd. Had the *body* bit even registered?

Clay turned away and proceeded down the steps. If a cop was stationed anywhere along the stairs it was going to be a really short story, but luck was on the journalist's side. The wooden path wended its way down the cliff, and finally the postcard-perfect landscape was laid out before him.

A long tract of clean yellow sand stretched out to the next bluff, a kilometre away; the remnants of limestone cliffs worn down by time and the elements intruding onto the beach, breaking it into segments. A choppy blue sea extended out to the horizon, with a handful of tiny islands protruding from the water. Under the unblemished sky, it was a wondrous sight. If only it wasn't so damned hot.

The problem with the picture was a section of the sun-bleached beach being cordoned off by police. More of the blue and white chequered tape flapped in the super-heated wind as two officers hovered around, checking watches and gazing forlornly up at the steps. They weren't the station heavyweights, for sure – their job appeared to be keeping stickybeak tourists and locals away from the crime scene. The tape at the top of the steps was doing the trick, but they couldn't be too careful.

As Clay descended the stairs, looking through the heat haze to the beach, he could see there were still plenty of people enjoying the waters of the Southern Ocean. The police hadn't gotten around to asking them to leave yet, but the beach-goers were either unfazed by what was going on or oblivious; Clay's own understanding of the situation sat somewhere between the two.

He watched the water rippling and lapping at the soft sands for a while before turning to scan the crowd at the top of the steps. Quite a few had turned up, maybe a couple of dozen, but they weren't the ghouls that come out for corpse action. They were everyday punters, either coming to the beach or leaving the beach. Word that a body had been found at the Bay of Martyrs hadn't penetrated the coast yet. These folks had gathered by accident and were trying to figure out what the hell the fuss was about. Clay was, too, but he wouldn't have bothered, certainly not today, if he wasn't being paid to poke around.

The deputy editor, undoubtedly sensing Clay's fragile state, had decided to punish him with a trip to Timboon, some twenty kilometres north of Peterborough. The drive had the prime purpose of covering a Sunday market, just the kind of banal non-story Clay had been asked to puke up with increasing regularity lately. Halfway through interviewing a droll bloke in a filthy beanie hat about his strawberry stall, however, the deputy editor had rang with a change of plan.

'Sounds like someone's washed up at the Bay of Martyrs, Clay.' The tone was that of a desperate editor who had a serious story on his patch, and only a limp-dick of a hack to cover it. 'Get your hungover arse down there as quickly as you can… and if you balls this up, don't come back on Monday. I'll give your job to that bloody work experience kid we had in, the one with the nice tits, that couldn't spell "Canberra".'

Clay had driven as fast as he dared, taking every dirt road shortcut through the lush, green dairy farms and patches of eucalyptus scrub that threaded the Great Ocean Road hinterland. It wasn't the threat of losing his job that fired him, they were far too common, it was the thought that maybe here was a tale worth telling.

On the sand near the taped-off pile of kelp, the two cops still looked nervous, lonely. It was a stroke of luck that Clay had made it here so early, beating most of the police to the scene. He stopped on the final step, as much to catch his breath as to look back up at the crowd again and check for the arrival of more officers, but with none in sight, he knew he was going to have to talk to the coppers at the water's edge. That meant continuing down to the bottom, trudging along the beach, and getting sand in his shoes. He'd probably be told to piss off, which would mean trudging back across the beach, getting more sand in his shoes, and climbing back up the steps again, all the while sweating his balls off and looking like a complete fool.

'Goddamn it,' he muttered as he continued clambering

down towards the crime scene.

In the back of his mind, Clay could hear the younger version of himself getting excited. When was the last time he'd covered a dead body washing up on the beach? Or anything half as interesting as this? Lately he'd been stuck writing obituaries for long-retired city councillors and rewriting federal government press releases about the proposed Warrnambool Airport upgrade. How many column inches had they devoted to that airport? Yes, it was big bucks, into the millions, but The Second Coming wouldn't get the coverage that airport had. This was a real story: life and death.

The older version of himself, the just-turned-forty and feeling sand slowly seeping into his shoes version, couldn't be bothered. Work was a drain on diminishing reserves of energy, and an inconvenience only to be tolerated between visits to the pub. Could he still muster the effort to give a damn about anything?

Sweat was starting to plaster his shirt to his back and his fringe to his forehead as he reached the cops. Clay swept his hair out of the way in a last effort to look presentable that had the side effect of bringing the cops into focus. Clay didn't recognise the female copper, but he picked out the other one as Eddie Boulton.

'Hey, Clay, good to see you dressed for the beach.' Eddie was a few years younger than Clay, but a relatively old contact from the days when their paths met on the crime reporting beat. The pair had got on, a rarity, and ended up sinking quite a few beers before Eddie got a move down the Great Ocean Road to Port Campbell.

'Yeah, I was just about to go for a paddle, Eddie. Care to join me?'

'Sorry, mate, no can do. I've got to make sure this pile of seaweed doesn't run away.'

The banter raised smiles.

Clay gestured to the notepad he was carrying. 'What have you got for me, mate?'

'I wish I knew. This got called in just under an hour ago by a tourist from the city. Down here with the kids, apparently. Bet they won't sleep tonight.'

'Mum and Dad won't be back in a hurry, either.'

Clay peered over the tape, squinted in the sunlight, then pointed to the ground. 'The office said you had a body; is that it?'

'To be honest, I dunno what we're looking at. It could be a movie prop for all I know. We got told not to touch a thing or go near it until the crime scene fellas arrive.'

'Male? Female?'

'Fellas are male, but I'm using the term generically.'

'Funny, Eddie, but I meant the...' Clay directed his pencil to the ground again.

'Your guess is as good as mine, mate.'

Clay leaned forward. So, there it was, buried in a pile of stinking seaweed – the grim visage of a once-was human. The decay of the ocean, the passage of time, and the hungry marine critters had all done their work. The eyeholes were empty and the rest of the body was partially covered by seaweed, but it looked like more than just the eyeballs were missing.

A pungent stench hit Clay in the face, something beyond the salty aroma of kelp, and he realised he'd moved downwind of the body.

'It doesn't smell like a movie prop,' he said. The hangover suddenly felt more serious, but he swallowed a couple of times and coughed. He hoped no one noticed and felt relieved Eddie was gazing up at the steps.

'Looks like the big boys are here. You might wanna make yourself scarce now, Clay.'

Clay followed his line of vision, looked up, and saw a parade of policemen clambering down the stairs. 'Shit. It had to be bloody Frank Anderson, didn't it?'

Anderson stood out in the crowd. He was fatter than the other cops present by a strong margin and was wearing civvies instead of a uniform. He was on the wrong side of fifty, with a thick moustache that might have been interpreted as a Chopper Read homage, if it wasn't for his position. He wore an expression that suggested he recognised Clay's skinny frame already, and that he was as pleased about this as someone who'd just had their flight cancelled.

The journalist turned to Eddie. 'Quick – you had any missing persons lately? A best guess as to who could wash up here?'

'Sorry, Clay, no idea who this is. You're going to have to wait for the boys and girls in the lab, like the rest of us.'

Clay glanced back at Anderson, who was moving from step to step with all the grace of a two-legged cow. It would be a solid minute before the beefy detective made it to the taped-off pile of seaweed. Clay pulled a small camera from his pocket – a digital point-and-shoot number – and walked back to where the greyish face poked out from the seaweed. He snapped a couple of quick shots before sliding the camera back into his pocket.

'I'm gonna pretend I didn't see that,' said Eddie.

'See what?' said Clay, offering the cop a cheeky grin.

Anderson was walking away from the bottom stair, negotiating the sand with only slightly more grace. He was heading straight for them.

Nothing to it but to do it, thought Clay. He made straight for Anderson, with his grin on full beam.

'Detective Sergeant Anderson, what a pleasure to see you again,' said Clay. 'What's it been? Five, six years? You're looking well. Have you lost weight?'

A few cops trailing in Anderson's wake suppressed smirks as they passed Clay on their way to the taped-off crime scene. Anderson's heavy brows drooped, his face contorted into a sour scowl that Clay was already familiar with. He'd succeeded in winding up the detective, but knew he still had a job to do.

'Go to hell, maggot,' said Anderson.

Clay turned and kept pace with the detective. 'Is that "maggot" with two Gs?' he said, pretending to write in his notepad.

'Which part of "go to hell" didn't make sense, Moloney? I can spell it out on your notepad if you like, ya bloody smart-arse.'

'Come on, Frank. I've just got a couple of questions.'

Anderson's scowl morphed into a slick smile. 'All questions must be directed to the police media unit,' he said, unable to keep the hint of smarm from his voice.

'Oh, give me a break. You know they're as useless as tits on a bull.'

'All questions must be directed to the police media unit.'

Anderson kept walking and Clay stopped. He gritted his teeth. Something about the dismissive slap down from Anderson cancelled out the effects of his hangover, made him want to run down the beach after him and slug it out for the story. Someone had died here; it wasn't the place to play games like this. For the first time in ages, something like ambition burned inside Clayton Moloney.

But if no one was going to tell him anything, he didn't have much of a story.

Chapter 3

At the break-up of the early-morning news conference, an animated hum charged the air of the meeting room and followed the trail of bodies back to desks. For a little after 9 a.m. on a Monday, this level of excitement for the day ahead unsettled Clay. It wasn't the manufactured enthusiasm he'd come to expect from colleagues who wanted to hold onto jobs in a rapidly shrinking industry; it was more than that, more than gut-wrenching curiosity, too. Death had visited, close to home, and these people now felt lucky to be among the living.

Clay passed around his camera; some were desensitised enough to want a look at the dead body captured in the tiny screen on the back. The photos hadn't been published – something about upsetting the relatives and the squeamish – but most of the hacks in the office wanted a peek. The indistinct images of a corpse covered in greying and rotting flesh attracted all the remarks he'd expected, and a few he hadn't. People were funny, but not the one in the picture: that one had nothing to laugh about. He felt strangely defensive of the unnamed body under discussion.

'Nothing like a corpse to liven up a newsroom,' said Clay.

A few titters followed. Clay goaded them again: 'It's ironic the way this place usually looks at this hour.'

'Says the Living Dead poster boy.' One of the mildly aggrieved spoke up.

'How is the hangover, Clay?' said another.

They were ganging up now.

Clay retreated. 'Touchy lot, aren't you? Sorry I spoke.'

He snatched the camera back, switched off the back screen and stomped to his desk. Clay turned over his notebook, shuffled the piles of press releases, looking for his contacts book. When he found it, lodged in the tip site of his desk's top drawer, he scanned the dog-eared index. He located Senior Constable Eddie Boulton's mobile number and dialled.

The officer picked up on the third ring. 'Hey, Clay. I don't think I'm supposed to be talking to you.'

'Oh, come on, Eddie, when has that ever stopped you before? Are you gonna let that tosser, Anderson, tell you what to do?'

'Well, there's the slight matter of the fact that he does outrank me.'

'Yeah, there's that, but he is a tosser, too.'

Laughter. 'There is that.'

'So, tell me what you know? The body's in Melbourne, right?'

'Off the record, yeah, it's probably on the slab as we speak.'

'Male or female?'

'No idea.'

'Has it been that long since you've been laid, Eddie?'

'Clay, the body was a wreck. Long time in the water, plus a few sharks and other assorted sea creatures had treated it like the all-you-can-eat buffet at Macey's Hotel. We've got a head, most of a torso, one and a half arms, and a stump that was once a leg.'

Clay scratched the details into his shorthand pad as the officer's description of the body grew in his mind.

'But, come on,' said Clay. 'If you were a betting man – which I know you are – male or female?'

'I'd go with female. The hair was on the longish side. Christ, I sound like my old man saying that. Look, I dunno.'

'What about marks or wounds on the body?'

'Aside from the massive shark bites?'

'Well, yeah…'

'I got nothing, Clay.'

'Age?'

'I dunno… youngish? Under twenty-five, I guess, but not a kid.'

'So who can I talk to on the record about all this? And don't say "Frank Anderson".'

Eddie's tone trailed into exasperation. 'Sorry, mate, but he's your man. And he's just gonna fob you off to police media.'

'Who are a pack of useless so-and-sos.' A pause. He reckoned there was still room to press the cop. 'Then tell me this – how long until an autopsy report is filed?'

'Months. Two at best, more likely four.'

'Damn.'

'But a preliminary one might get filed in a week or so to help speed along the investigation.'

'Where does that go when it's filed?'

'Anderson will get one and he'll pass it around the criminal investigations unit in Warrnambool. And one will probably go to the prosecutions office so they can keep up with the case for future reference.'

'The Warrnambool prosecutions office?'

'Probably Melbourne. But one might go to the prosecutors in Warrnambool. If you're lucky.'

'Here's hoping. Thanks, Eddie. I owe you a beer.'

'You owe me many beers, you cheap bastard.'

Clay hung up. Bradley Tudor was heading his way, with a woman he didn't recognise. He was pretty sure the editor couldn't read shorthand, he probably couldn't even read joined-up writing, but he closed over his notepad on instinct. Clay quickly lost interest in the approaching Tudor and focused on the woman. She was average height, with dark brown hair and matching, but darker, eyes. There was something quietly confident about her and the way she walked through the office in her torn Levi's and faded T-shirt. Clay put her at early thirties, but with a self-assurance that suggested she was closer to his own age – though admittedly wearing it a lot better.

'Clay, this is Bec O'Connor, the new photographer,' said Tudor. 'You two can get to know each other on the way out to the airport.'

Clay and Bec exchanged a quick, and somewhat awkward 'hi' before both turning back to gaze at the editor.

'What's at the airport?' said Clay.

'Planes,' said Tudor, smirking at his pathetic idea of a joke.

Clay's expression remained unchanged while Bec smiled politely.

'But seriously,' continued Tudor, oblivious, 'Wayne Swanson is landing out there shortly. You need to ask him about what's going on with the airport redevelopment he promised in the last election and you also need to grill him about the Gold Coast deal that was all over the nationals.'

'What Gold Coast deal are we talking about?' said Clay.

Tudor's humour was replaced with disdain. 'Don't you read the papers? Or listen to the news in the morning?'

'I've been busy.'

The editor glowered; something like a riposte was clearly forming on his lips, but it seemed to slip away from him. 'The metros are alleging some kind of backdoor deal was done between Swanson and Fullerton Industries on a new hospital on the Gold Coast. Fullerton's got local connections, too, not to mention truckloads of the green stuff, so it could be a good yarn for us. Do your research on the drive out.'

'If I must,' muttered Clay.

Tudor seemed to be pretending not to hear; he turned to Bec. 'All the equipment you'll need is over in the photography department, Bec. Go and see Damian, he's desking the jobs today, and he'll sort you out with a camera and all the rest of it.'

'Thanks for that.' Bec wandered off in the direction of Damian's desk and Tudor perched over Clay like he was about to take a bite out of him.

'This is a good story, Clay. Local politician, locally connected business, deals for the boys... how about a bit of enthusiasm? Or have you had enough of this caper?'

Clay sank further into his chair. 'Settle down. I'm just a bit out of the loop this morning, that's all. Big day, yesterday, what with me writing the front page about a bloody body washing up at Peterborough. Or did you forget that, Tudor?'

They were talking low and close, but Clay sensed a few heads around the office were turning in their direction.

'One sunny day doesn't make a summer. I have cadets on the payroll putting in higher word counts than you, and guess what? They do it for a lot less.'

'I'm sure the quality of their copy's spot on, too.'

'Watch it, *mate*,' said Tudor. 'Word is the boys in Sydney might be swinging the axe at the regionals soon and it ain't gonna be the enthusiastic young journos on low pay that get the sack. It's more likely to be the cantankerous ones who do one front-page story a month, have a few warnings about their behaviour on their record, and are on good pay 'cos they've been here for twenty years.'

'Well, if all Sydney wants is fresh-out-of-college fodder to rewrite Hungry Jack's press releases, then I'm sure you'll all be very happy in your Brave New World, and I, on the other hand, will gladly jog on, *mate*.' Clay took a deep breath, but couldn't take any of the bite out of his voice. 'Now, if you'll excuse me, Mr Editor, I have a politician to interview.'

Tudor stepped out of the way as Clay rose. A further exchange of words looked imminent, but as Bec appeared, camera case in hand, Tudor clamped his mouth shut.

Chapter 4

'That was an interesting scene.' Bec spoke with an Irish lilt that recalled Clay's university years and the memories of international students and backpackers.

'That's an interesting accent.'

Bec had the wheel of the office Subaru, following Clay's directions to the airport. 'Is that what you call avoidance chat?'

Clay pored over the metro papers, caught up in what he'd missed about the member for Warrnambool, Wayne Swanson, and his friends at Fullerton Industries. It seemed Swanson, in his role as federal infrastructure minister, was being accused of less than scrupulous management of a new hospital tender that Fullerton had landed. The story was patched together from leaked documents and unnamed sources, but the inference that Swanson had greased the deal was plain, and Clay could see how it all added up to trouble for the politician.

'I'll take that silence as a yes,' said Bec.

Clay didn't look up from the newspaper. 'I'm not sure what you're talking about.'

'Well, I've worked at a few papers here and there, and usually when an editor and a journo have an up-close-and-personal moment like that, it means bad things are going down. Or they're about to shag in the supply room. Maybe both.'

'Tudor and I don't see eye to eye on most things.' He closed the newspaper and folded it up before tossing it at his feet. 'So... you're from Ireland, hey?'

Bec took the hint and shifted conversational gears. 'Yes. From Dublin.'

'And where are you living now?'

'I'm renting a little farmhouse out the other side of Koroit. It's pretty.' Her face lit up at the mention of the place.

'Why the hell are you living all the way out there?'

'What do you mean "all the way out there"? It takes me less than twenty minutes to drive to Warrnambool.'

'Yeah, but I can walk to work in five minutes. And I never have to pay for a taxi to get home after the pubs.'

'Some of us don't live our life around "the pubs".'

She didn't take much to thaw out, Clay liked that about her. 'What's the matter? Too old to party?'

'Some of us have done our fair share of that already and grew out of it.'

'Some of us sound like an old person when they're probably younger than me.'

Bec offered a scoffing laugh in response. 'I doubt it. I'm thirty-nine. And what are you?'

'Just turned forty, actually.' He still hadn't adjusted to the number. It sounded too far off, like hip replacements and blending your food. 'I could have sworn you were about thirty-four at the oldest.'

'Er, thanks. But I'm not that hung up on my age.'

An awkward silence played. Both parties seemed more comfortable with sly insults than compliments and the forty count was still a sore point for Clay. In an attempt to take the edge off the conversation he moved away from the subject. 'You do know they have an Irish festival in Koroit every year?'

'Yes. It's part of the appeal.'

'Really? You come all the way across the world from Ireland to end up in perhaps the most Irish town in Australia?'

Bec was quiet for a moment. 'I guess it feels like home in a way, but without actually being home.'

'I see.' For the second time in less than a minute there were uncomfortable thoughts in the air, and the silence descended again.

It was the landscape that broke the lull. 'Turn left here.'

Bec flipped on the blinkers, turned the wheel.

The Warrnambool Airport lay beyond the edges of the city, among the fertile pastures of Mailors Flat. A small red brick house and an assortment of sheds made the place look like a farm at first, especially given its location amid a landscape dominated by paddocks full of Friesian cows, happily chewing their cud.

'It's not much of an airport,' said Bec, as she parked the Subaru.

'No kidding. Some of these shacks will be worth top dollar when the airlines start landing.'

'They're really putting in that kind of development here?' She stopped in the dry, dusty road and looked around.

The windsock flapped forlornly in the weak westerly that had replaced yesterday's harsh northerly, returning the region to a more pleasant and bearable version of summer. A handful of large sheds served as hangars and four runways crisscrossed each other in the shape of a hashtag. The terminal looked more like a settler's hut than a place where passengers checked in, and the refuelling truck wouldn't have been out of place in a Norman Rockwell painting.

'Swanson made some million-dollar promise, but you know what they say about a politician's promise,' said Clay. 'The clever bastard bragged he'd put Warrnambool on the map by pumping money into this place. Bring even more tourists here to go up and down the Great Ocean Road. Internationals flying in from all over the place. I'll be very surprised if anything ever comes of it.'

A droning sound off in the distance caught their attention and Clay and Bec turned their gaze to the east, where a light plane had appeared. They watched as it circled around to the north of the airport, eventually beginning its descent.

The first man off the plane moved slowly, the sallow skin and drawn cheeks signalling heavy fatigue. Grey hairs were migrating upwards from his temples, while his jowls were migrating downwards. Swanson seemed to have aged prematurely by at least a decade. Clay, in his age-obsessed state, congratulated himself on avoiding politics as a profession.

Bec snapped away as Swanson walked from the plane, mopping his brow with a handkerchief, heading for the hut-terminal. At the front door of the building he spotted the pair from the newspaper.

'Clay, good to see you again,' said Swanson, extending a sweaty palm and giving Clay the too-firm handshake of the overcompensating. 'And it's good to be back in the 'Bool.'

'What can you tell me about your airport promise, Wayne?' Clay removed his notepad, yanked a pencil from the spiral. 'You said there'd be funding in the next budget for a major upgrade.'

'I'm glad you asked me that, because we're moving forward with the upgrade and I'll tell you who the successful tender winner is soon… obviously following due process.'

Swanson went into the benefits an airport upgrade was going to have for 'the good electorate'. Clay was barely listening, half-writing the article already. When he noticed Swanson slowing he seized the chance to change tack. 'Wayne, I want to ask about the Gold Coast hospital allegations with Fullerton Industries.'

Swanson waved a hand as if shooing a blowfly. 'It's a beat-up. Due process was followed, any allegations suggesting otherwise are bloody lies.'

'But you are friends with Lachlan Fullerton, aren't you?'

'I know lots of people. Lots of CEOs and business folks. And yes, I know Mr Fullerton. He's from my home town – he's a good Warrnambool lad – so it'd be strange if I didn't know him, given the size of the place. But that doesn't mean he's been favoured in a tender process, now, does it?'

'You're not aware of any secret payments to your department?'

'God, no.'

'What about threats to competitors from Fullerton?'

'That's bloody ridiculous.'

'And you'd swear in court that you didn't get any advantage from Fullerton landing the tender?'

All smarm was gone from Swanson's voice. It sounded like he was now forcing civility; he raised a hand, levelled it at his breastbone. 'I'd swear on a stack of Bibles this high.'

Clay shot his best just-doing-my-job smile – a wry, almost gummy grin he reserved for the easily pleased, or easily fooled. 'Sorry to ask all that, Wayne, but you know I've got to.'

Swanson's features softened once back in the familiar territory of flattery, albeit with beads of sweat at his temples. 'I know, I know,' he said. He slapped Clay playfully on the shoulder and turned to walk to the approaching car. 'If you're done breaking my balls, I'll be off. This Rotary Club luncheon speech isn't going to give itself. I might see you at the Warrny for a beer later.'

One of Swanson's minders, quickly exiting the black government sedan, rushed to open the car door and Swanson dropped himself into the back seat. As the car pulled out, revving hard, the politician looked to be barking orders at the driver: Clay guessed he wanted the air-con on full.

'Do you really go drinking with him?' asked Bec.

'Not if I can bloody well help it,' said Clay.

Chapter 5

Autopsy done. See Gabby.

The text was from Senior Constable Eddie Boulton. Forcing thumbs onto too-small keys, Clay tried to reply on his antique Nokia:

Thanks mate. Make that two beers I owe you.

Clay was grateful for Eddie's update, because Detective Frank Anderson could hardly be bothered to pick up his phone. Ten days had passed since the body washed up at the Bay of Martyrs and the story was in danger of becoming old news.

'Watching you text is painful,' said Bec.

'How about you watch the road instead,' said Clay.

They were on their way back to Warrnambool from Port Fairy, where the day's story was a local woman celebrating her hundredth birthday. Tudor was torturing Clay, he knew it. The poor old dear had lost her marbles years ago, so there was nothing for a reporter to report.

'Seriously, watching you text is like watching a monkey play that board game, *Operation*,' said Bec. 'Do you have that game here? You know, the one where you get zapped when you touch the sides while trying to remove a bone or kidney or something?'

'Yes, we have that game here. The analogy isn't wasted.'

'Good. Because it's a good analogy. Accurate.'

Clay smiled in spite of himself. Tudor might have been punishing him by sending him on increasingly inane jobs – a man who'd found an egg with three yolks in it had been the worst so far – but at least Bec was there to lighten the load.

'We need to make a detour. Take me to a bakery, then take me to the cop shop,' said Clay.

The town's police prosecutors were housed in a separate building from the rest of the force. While all the other cops were in the new glass and chrome police station next to the equally flash new courthouse, the prosecutors were stuck in a badly renovated unit nearby. The heating system didn't work, the cooling system didn't exist, and the tiny building seemed like it was held together by huge grey filing cabinets, ageing desks, and an invisible will power.

Clay was about to chance his luck, he knew it, but buried his nerves as he knocked on the door. A speaker box near his head squawked to life, almost making him drop the box of fresh bakery biscuits he had under his arm. He could sense Bec watching him from the car and tried to regain his composure.

'Yes?' said a voice shrouded in lo-fi distortion.

Clay pushed the button marked 'talk' and moved his mouth closer to what he presumed was the microphone. 'Ah, it's Clayton Moloney. I'm here to see Gabby.'

There was a long silence and Clay's fears rose up. *What if she doesn't want to see me? Did we end on bad terms? I can't remember. I don't think we ended on bad terms. Maybe she's been told not to speak to me. Maybe Frank Anderson told her not to speak to me.*

The door made a loud clicking sound and opened a fraction. Clay took a deep breath and pushed it open, stepping into a small entrance hall that was even warmer than the summer's day outside.

The door swung closed behind him, clicking back into place. He stepped forward out of the atrium and into the main room of the apartment. At some point, the room must have been a lounge and a bedroom, but a wall had been removed and about twenty tonnes of paperwork and a few desks had been installed.

No one was sitting at any of the desks except for a young woman with a bob haircut that was dyed the colour of Merlot. She had small features to go with the bob, giving her a vaguely pixieish appearance when paired with her petite frame. A nose ring in her left nostril added to the exotic look.

'Hey, Gabby.'

'Clayton Moloney. What's it been? A year?'

'I would have said a couple of months, but then my memory never has been good.'

'Right.'

'I thought you moved away.'

'No. You just stopped calling me.'

Clay winced. 'I'm sorry… things have been busy.'

'For a year?'

'Umm. Yeah.'

Gabby let out a huge laugh that made Clay jump a little. 'You're a dag. I'm just messin' with ya. I'm not gonna break your balls.'

'You're not?'

'No! Why should I? We had some fun, we moved on. Whatevs.'

Clay repressed a sigh of relief, while simultaneously cringing at the trendy mangling of the word 'whatever'. It served as a reminder of one of the reasons why he'd stopped seeing Gabby Petrie – the age difference of twelve years had become increasingly evident and gone from being a cute and playful thing to a general annoyance.

But he still liked Gabby. She was fun, a free-spirited young woman, and he was glad she didn't hate him, if only because he wanted something from her.

'I brought you a present.' Clay placed the box of biscuits on her desk.

'Ooh!' she squealed. 'Chocolate chip cookies. You remembered they're my favourite.'

She called them cookies, Clay thought. Aussies called them biscuits. Damn Americanisms. That was almost as bad as 'whatevs'.

Gabby's face took on an expression of playful suspicion. 'Wait a minute. What do you want? I don't just roll over for chocolate chip cookies. That at least costs cookies, a cake, some dinner, and probably a bottle of wine.' She laughed that huge laugh again, although this time Clay didn't jump.

'Ha, sorry, Gabby, no, I'm after a report. A certain preliminary autopsy report.'

'An autopsy report? Well, this is serious. I'm afraid that's going to cost you a lot more than a box of cookies.'

Clay suppressed a laugh, but wondered what he was getting himself into.

Bec had all the windows down on the Subaru; one arm on the ledge soaking the sun, fingers tapping to Johnny Cash's *Folsom Prison Blues*. The sound of the passenger door startled her.

'Well, that went well,' said Clay. He expanded on the escapade.

'You swapped some biscuits for an autopsy report?' said Bec.

'And dinner. I have to take the prosecutor's assistant out to dinner.'

Bec laughed deep. It was a whole-hearted laugh, a foreign laugh that Clay had never heard before. It was a laugh that seemed out of place in the 'Bool that had become so ordinary to him.

'You whore,' she said between gulps.

'It's a dirty job, but someone's got to do it.'

Clay's plan was to duck out of the office at lunchtime and read the autopsy report at the café beneath his apartment, but Bec insisted she tag along, so he directed her to Cannon Hill. He wasn't really sure why he'd picked that spot. At night, it was *the* make-out point, but by day it had the best view in town, sweeping out across the winding channels of Lake Pertobe, rows of Norfolk pines, and the cool blue waters of Lady Bay.

'What a view,' said Bec.

'As good a place as any for sandwiches and some not-so-light reading, I thought.'

Clay opened up Gabby's photocopy of the report; it was three pages long.

'Bit brief…' he said.

'You did say it was only a preliminary report, but three

pages does seem a bit short. Anyway, hurry up, give me the pages as you read.'

Clay passed each page on to Bec when he'd finished it. After reading the whole report, both sat in silence. The view seemed to have lost some of its appeal to Clay.

'There's something not right about all that,' he said.

'I agree.'

A full minute passed.

'Give me another look,' said Clay.

Bec handed the pages back to him and he slowly went through the report again, line by line.

'Warrnambool girl, Kerry Collins,' he read. 'Eighteen years old. Death by drowning. Victim appears to have been in the water for approximately seven days.'

'The toxicology screens are clean, no drugs or alcohol, although it notes that alcohol would have passed from her system in seven days,' said Bec.

'You get the loss of limbs, believed to be a result of shark attack, occurred posthumously.'

'Yeah, I saw that.'

'But some bruises on her forearm and a wound to the back of the head *appear* to have occurred prior to death. Head wound *possibly* caused concussion, likely followed by death by drowning.'

'So she hits her head and drowns,' said Bec.

'On what? Some passing driftwood? And what are the bruises on her arm?'

'OK, she hits her arm and her head. What am I missing here?'

Clay looked up from the report and out across the bay. 'Probably nothing. It's probably a simple, straightforward accident. The cops will ask a few questions of friends and family and the coroner will issue a nice and easy finding. Accidental drowning. Probably fell off a boat. Whacked her head on the way down. Drowned. Shark bait. The end.'

Bec looked at Clay. Could she hear his brain ticking over? It wasn't the end, nothing like it.

'But… I'm hearing a *but*,' said Bec.

'*But* how did she end up in the water?' said Clay.

'You said a boat.'

'Was she on the boat by herself?'

'I guess so.'

'I don't know many eighteen-year-old girls who go sailing by themselves. And if they did, they would be the safety-conscious competitive boating types. Life jackets, that sort of thing. But, more importantly, she would have told someone she was going out sailing.'

'And let me guess – in the week prior to Kerry Collins washing up, no missing sailors were reported?'

'Spot on. A sea rescue is a big deal around here. People come running from all around – the water police, the regular police, the rescue chopper, marine rescue, state emergency service. You name it, they're there. We haven't had one of those for a long time. And by my calculation she went missing between Christmas and New Year's Eve. That's the paper's quietest time of the year, because just about everything's closed. A girl in a boat reported missing at sea would have been front page news.'

'So she wasn't on a boat by herself. Maybe she was swimming by herself.'

'Possible. We can't rule that out. But then what did she hit her head and arms on?'

'Rocks?'

'Maybe. But what if she wasn't alone? Maybe she was swimming in a group. Or on a boat with other people.'

'There still would have been a search.'

'Right. So, we know there wasn't a search – we would have heard about it at the paper – so that means someone perhaps didn't want a search.'

'Surely someone would have notified the authorities she was missing.'

'If they did, I'd like to know when that call went through. It could tell us a lot. Because I'm seeing a few possibilities here.'

Bec looked into Clay again. He knew she was reading him.

'You're pretty worked up about this, Mr Reporter…'

'If I am, I'm the only one.'

'That doesn't sound right.'

'It's not bloody right… pretty far from it.'

Bec folded over the report, handed it back. 'I meant, you're not the only one who's worked up about this.'

Chapter 6

Clay hated the death knock. Even when Tudor ladled on the false flattery, telling him he was good at them, Clay always felt the unwholesome flutter of guilt that came from poking your nose into the privacy of grief.

He preferred the old-fashioned approach of visiting the home, rather than hiding down the phone line. It felt more sincere, more human. And if it meant burning a whole afternoon with a poor old dear who wanted to talk about losing the love of her life, so be it. He had precious few opportunities, beyond tipping waitresses and wearing a poppy, to feel good about his actions these days.

'You set?' he said.

Bec raised her camera case, nodded. 'As I'll ever be.'

'You've not done too many of these, have you?'

A frown. 'Not on the job. But I'm Irish. This sort of thing's a national pastime.'

Clay knocked on the frosted glass. He'd doorstepped plenty of relatives of the recently deceased, but could never say he'd got used to it. No two were the same. You never knew whether you were turning up to tears and hearts turned to mush or walking in on a wake – which he'd managed once, taking a drink and pretending to be an old friend of the departed.

'We can't compare down here, then?' said Clay.

'How could you, with all this sunshine? We have the Holy Trinity of grey skies, Arthur Guinness, and "Danny Boy".'

'Sounds like a barrel of laughs.'

'Trust me, I know, there is nothing like an Irish funeral.'

'Something you want to talk about?' He'd made the remark flippantly, but Bec's expression said it hadn't been taken that way. 'Sorry, did I touch a nerve?'

Bec narrowed her gaze. 'I think we'll leave it there for now.'

Clay brushed down his shirtfront as he spied movement in the house. Usually, by the time he arrived, the family members were resigned to the deceased's passing. A quiet acceptance kept what he'd seen of the grieving measured and thoughtful. The departed were always missed, but it was their time; hopefully they'd had a good run; hopefully they were somewhere better. As Brian Collins opened the door Clay knew he was dealing with a different situation entirely.

'Thank you for coming,' said Brian, once Clay had introduced himself and Bec. Kerry's father's gaze was unfocused, wandering the room, whilst his hands seemed to be searching for something to touch. He acted as though he had invited Clay and Bec to his home, not like they'd just shown up unannounced, looking for a scoop.

Clay saw Brian's grief was wild and unhinged. This was a new kind of loss – the Collins family's hurt was raw and tangible, hanging in the air like a pall. The house was unnaturally silent, and here and there were the traces of a family out of its usual routine – unopened mail, dirty dishes, limping houseplants.

'Through this way, please.' Brian led them into the lounge room. It reminded Clay of his parents' house back in the early Nineties: lots of polished pine, decorative plates, and softly-coloured walls co-ordinated with the drapes. Framed photos everywhere, pictures of Brian, his wife, two boys, and a girl who appeared to be the youngest member of the clan had to be Kerry. She had an infectious teenage smile that told Clay she was likeable, the girl next door, taken too soon; he looked away quickly.

'We're sorry for the intrusion,' said Clay. 'I realise the funeral was only yesterday, but we thought you might like to tell us a little about Kerry so we can share her story, particularly for those who couldn't make it to the funeral.'

The funeral had been hastily arranged. It had taken place the same day Clay and Bec had read the autopsy report. The Collins family had been told about Kerry's death only two days earlier, just as the body of their only daughter was arriving back in town following the post-mortem in Melbourne. The Collins wasted no time in sending off Kerry, who had already been missing for more than two weeks.

'Yes… Yes, I'd like that,' said Brian, in a clear, gentle voice. He trailed a hand through his dark, thinning hair. 'We have family up in Queensland who couldn't get down in time. They'd like to read about Kerry. I have a copy of the eulogy here somewhere you can have. It might be useful. She was such a bright kid.'

Brian walked into an adjoining room, returning soon after with a folded square of paper, which he handed to Clay. As he read, the room's heavy silence was interrupted by a clock on the mantelpiece; it seemed to take an age between each tick.

The eulogy was the usual – it would make Clay's job of writing up a tribute piece all the easier. Kerry was adored by her family and everyone who knew her. She was kind and generous. She was funny and caring. And like all those who die young, she was filled with a potential that would remain forever untapped.

Brian wrapped his hands together, looked at Clay as he read, then rubbed the back of his neck. It was as though he would never sit still again. 'She was working as a waitress,' he said. 'Kerry always had a good work ethic. She used to work at the ice cream shop here in Port Fairy on weekends and on school holidays, and then she started waitressing.'

'Where was she working?' said Clay.

'She worked at a few places. Fishtails Café some days, Proudfoots Restaurant at night, and she did some function work on the side. I think she was heading out to waitress on the last night anyone saw her. It was just after Christmas.'

'Do you know where?' Clay was straying from the newspaper tribute now, fishing.

'No, I don't. Sorry. The police asked me that, too.'

Clay wondered if the cops might be thinking the same as him after all. 'I guess you've seen the police a lot over the past couple of weeks.'

'Yeah. They were here this morning asking questions. They were here a few days days ago to tell us it was her body they found at Peterborough. They were here before that when we reported her missing.'

'When did you last see Kerry?'

Brian patted his hands together again. 'I think Kerry was working at a function on a Sunday night. I remember thinking it was weird, like "who has a function on a Sunday night?" She didn't say where. We didn't ask. She came out here for lunch that Sunday. Last time we saw her.'

Clay felt his questions were sounding more and more like a cop's, but Brian didn't seem to mind. 'And when did you realise Kerry was missing, Mr Collins?'

'Not until the Tuesday. Her housemate called. Said she hadn't been home for two days. Wondered if she was here.'

'Must have given you all a fright.'

'Everyone was calling everyone. It was frantic. We called all her friends, but nobody knew anything... That's when we told the police and they started looking around for her. Then a bit later on, the following Sunday, she... she washed up in Peterborough.' Brian let out a deep exhalation and sat still for the first time since he had opened the door. His hands rested quietly on his round belly.

'I knew it was her,' said Brian. 'As soon as I read the story in the paper.' His eyes swam, then locked onto Clay. 'You wrote that story, didn't you?'

'It was mine, yes.'

Brian Collins nodded. 'I knew it was her,' he repeated in a low voice. 'They only confirmed it the other day, when they told us. But I knew. Dorothy didn't want to believe it. I played along with her. "You're right, Dottie," I said. "It can't be her. Our Kerry'll turn up. She'll be OK."' He turned and looked at a closed door in the hallway beyond the lounge room. 'Do you know my wife hasn't left the bedroom except for the funeral?' He shook his head. 'Poor Dottie.'

The whirring of Clay's dictaphone and the tick of the clock

on the mantelpiece were the only sounds in the room for a few moments, until Brian started sobbing. He was lost to himself, the others in the room an irrelevance. Clay could think of no clearer picture to symbolise a family's heart-torn grief. He wanted to reach out, offer comfort, but he knew the situation was beyond retrieval by the blandishments of a stranger who'd only just walked through the front door.

He reached down and turned off the recorder.

Chapter 7

Clay had hardly slept.

The fact that Gabby Petrie was in his bed beside him, snoring gently beneath her mess of red wine-coloured hair, had a little bit to do with it, but his insomnia was predominantly related to Kerry Collins.

He'd stayed back late at the office working on her obituary, turning the taped interview with Brian Collins into a touching article he was proud of. After that, he'd been in need of drink and called Gabby, making good on his promise.

But much later that night, when he'd put his head down to try and sleep, he could hear Brian's words and low sobs playing over and over in his head. He must have drifted off at some point, if only for a matter of minutes, because he was aware of a dream. He was sitting in the Collins' house in Port Fairy, right where he'd sat in the lounge room that day, with Bec beside him and Brian opposite in the comfy leather chair. In this dream, Clay's eyes were drawn to one of the framed photos of Kerry on the wall, but the more he stared at it, the more it changed. Kerry's skin went pale, bloodless. Her mouth opened into a silent scream and her lips rotted away. Her eyes shrivelled and were gone, leaving behind two black craters. It was the face of the body in the seaweed at the Bay of Martyrs. It was a face that hadn't bothered him until now. Now it was a person. Now it was haunting his dreams.

Clay shivered in the early morning light. He was drenched in sweat.

He rolled out of bed, careful and quiet so as not to disturb Gabby, and pulled on a pair of grey tracksuit pants before walking into the lounge room. The coffee table, a strange looking wooden hexagon he took a degree of pride in, was covered with the detritus of the night before: two empty wine bottles, an overflowing ashtray, records out of their sleeves, half a joint, and a small bag holding a couple of buds of weed. Clay liked Gabby because she was fun and she liked to party, but the trade for the preliminary autopsy report had grown into a lot more than just dinner and a pack of biscuits.

Clay opened the curtains to better survey the aftermath of the previous evening. A storey below, Warrnambool's main drag – Liebig Street – was starting to stir. The breakfast cafés and coffee hotspots were swinging into action. Tables and chairs getting set up on footpaths. A street sweeper making a final pass. A magpie calling in one of the leafy trees that threw stark morning shadows onto the shopfronts.

Clay heard the soft rumble of kitchen machinery below his lounge floor. The ever-present hum of fridges was joined by the gurgle of a coffee maker and the blitzkrieg of a blender, all muffled by the sandwich of ceiling, wiring, floorboards, and carpet beneath his feet. Already he was starting to feel a bit better. The normality of daily waking life and its soundscape was like placing a hand on a wall to steady himself after the unsettling tremors of his attempts to sleep.

He pulled a cigarette from a near-empty pack and lit up as he cleared away the mess. Bottles in the recycling, ashtray emptied, records back in their sleeves. By the time he'd finished the smoke, the lounge room and Clay's mind were almost back to normal.

A sleepy stumble of feet on carpet caught Clay's attention as he flicked ash from the cigarette into the clean ashtray.

'Hey there, cowboy,' said Gabby. She looked dishevelled as she struggled back into the eye-catching black dress she'd worn the night before. At dinner it had shimmered – this morning it looked like lifeless fabric. Gabby's hair had been suppressed into a loose approximation of order, but the remains of her eye make-up scrubbed the illusion of control.

'Hey, yourself. You sleep all right?'

'More like passed out. I'm still wrecked.'

'Just like old times, Gabby.'

'Funny... Zip me up.' She spun around, wobbling a little as she completed the one hundred and eighty degree turn.

Clay got up from the couch and walked towards her. The sight of her bare back and the obvious lack of a bra strap threw up flashbacks of last night's activities. He zipped up the back of her dress with care, catching a whiff of the last hints of a familiar perfume; it was now mixed with cigarette smoke and boozy sweat into a scent that somehow still managed to be alluring.

Gabby turned and they were standing close together. She perched up on her toes and pressed a brief kiss onto Clay's lips. 'I gotta get to work.'

'Me, too. Thank the gods it's Friday, right?'

She gave him another peck. 'You should quit smoking.'

'So should you.'

Another kiss. This one longer and with eyes closed, accompanied by heavy inhales and the space between their bodies disappearing.

Clay pulled away first. 'Work.'

'Right.' She turned and headed for the door. Fetching her high heels and handbag from the hallway floor on the way, she waved a hand over her head without turning around. 'Thanks for dinner. I'll call ya.'

'Bye, Gabby.'

The door clicked closed behind her as Clay stumbled into the bathroom. When the first jets of the shower hit his face he silently cursed himself. He hadn't meant to sleep with Gabby. But he hadn't been able to stop himself. It was always the way after a few drinks and a few joints, and it had caused him plenty of troubles in the past, including with Gabby.

There had been references made to that during and after dinner, and Clay had started to recall a tricky extrication a year ago. Gabby had wanted an exclusive relationship, Clay didn't want a commitment. It was the usual clichéd story, and it was such a regular occurrence for Clay that he'd become something of a master of the tricky extrication. Not that he was proud of the fact, but it was a fact.

He wondered what he was doing now, what new depths of trouble he was digging for himself. Gabby was good fun and bloody useful, but while Clay still didn't want to get involved he doubted she was thinking the same way. She was as bad as him in her own way; she knew the score, but that didn't make it any easier.

Dried and dressed, he made his way out the door, down the stairs, and through the café's back door. Kitchen staff waved hello as he weaved his way between them and out past the counter, where his morning order – a double-shot black coffee, half a sugar – sat waiting for him.

'You're a gem, Wendy,' he called to the middle-aged woman at the coffee machine, raising his disposable cup in salute.

'I'm surprised you're on time this morning after seeing that red-haired thing doing the walk of shame through the car park with her heels in her hand,' said Wendy, giving him a fake look of disapproval.

'I'm sure I don't know what you're talking about,' he said, as he plonked some coins on the counter. He knew full well, and that feeling of having acted a little less than perfectly towards Gabby poked at his conscience again. Bec would call him a user. She'd be bang on the money, too.

Clay headed for the door, eyes down to avoid Wendy. He was almost out when he saw it. A copy of the day's paper lay face up on an empty table, and there was the face of Kerry Collins. She was the image of innocence, with her sweet smile, button nose, and youthful face, bordered by an angelic veil of blonde hair.

Clay halted, drew steady breath. There was something about seeing a story in print that made it real for the first time. The visit out to the bay, the talks to cops, fishing for more detail where and when he could, none of it seemed like anything more than a job, another day at the office. The first sight of the paper made everything real. This was news, a tragedy in his own town. When he picked up the paper he was the kid who'd just heard his dog had been run over, tasted his first hurt in life. Clay's mother had broken the news then, but it hadn't sank in; he didn't cry until the policeman came to the door with Bindy's collar. He cried then, and for a long time after. There were some wounds that just didn't heal.

'SHE WAS ONLY 18' read the headline. Still a kid herself, it smacked him now. She'd lost out on so much of life. He lowered the paper, looked away. Sun split the leaves of the trees, blasted the asphalt with fierce white light.

'Christ... eighteen.'

What kind of an age was that? He knew exactly: it was the same age as his own daughter.

Chapter 8

Bec pushed open the doors of the Hotel Warrnambool.

It was 5 p.m. on a Friday and the place was already packed with the post-work crowd, suits and business frocks, the first beers and wines of the day, the babble of banter over the sounds of some acoustic Eighties-sounding balladry Bec couldn't identify coming through the speakers.

Clay had raced out of work a few minutes before her and had been adamant they meet up at The Warrny for a drink after work. He hadn't given her time to say no.

She scanned the crowd, but couldn't see him. This was the last place she wanted to be. It had been a long week and yesterday's death knock at the Collins' place had taken her last vestiges of vitality. She was not opposed to the idea of a drink, but she would much rather be doing it on the porch of her rented farmhouse on the edge of Koroit, far away from the bustle of a busy pub.

Bec weaved her way through the bar with practised ease. While her photographic skills had taken her around the world, she'd also done a bit of bar work here and there to help pay for the next plane ticket or the next week's rent. Working in pubs taught her many things, not least of which was the instinctive ability to find a path through a crowded room.

She made it to the bar and ordered. One wine, only *one* wine. See why Clay was so keen for her to be here. Then drive home. Maybe another glass of wine in the bath. Read a few more chapters of *The Dressmaker*. Fall asleep. Yeah, that sounded nice.

The barman, a round man with a jolly face and a cheery-looking white moustache, returned with a glass of the house red. It was enormous, probably the equivalent of two glasses in one. Aussie measures, she thought, they sure don't let you go home thirsty here.

Scanning the crowd once more, she spotted Clay. He was out in the smoking area, a partially undercover balcony at the rear of the pub, visible through two large glass doors. It looked a lot less crowded out there. Clay was by himself, sipping a pint of beer from one hand, a lit cigarette burning in the other.

'I didn't know you smoked,' she said as she reached him, sitting her glass of wine on the high table he was leaning on.

'There's probably a lot you don't know about me. Want one?'

'God, no. Only idiots smoke.'

'You got that right.' He hadn't even looked at her. His gaze was drawn to the bank of huge TV screens up on the wall, each one tuned to a different sport. He appeared to be watching the cricket and the fact he hadn't even glanced at her seemed rude.

'Did you invite me here to watch the cricket?' she said, unable to prevent the edge from creeping into her voice.

Clay sucked on his cigarette and turned away from the TV, meeting her eyes briefly before seeking out the ashtray. 'Sorry. I don't think I was even really watching that. I just kinda vagued out.'

Bec noticed the darkness under his eyes, the haunted look within them. 'Are you OK?'

He creased up his face, then let it settle back to a more familiar form. 'Yeah, I'm fine. Sorry. I invited you here because I thought you might want to meet someone. It's about the Collins girl. Ah, here he is.'

Before she could say anything, they were joined by a handsome man with short-cropped blonde hair. He looked to be in his early or mid-thirties and carried himself with a quiet strength to match the lightly muscled frame beneath his red polo shirt.

'Bec, this is Senior Constable Eddie Boulton. Eddie, this is Bec O'Connor from the paper.' Clay tipped the last of his pint down his throat. 'Now, about that beer I owe ya...'

'Yeah, a pint of something that's not crap would be great,' said Eddie.

'I'll be right back.'

Clay headed into the bar, leaving Eddie and Bec to share a little awkward smile.

'So—'

'How—'

The simultaneous attempt to start the conversation added to the uncoordinated feeling of the moment, like they'd just bumped heads trying to pick up the same dropped dollar.

'Sorry, you go,' said Bec.

'I was just going to ask how long you've been at the paper,' said Eddie.

'Two weeks. I only came to Australia about a month ago.'

'Your accent? Scottish?'

'Irish.'

'Beautiful country. What made you leave Ireland and come to Australia?'

'Oh, no, I haven't been in Ireland for a long time.' She froze for a second, assailed by the memory of her last visit. The funeral. The anger. Her mother, always her mother.

She sipped wine slowly as she gathered her thoughts. 'I was in South East Asia before coming here. Change of pace, and all that. How about yourself? What's your story?'

She listened in polite silence with the appropriate amount of nodding as Eddie gave a quick rundown of his career in the force, and was glad when Clay returned with two pints of beer – not because Eddie bored her, more that her reserves of small talk and polite chit-chat were running low and had been for some time. She was too used to being on her own. Still, Eddie seemed like a nice guy.

'Thanks for the beer.' Eddie nodded at Clay. 'I wasn't expecting you to come good on that.'

'Hey, I'm good on my word.'

'Right.'

'Plus, I wanted to pick your brain on something.'

'Here we go. Ulterior motive. What is it now, Clay? If it's about Gabby Petrie, I hear you're already handling that situation pretty well.'

Clay looked at his shoes in a manner Bec took to be embarrassment, before reaching for his cigarettes. He made what appeared to be a concerted effort to avoid her gaze. He was hiding something, so she called him on it.

'Who's Gabby Petrie?' she asked.

Clay sipped his beer and set it down, then lit his smoke, all in one deft move that seemed to be about keeping his mouth occupied. Eddie answered for him: 'She's a pretty little thing in the prosecution office. Word around the force is that Gabby and Mr Moloney here were seen out for dinner last night. And word is she spent the night at Clay's.' Eddie laughed a little at his friend's discomfort.

Bec's gaze filled up with a wide-eyed surprise. She felt a hint of disdain creeping into her expression, but she tried to hide it. She was looking at Clay, not Eddie. 'Really?'

'Good to see the constabulary are focused on the big issues.' Clay was still avoiding Bec's eyes. 'Anyway,' he said, sharpening his tone in an attempt to regain control of the conversation, 'I wanted to ask you about the Kerry Collins case.'

'Aww, jeez, Clay, come on, you know I'm not supposed to talk to you about that.'

'Eddie, it's OK. We're just a couple of old mates talking about work over a beer. No big deal.'

Eddie was looking around the smokers' balcony. It was a large area, with only a couple of dozen people in it, and Bec watched as the cop assessed each and every one of them in a split second. Comfortable there was no one around to cause him concern, he seemed to relax a little into his beer.

'What do you wanna know?'

Clay took a drag of his smoke. 'Is it being treated as a murder investigation?'

Eddie almost spat his sip of beer out at Clay's question. 'What? God, no. Why would it be? The preliminary autopsy report suggested it was an accident.'

'So how did she die?' said Clay.

'I'm pretty sure you saw the report. She drowned. Probably banged her head and then drowned.'

'The report didn't mention what she was doing prior to that.'

'The boys at the Warrnambool station are writing it off as a swimming accident. Death by misadventure.'

'She was last seen heading to work, waitressing at a private function, not heading to the beach.'

'What? She couldn't have taken a late night dip after work?'

'By herself?'

'Stranger things have happened, Clay.'

The reporter paused, turned the volume down a notch. 'I checked the weather reports. On the night she went missing, the temperature got down to six degrees. Not exactly swimming weather.'

'Maybe she was high.'

'Tox screen found nothing.'

'She was in the water for a week.'

'Fair enough.' Clay raised his drink, Eddie followed him. They looked at each other over their beers and Bec found herself oddly intrigued by the conversation's rally. What had she just seen here? Locals in banter or was it really heating up?

'Let's try this on for size, Eddie,' said Clay. 'Given we know it was cold, and given that most eighteen-year-old girls don't go night swimming by themselves, that leaves us with one missing puzzle piece that I can't shake.'

Eddie frowned. 'And what's that?'

'If she was swimming or on a boat or somewhere near the water, it seems more than likely she wasn't alone. An eighteen-year-old girl, in summer, near water – they're rarely by themselves, am I right?'

'Well...'

'Come on, Eddie, you work in Port Campbell. You worked in Warrnambool. When was the last time you saw a teenage girl at night by herself on the beach, or swimming alone, or on a boat by herself?'

He put down his pint, raised flat palms. 'OK, you got me.

Never.'

'So she was with someone. Which means that if it was an accident, someone would have reported it and got the search and rescue people in action. But they didn't. Someone was probably there with her when she died, and they didn't report it. Her folks called it in on a Tuesday and no one had seen her since Sunday. Doesn't that sound odd to you? Someone was with her and they didn't report it.'

Eddie didn't respond. He picked up his beer and looked up at the bank of TVs on the wall. Clay took another drag on his cigarette.

'Suicide.' Bec offered the word slowly, in a low voice.

'*What*?' said Clay.

'You're ignoring the possibility she may have killed herself. She could have thrown herself off a cliff and ended up in the water. That could explain the head trauma, too.'

Eddie nodded, returned his focus to the high table and leaned on his elbows. 'Look, suicide's the second most common cause of death among teenagers after car accidents. Hardly a day goes by that the Warrnambool station doesn't get a call about a troubled kid trying to top themselves.'

'No way she killed herself,' said Clay. 'Happy-go-lucky kid, loved by her family, popular, outgoing, confident...' Clay trailed off. Bec could see the wheels turning in his mind as he realised it was a possibility he could never rule out, no matter how gregarious and in control Kerry seemed to the world at large. Clay shook his head. 'No. I know it's possible, but I don't think it's plausible. I reckon there's foul play involved.'

'Forget it, Clay,' said Eddie. 'Anderson and his boys in CIU have closed the book on this one. There's no motive, no evidence, no witnesses, nothing says murder about this, aside from you and your guesswork.'

'Sorry, mate, but I don't buy it,' said Clay. 'How come no one knows where she was working on the night she disappeared?'

'Because maybe your Irish friend here is right. Maybe there was no function. Maybe it was just a way to get everyone off her tail so she could slip away quietly. I mean, who has a private function on a Sunday night?'

Bec surveyed both their faces. Eddie looked almost sad about being right, as if he felt sorry for shooting down Clay's theory. Clay appeared to be clenching his teeth, unwilling to accept defeat.

Eddie nodded to some people entering the smokers' area. 'Now, if you'll excuse me,' he said, 'I've got some colleagues to catch up with.' He smiled to Bec. 'Nice to meet you. And thanks for the beer, Clay.' Eddie drained his pint glass and wandered off to a raucous greeting on the other side of the balcony.

'Thanks for backing me up there, partner,' said Clay, his voice a low growl.

Bec was taken aback. The comment felt like a slapdown for something she didn't deserve. 'What the hell does that mean?' she said. 'Was I supposed to abandon logic and reason and shut my pretty mouth like a good girl? Or wave some pom-poms like I'm your bloody cheerleader?'

Clay's jaw relaxed and a wash of tiredness slid across his face. 'I'm sorry. You're right. You were just playing devil's advocate. All apologies.'

'It's not that your theory doesn't hold water, it's that there's nothing to back it up,' said Bec. 'I'm not saying you're wrong, but you need a bit of evidence.'

'That should be the police's job. Doesn't it bother you that the cops have already pulled the pin on this one?'

Bec weighed up the question as she returned to sipping her wine. 'I don't know how the police operate in this part of the world, but I can only assume they've done a thorough investigation.'

'Ha. Frank Anderson wouldn't know *thorough* if it bit his fat arse and kicked him in the tackle.'

'What a charming mental image.'

Clay relaxed enough to release a spontaneous smile; it was the first time he'd done so since Bec arrived at The Warrny.

'Sorry for being a dickhead,' he said. 'I didn't get much sleep last night.'

'Does that have anything to do with a girl named Gabby?'

Clay winced. 'Yes and no.'

He pulled out another cigarette and lit it. Bec assessed her glass of wine, which was already half gone.

'Well, thank you for the evening's entertainment,' said Bec, 'but if I finish this glass I shan't be able to drive home.'

'What? No! Sod that. Just get a cab. Or you can crash at my place. Your car will be safe in the car park.'

Bec eyed Clay but didn't detect anything untoward.

'Come on,' he said. 'Stay and have a drink with me. If you're going to be my partner you really should stay and have a drink with me.'

'Who said anything about being your bloody partner?'

'Whatever. But stay and have a drink or three with me. It's Friday night. It's been a rough week.'

Bec took a deep breath. 'All right. But you have to answer one question for me: did you really sleep with someone in exchange for an autopsy report?'

Clay grimaced and bit his lip all at the same time. 'It wasn't my intention. But, yeah, I guess I kinda did.'

Bec shook her head, laughing. 'You whore.'

Chapter 9

Bec awoke with a strange smell in her nostrils. What is that: weed? These aren't my bedclothes, it's not even my bed. Where the hell am I?

She wasn't worried. Twenty years of travel had led to her sleeping and waking in many strange places over the years. A bus stop in Barcelona. A beach in Thailand. A backyard in Berlin. A bathtub in Paris. She had grown less concerned about it. Clarity usually trickled in soon enough.

She was clothed. She was on a couch. A not-too-ratty blanket had been placed over her. A glass of water was on a nearby coffee table.

The previous night came racing home, but opening the door to it in her mind appeared to let the first tinglings of a hangover in, too. This was Clay's house. A couple of empty bottles of red sat on the coffee table next to the glass of water.

She grabbed the glass and skolled its contents. Snippets of conversation and flashbacks of the evening swam into focus in Bec's mind. Did I have a cigarette? Did I dance in Clay's lounge room to The Cure's 'In Between Days'? Did Clay tell me he had a daughter?

The mental image was there, clear, sharp, solid as a metal cube she could pick up and hold. Clay had gotten very serious at one point in the evening and talked about a daughter he'd never met. She'd be eighteen now, he'd said. Same age as Kerry Collins, he'd said, staring wistfully into nowhere. Bec had reached over to put a reassuring hand on Clay's knee and knocked a glass of wine flying. It had broken the spell of Clay's seriousness and he went back to making jokes and asking questions. Bec was thankful she hadn't reached his knee. God knows where that would have led.

'Morning. How's your head?'

Clay stood at the door holding two takeaway cups; the aroma leaking into the room spelled coffee. He looked unwashed and unshaven, his hair an unstyled bird's nest of sorts, but somehow he seemed fresh and lively. He was a poster boy for the day ahead, bursting with positivity. It was almost too much for Bec to take in.

'My head's starting to hate me. Yours?'

'Fine. I'm well-practised. Match-fit.'

'Right.' Bec took the coffee he offered and cradled it like a precious gem while she gathered the strength to stand.

'Good night, hey?' said Clay. 'That was fun. You're all right, O'Connor. I knew your partying days weren't over yet.'

'Thanks for the vote of confidence.' Her voice croaked, rattled in ways unfamiliar to her ears. 'Right now, I'm wishing those days were well behind me.'

They sipped their coffees in silence. Clay leaned on the wall, eyed the chair but seemed to have too much energy to stay still. He loped across the room and opened the blind. Drizzle speckled the window and a grey sky hung over Liebig Street like a dark shadow.

'First rain in two weeks,' said Clay, staring out into the drab summer's day.

'Last night... you said something about a daughter.'

Clay didn't turn around. 'Did I?'

'Didn't you?'

'Yeah, probably. I sometimes get a bit emo when I drink.' He tried to deflect the question and put a brake on the conversation, but with just a stare Bec told him she was having none of it. 'Mostly I'm a laugh riot, but I'm not averse to the odd deep-and-meaningful.'

'So it's true,' she said.

'It's true.'

'What happened?'

Clay turned to face her. He sighed as he spoke, 'You really want to hear this first thing on a Saturday morning?'

'It'll take my mind off my hangover.'

He sat down in an old leather armchair. It was so battered it might once have been worked over with a baseball bat; Bec sympathised with the armchair – her head spun as she sat up on the couch to face Clay properly. The room was cold, matching the look of the day outside. As she wrapped the blanket around her, Clay reached for a pack of smokes on the coffee table between them. He lit up before he began.

'Back when I was nineteen, I was living in Sydney. I met a girl, we fell in love, she got pregnant. Her parents were adamant that she keep it. They were of the God-fearing persuasion, so I tried to do the right thing and married her. In hindsight I'm not sure if it was the right thing, but nonetheless, we tied the knot in one of those registry office-type ceremonies. Seven minutes, no muss, no fuss.' He paused, sneering, 'Took longer to conceive the damned kid. Anyway, two months into the marriage and seven months into the pregnancy, she skipped out. We were living in a share house at the time. It was hell, but we couldn't afford any better. I was studying journalism at uni and she wasn't having the best of times with her pregnancy, so we were both living off government handouts. It was a bad time. I don't blame her for bailing.'

He inhaled his cigarette and blew a lazy smoke ring that wafted against the window like it was trying to escape.

'So, she took off,' he continued. 'I figured she'd go to her parents, so I rocked up there and talked to her dad, but he wasn't having a bar of it. Told me to beat it. Blamed me for ruining his daughter's life. I got angry and broke a window. He said he was going to call the cops, so I left. I then proceed to get blindingly, fall-down, off-your-face drunk for a week straight. I sobered up in between enough to go around to her parents' house. Sometimes I'd go around there while still smashed. It didn't make a difference. I went there in tears, I went there angry, I went there begging, I went there politely. Nothing changed. I never got to see her again.'

Clay inhaled once more and sat in silence for a minute as if trying to figure out how to tell the next part. Bec sensed the hurt he had been carrying around; it was still there, after all these years. Did that kind of pain ever go away? She'd borne her family's wounds for long enough, but that was different. Families were always with you, in the folds of your mind; you never escaped them because, in truth, they were a part of you. The irrits they gave you, they put them there.

'You know, I'm not sure if she was even there at her parents' place,' said Clay. 'I didn't see her there, and her parents never directly told me if she was or not. For all I know she was staying with friends, but for some reason that never entered my mind.

'I visited the in-laws' house every day for a month. On the last day, which I figure was only a couple of weeks before the baby was due, her dad hands me some divorce papers and tells me they're moving away. Won't say where. One more time, as nicely as possible, I tell him I still love his daughter and that I want to be a father to our child. "Please," I say to him. "Please let me see her." He just shoves the divorce papers in my face again and tells me to sign them. I don't know what else to do. So I give up. I sign them. And do you know what he says to me? "God have mercy on your soul." Then he closed the door and that was it. I got drunk again, for two days straight, and by the time I went back to the house they were gone. They'd moved. I didn't know how to find out where. Haven't seen her or her family since.

'A couple of months after that I bump into a mutual friend who tells me my ex-wife had a baby girl. No idea what the name was. But he said he was sure it was a girl and that she was living with her parents in Newcastle. I drove up there the next day and spent a couple of days driving around trying to find her. I went to the hospital, I checked the phone book, I asked around. Of course I didn't find them, it was like looking for a needle in the proverbial, but that was the last I heard – that she'd had a girl. I don't even know if it's true. But I feel like it is.'

Bec and Clay sat facing each other while he finished his cigarette, only the burn of dry paper and tobacco interrupting the silence.

'Have you tried finding her since?' said Bec.

'You mean through Facebook and Google and stuff like that? Sure. I mean, I'm pretty technologically inept, but I've tried. No dice.'

Another awkward silence opened up, loomed above the room like the threat of more heartbreak to come, but this time it was cut short by a knock at the door. The shrill sound of crying hinges was followed by a female voice calling, 'Yoo-hoo. Anyone home?'

Gabby Petrie appeared in the door of the lounge room carrying two takeaway cups of coffee. Her eyes blackened when she looked at Bec, wrapped in a blanket on the couch. 'Who are you?' She spat the words.

'Hey, Gabby,' said Clay, rising from the armchair and turning to face her. 'This is Bec, my friend from work. Bec, this is—'

'Did she sleep here last night?'

'Yeah, but—'

With one quick movement, Gabby strode towards Clay and swung one of the cups of coffee like she was pitching a softball. Clay wore it like a bad first attempt at action painting.

In another swift manoeuvre, Gabby pirouetted on her ballet flats, her black skirt spinning up with a dainty flash, and she was gone. The slamming of the door shook through the apartment, followed by the dull thud of footsteps stomping down the back steps.

Bec was stunned. Clay, for some reason, didn't look totally surprised. He licked coffee as it dripped from his top lip. 'I think that autopsy report's costing me a lot more than I anticipated.'

'Cookies. Dinner. And now a T-shirt…'

Bec was racked by uncontrollable laughter as Clay sifted the sugar and brown liquid from his stubble.

Chapter 10

Radio had the story first, which annoyed Clay no end.

'Warrnambool-based company Fullerton Industries has won the contract to undertake the one hundred million dollar upgrade of the Warrnambool Airport,' said the newsreader. It was the 10 a.m. bulletin but the newsreader had already been heralding the item as an exclusive since 7 a.m. Clay had missed the boat – or plane, as it was in this instance – completely.

'Member for Warrnambool Wayne Swanson announced the tender this morning during our breakfast programme.'

The broadcast switched to a voice grab from Swanson, who sounded like someone who was weary trying to play upbeat. Clay groaned inwardly as the MP mentioned jobs, benefits, and the phrase *moving forward* on three separate occasions before praising Lachlan Fullerton for *putting Warrnambool on the map*.

Clay found the newsreader's voice grated as he pointed out, in an annoyingly cheery tone, that a date was yet to be set for works to begin, before moving on to the next item – a dead whale had washed up at Levys Beach.

'Amateurs,' said Clay, slapping the off button on the car radio.

'Amateurs?' said Bec. She was in the driver's seat of the office Subaru, bound for Port Fairy. They were off to track down Swanson for an interview; Clay knew he was now playing catch-up, but his piece would at least be professional and ask the right questions. They'd also been told to grab some cheesy photos of holidaymakers for another space-filler story, which Clay was expected to write up as well, and he resented this as more punishment from the editor.

'Of course they're amateurs. There was no mention of the fact Fullerton and Swanson are already being investigated for the Gold Coast hospital deal. It's just lazy journalism. They were too busy gloating about the scoop to do any real reporting.'

'I don't get it,' said Bec. 'If Fullerton and Swanson are already being investigated for one deal, why would Swanson award Fullerton another? That doesn't make sense.'

'It's either a stroke of genius or the dumbest thing I've ever heard of. But I can't tell which.'

'Explain.'

'Well, Swanson giving Fullerton the Warrnambool Airport deal could be Swanson's way of saying "I've got nothing to fear – here, look, I'm so unfazed by your puny investigation I'm going to give Fullerton another contract, right in front of your face." If everything's legit, he's got nothing to worry about and it's business as usual.'

'Or...?'

'Or Swanson is so bloody-minded and pig-ignorant that he thinks he's bulletproof and he can keep throwing dodgy deals around because he reckons he'll never get caught. Like I said – stroke of genius or the dumbest thing ever.'

'So which do you think it is?' said Bec.

Clay stared out the window at the farmland. Irrigators dotted the paddocks, working overtime in the heat to try and keep the potato crops from failing. He ran his hands through his dark hair again, grabbing clumps in his fists to show his frustration. 'I really don't know,' he said. 'I usually have a gut instinct on this kind of stuff, but this is such an abnormal political situation. It's the middle of summer; Parliament's not even sitting at the moment. The news cycle is so slow that releasing the contract winner at this time of the year is like making an announcement from every rooftop and every town corner. You can't hide this. That's why we're doing some stupid story about holidaymakers, there's nothing else happening. Swanson's made himself a target with this announcement, so he must have a bloody good reason.'

They found Swanson where his PA had said he'd be – touring an abalone farm just outside Port Fairy. He was ostensibly on holiday, but had tipped off the media to a full day of visits in the small seaside town. Clay suspected the politician was suffering withdrawals after a short period of not being in front of a camera or a microphone.

'Clay, good to see you again,' said Swanson. They were in the car park outside the processing plant, where the unmistakeable seafood smell seemed to cancel out all other senses. Clay was barely aware of the too-firm handshake again or the rising heat. It was going to be another day above thirty degrees. Swanson was sweating in heavy patches, and looked a touch more wan than he had two weeks before.

'How's the holiday going, Wayne?' said Clay.

'Good, good. Always a good time when I'm in Port Fairy.' He turned on the smarm. 'And I see you've brought your Irish friend with you again.'

Bec offered a polite smile. 'Bec O'Connor, nice to see you again, sir,' she said.

'Please, call me Wayne. Now, what do you want to talk about, Clay? Something tells me it's not abalone farms.'

There were no other media outlets around. The metro papers were three hours away and either hadn't arrived in the region yet or weren't coming. Maybe I'm reading this whole thing wrong, thought Clay. Maybe I've been so focused on Kerry Collins it's thrown my news sense out of whack.

'No, Wayne, I want to talk about the Warrnambool Airport deal.'

'Of course you do. Well, go on, fire away.'

'The integrity of the Fullerton Gold Coast deal is being investigated and you've just gone and given Fullerton another deal. Some people are questioning the timing of today's announcement.' 'Some people' being me, he thought.

'So what does that tell you, Clay?'

'To be perfectly honest, it tells me you're either a man of honour or a bloody idiot.'

Swanson didn't appear stunned so much as wary, raising an eyebrow on his moist brow. Clay watched him dab his forehead with a handkerchief, which looked like the equivalent of bailing out a boat with a thimble. 'And which one do you think I am?'

'Not my place to say, Wayne. And time will tell, I guess.'

Swanson eased back his shoulders, straightened his spine. 'I have full confidence in the due processes involved in both these tender selections and I have no doubt that confidence will be vindicated. As I have nothing to fear in these matters and I am certain due process has been done, it seemed prudent that, moving forward...'

Clay felt the life draining from him; the man was a walking media release. He spouted platitudes like a fairground fortune teller and you didn't even need to drop a buck.

'I can guess the rest,' said Clay.

'Let me finish... *moving forward*, we could get the ball rolling on this deal to ensure the future growth of the region, benefitting the region and its constituents with jobs, infrastructure, tourism, and other economic benefits.'

Clay held up his notepad to show he hadn't written down any of Swanson's prepared lines. 'Some people are questioning the need for this airport revamp in the first place, Wayne. Warrnambool is a city of thirty-five thousand and no one has been crying out for more planes to land here. They want better roads and better trains. Some people are suggesting this is a waste of money.'

'These people, these *some people*,' hissed Swanson, 'aren't visionaries. They're stuck in a cycle of whingeing and aren't thinking about the future.'

'Are you saying you're a visionary?'

'What I'm saying, *Moloney*, is it takes bold action and big ideas to grow the future.'

'Some people are saying this isn't so much a big idea as a big boost to your mate Lachlan Fullerton's bank balance.'

That one hit home, and Clay knew it. Swanson took a step forward, which would have been menacing if he hadn't been half a head shorter than Clay. In the periphery of his vision the journalist could see Swanson's minders, who had been hiding in the shade next to the minister's car, but now started to move in to find out what the hell was going on.

'I thought you were one of the good guys, Clay.'

'I'm doing my job, Wayne. That makes me one of the good guys. And either way you look at this airport deal, it takes balls the size of watermelons to make the announcement you did today. That tends to worry people. That means journos need to ask questions. Are you going to be able to handle all the questions? Because the big question is, "How did your mate just get a hundred million dollar contract for an unnecessary project?" And I don't think you can keep answering that one again and again without looking like a moron.'

If Clay didn't know better, he could have sworn the politician's sweat glands had just burst open – the damp spots on his shirt were spreading. His breathing was up, too; he panted like a farm dog as he leaned in further, one skyward-pointing finger signalling he didn't intend to take any more crap.

'Listen here, Moloney – and this is off the record – but I'm not a moron. And I can take it, whatever peanuts you in the press gallery throw at me, I can take it. But you might want to be careful. There aren't many truly powerful people in the south-west of Victoria, but you're starting to piss a couple of them off. So just keep that in mind.'

'Are you threatening me?'

'Of course not. Don't be ridiculous.' He let out a piranha smirk; it looked practised, if not well-used. 'I'm trying to help you.' Swanson's minders were at his side, and he took that as his cue to leave. 'See ya, Clay, can't wait to see the story in tomorrow's paper.'

'What the hell was all that about?' said Bec as they trudged back to the Subaru.

Clay watched as Swanson's car spun up a cloud of dry red dust as it left the abalone farm's car park. 'I was trying to rattle him. I wanted to see what happened if I pushed him a little bit. The daft bastard's had it too easy from us for too long. Something's not right here.'

'You said before that the airport deal could be either a stroke of genius or the dumbest thing ever. I take it you're siding with the latter now. Do you smell a rat?'

'A fat one. Let's face it, given the choice between an honest politician or a dumb politician, it's pretty obvious which one is more common.'

'So what do we do?'

'Let's go and pay Lachlan Fullerton a visit.'

'Clay, we've got holidaymakers to interview. Tudor said—'

'I think this is a bit more important, don't you, Bec? Come on, I'll show you how the other half lives down here.'

Chapter 11

No bad houses overlooked Port Fairy's East Beach.

Even the lesser ones, the old fishermen's shacks given a lick of paint, a modern kitchen and an indoor toilet, were worth close to a million dollars. It was all about the view. To the far right was the lighthouse, and everything to the left of that was open water and a semi-circle of beach. On a clear day, you could see all the way across the bay to Warrnambool, and off to the left the long extinct volcano-turned-nature reserve known as Tower Hill. The real beauty of the East Beach properties was no one could ever build there again – all the houses along the three-kilometre stretch were built before the environmentalists got involved and started forbidding such things as erecting McMansions on sand dunes.

Lachlan Fullerton's house did not look like a renovated fisherman's shack. It was a three-storey monstrosity on a block that reached from the top of the dune and down towards the Moyne River on the other side. The bottom-level three-bay garage was practically carved into the sand dune, and on the top level was a huge outdoor undercover decking to maximise the house's party potential and the prodigious view. From the outside, everything looked expensive – lots of glass and brass. Even the door appeared pricey, probably made out of some centuries-old tree cut from a Tasmanian heritage-listed wilderness area, thought Clay as he rapped on it.

'What are the odds he's actually home?' said Bec.

'He's home,' said Clay. 'He's got houses all over the country that I couldn't account for, but when he's here, I know.'

'How?'

'Even billionaires have to book a round at Port Fairy Golf Club. I checked with a friendly receptionist before we left.'

As if on cue, the door opened and there stood the CEO of

Fullerton Industries. Clay gauged him to be about forty. He was a little shorter than Clay, but with a better tan, whiter teeth, and swept-back black hair that was beginning to recede at the temples, where it seemed to have been dyed to hide the creeping grey. Fullerton looked fit and was dressed for the golf course.

Clay introduced himself and Bec, half expecting the door to be closed in his face. Instead, Lachlan Fullerton invited them in with a wave of his hand.

The exterior's impression of wealth was not merely a façade; inside looked like a shot from *Lifestyles of the Rich and Famous*. Clay and Bec were asked to sit on one of two large white leather couches in a vast open-living area, with a sunken lounge and a mezzanine overhead. The room wasn't high enough to get the sea views, that was reserved for the top floor, so the windows opened out the other way, across the river and the wharf. The main draw was a life-sized statue of Athena in white marble and gold filigree detailing that dominated the floor space, drawing attention from all around. The paintings on the walls tried to compete but failed, even though they were instantly familiar as the works of well-known Australian artists: a John Brack, a Brett Whiteley, a Sidney Nolan, a Ben Quilty.

'You're doing a story for the paper about the airport deal, right?' asked Fullerton as they sat. Despite being born and raised in Warrnambool, he spoke with the more formal accent of a Sydneysider, Clay noticed.

'That's right. We've just been talking to Wayne Swanson.'

'Good man, Swanson. What did he have to say for himself?'

'Well, he was, ah, a little annoyed by my line of questioning.'

'Let me guess – deals for mates, why spend so much on an airport in Warrnambool, Gold Coast hospital, blah, blah, blah, et cetera, et cetera?'

'Something like that.'

Fullerton perched himself on the arm of the opposite couch and a small paunch revealed itself above his belt. 'And now you're here to ask me the same questions, no doubt.'

'Well…'

'Tell me, Mr... Moloney, wasn't it? Tell me, Mr Moloney, what would you like me to say? Because I'm going to tell you the same thing Mr Swanson told you – that everything is above board, that this is a good investment for the region, and that I fear no investigation, into either this deal or the Gold Coast one. So unless you have something else to ask, I'm afraid we're only wasting each other's time.'

Clay looked at Fullerton and then let his gaze wander around the room. The sound of the sea rolling onto East Beach could be heard, punctuated by the cries of seagulls. It wasn't a bad spot to soak up your days.

'It's a hell of a place you've got here, Mr Fullerton,' said Clay. 'How often do you get back to south-west Victoria?'

'If I could, I'd get back here every weekend, but alas, it's more like once a month.'

'Did you grow up in Port Fairy or Warrnambool?'

'Warrnambool, but every school holiday was spent here. This was the site of my grandfather's home-away-from-home – his fishing hut, he called it. We tore it down after he died and built this. Indoor plumbing's a hell of a thing.' Fullerton offered a relaxed smile but Clay was starting to dislike him more by the second – the stench of wealth was getting up his nose. 'I loved spending time here as a kid. We'd go fishing every day, either on the river or out at sea if it was calm enough to take granddad's tinny out on the bay. Of course, nowadays, I have a slightly better boat than an old tinny.'

'Probably a couple of boats, I'd wager.' Clay kept his tone even, disguising his disgust.

'Four, actually. One here, one in Warrnambool, one in Sydney, one on the Gold Coast.'

'And a couple of houses?'

'Four or five, yes.'

'And a couple of planes?'

'Ha, no, just one of those. You only ever need one plane, Mr Moloney. Anything more is excessive.'

Clay didn't think Fullerton had a proper grasp of the

concept of excess. He could see that enough was never going to be enough for this man. He worshipped wealth, wore the robes of a religion that was a mystery to the uninitiated. 'And you're not an excessive man.'

'I'm a practical man, Mr Moloney. That's how people like me make their fortunes. By being practical. By assessing situations and deals and working out the practicalities for both parties.'

'I'm sure it doesn't hurt to have friends in high places.'

'It never hurts to have friends, whether they be in high places or low.'

The two men sat staring at each other; opposite ends of a class divide that was continually widening. Fullerton's face showed nothing but measured patience, and it infuriated Clay even more. This guy is a rich, smug bastard, he thought, with his own private fleet and his four or five houses. Take that away and he's nothing, the same as everyone else. Clay was sure Fullerton would die – or kill – before he let that happen, though.

'You obviously have a good eye,' said Clay.

'A good eye?'

'Well, the art on your wall, for one. And the design of this house. The furniture in it. Everything looks amazing. It looks a million dollars. You obviously give some thought to the way things look.'

Fullerton nodded. 'I suppose so. Doesn't everyone?'

'True. So how do you think this airport deal looks? From the outside, I mean.'

'I don't follow...'

'You're being investigated over the Gold Coast hospital deal. There's nothing to be gained by Swanson giving you the Warrnambool Airport deal right now. There's no political imperative, no desperate need for the infrastructure, and it will attract the kind of attention the Right Honourable Member for Warrnambool doesn't really need at the moment. So how do you think that looks... from the outside?'

Clay thought he saw Fullerton's mask of serenity flicker, revealing a layer of something else beneath. Annoyance? Contempt? Hate? But it was a nanosecond. To the untrained eye, Fullerton was calmer than a Buddhist temple on meditation day.

'From the *outside*, Mr Moloney, it looks to me like a lot of jobs, a lot of tourists, and a lot of benefits for south-west Victoria. How does it look to you?'

Clay attempted to return Fullerton's beatific smile. 'How did you put it before? Deals for mates? Yeah, that's it. But your point about practicalities was interesting, especially about making deals work for both parties. I see how this works for you, but not Swanson. And that makes me suspicious. Forgive me, but I trust politicians about as far as I can kick them, and I haven't played footy since I was in high school.'

'As a member of the fourth estate, I would expect nothing less.' Fullerton stood. 'I have enjoyed our little chat, but I'm afraid you're making me late for eighteen holes at the Port Fairy Golf Club.'

Bec and Clay rose and walked to the door. 'Thank you for your time, Mr Fullerton,' said Clay. 'I'm sure you'll read tomorrow's paper with interest.'

'Well, I didn't see you use your notepad once, so I sure hope you quote me correctly.' Fullerton ushered them outside. 'Thanks for dropping by. Feel free to do so any time.'

The door closed before Clay or Bec could say anything more and they trudged back to the car.

'That went well,' said Bec.

'You were quiet in there.'

'You were doing fine all by yourself. Besides, I'm the photographer, you're the reporter.'

'I didn't see you taking any photos.'

'What did you want? A *Cribs* shoot?'

'I'd settle for a smoking gun.'

'Did you really expect to just ask the right question and he'd blurt out a confession? "You've got me, I admit it! I'm giving

Swanson brown paper bags full of kickbacks every week."'

'No. I just wanted to see the look on the smug bastard's face so I can remember it when I take him down.'

Chapter 12

'What do you mean, you didn't interview any holidaymakers?'

Deputy editor Terry Kenna was angry. He was 'step into my office and close the door' angry, although Clay was uncertain as to why he was getting berated by Kenna and not the editor. Tudor must have been in one of his seemingly endless meetings.

'I mean we didn't interview any holidaymakers, Terry. Not sure how I can spell that one out any clearer.'

'Don't be a smart-arse with me, Moloney. Why?'

'Why what? Why shouldn't I be a smart-arse?'

'No, bloody hell, why didn't you interview any holidaymakers?'

'There's a multitude of reasons, Terry, some complex, some straightforward... I'm not sure you'll be able to grasp it all, but I can bring in one of the whiteboards if it will help.'

Clay loved winding up Terry Kenna. If winding up Terry Kenna was an Olympic sport, Clay fancied himself for the gold. They'd both been at the paper for about the same amount of time but had taken very different paths. Clay had been a good reporter with a nose for hard news, but masked his growing disinterest and cynicism with snide humour and a deprecating wit. Kenna was a below-average sports reporter who had risen through the ranks to deputy editor largely through brown-nosing and the fact that no one else wanted the gig.

'Don't be a smart-arse, Moloney. You were sent to Port Fairy to interview Swanson about the airport deal, then head to one of the caravan parks and get us a nice page-three pic story about some wankers from Queensland who've come down to sip lattes on East Beach, or some such crap.'

'We did the airport story. It took longer than expected. We went to Lachlan Fullerton's house. Didn't leave time for latte-sippers. Bec had other jobs to get to back in Warrnambool. So we hit the road.'

'Now I've got no page-three pic story. And as much as I'd love to chuck a page-three girl on there, that kind of thing is frowned upon. So for all intensive purposes, we're screwed.'

Intensive purposes. Hearing that from a fellow journo made Clay's blood pressure spike; he promptly felt justified in not only ditching the story, but being unapologetic about it to Terry Kenna, too. The solution was simple enough, but Kenna didn't have the gumption to figure it out for himself. How did this man climb the steps to the office every morning?

'We're not screwed, stop being melodramatic, you idiot. Just get one of the photogs to go take a weather shot, maybe get some holidaymakers down at the Warrnambool beach. Hell, you might even get a bikini shot out of it.'

Terry seemed to take to the idea. Nothing like the mention of bikinis to distract him, thought Clay. It was the journalistic equivalent of raising a ball for a dog and bouncing it off the wall; if that didn't grab the required attention, nothing would. He watched the deputy editor for a bit as Terry sat there with a dumb grin on his face. It faded after a time and Terry leant forward, trying to adopt a more serious look. He tapped the eraser-end of a yellow pencil on the desk as he spoke. 'I don't mean to break your balls, Clay. I mean, we're mates, after all. I just happen to be deputy editor.' Clay resisted the urge to roll his eyes. He didn't consider Terry a mate. He was a workmate, nothing more. A sexist, a casual racist, and a meathead who happened to outrank him, if only by default, but not a mate. Terry's idea of mateship was tied up with ape-like chanting at the footy match or shooting roos at dusk.

'But I feel like I should warn you,' said Terry. 'As a mate.'

'Warn me?'

'Not official like. Not an official warning or anything. I mean, I feel I should give you a heads up. As a mate.'

'Spit it out, for Chrissake, Terry.'

'Tudor's got it in for ya. And skipping out on jobs like you did today, well, that's the kinda thing he's looking out for. The bosses in Sydney say we're overstaffed, so they're squeezing Tudor's balls, and he's gunna have to squeeze someone else's balls in return.'

Clay couldn't restrain a laugh at Terry's vivid imagery, but Terry waved him down with the utmost sincerity.

'This is serious, Clay. Tudor wants to axe someone, and you're the chook that's first in line for the chopping block.'

'Terry, we're the only two people in the office that have been here longer than two minutes. He's not going to sack me.'

'Don't be so sure, mate. Us old-timers, we get paid more. Sacking you puts a bit more cash back into the bottom line. Hell, they could sack you, hire that cadet with the nice tits that couldn't spell "Canberra", and still turn a profit on the whole thing.'

'I don't believe it.'

'It's fair dinkum, Clay. Your arse is over a barrel, and Tudor is just waiting for a cock-up.'

Clay was impressed by the Carry On-style double entendre until he realised Terry was completely oblivious he'd even done it. 'Thanks for the rather vivid advice, Terry,' said Clay.

'You're welcome,' said Terry, still failing to twig.

Bec had noticed Clay skulking around the photographers' desks for the last ten minutes, obviously waiting for something. It turned out he was waiting for the other photographer to leave so he could have a quiet word with her. He zipped over, swerved excitedly between the desks and started to rub his hands together.

'Fancy a knock-off drink, Bec?'

'Clay, it's Monday,' she said. 'Can't you lay off the booze for one day?'

'I said "*a* drink". Not "let's get shit-faced". Although you're more than welcome to sleep on my couch again.' A roguish grin appeared on Clay's face.

'Spare me. Took me two days to recover from that last time.'

'Ha. Look, I promise you'll be able to drive home after this.

Plus, I kind of need you to drive me to where we're going for a drink.'

Suddenly the image he was painting altered.

'Where are we going for a drink?'

'I'll tell you when we get in the car.'

Bec smiled and caught herself. Clay was the kind of guy you had to watch, she told herself. Charm usually hid something; plus, it never lasted. She'd moved to south-west Victoria for a less complicated life, and a man like Clay inevitably complicated things. Even when he wasn't trying to.

'All right, fine,' said Bec. 'Let me finish up and log off and I'll meet you in the car park.'

Clay was leaning against her car, a beat-up red Mazda from the Nineties, when she got out to the car park. 'This your wheels?' he asked.

'How did you know?'

He looked around, waved a hand in desultory fashion. 'This one seemed like your car. Sturdy, reliable, probably had a bit of zip back in its day, bit rough around the edges now but still kinda cute.'

'I have no idea how to take that. I think I'm insulted.'

'That was a compliment.'

'Really? Take a mental note, hotshot – never liken a woman to a car. And especially never use the word "sturdy" when describing a woman.'

'I wasn't describing a woman. I was talking about your car.'

'Just get in.'

The Mazda started with the slightest of coughs – it obviously wasn't as fresh as it used to be – but worked steadily through the gears.

Clay refused to tell Bec their destination, instead directing her eastwards along the highway that ran through the middle of Warrnambool. Between the two dual carriageways, massive ancient-looking Norfolk pines lined the median strip, their long rod-like needles banking up in the gutters.

They turned between the trees when they reached the old

Fletcher Jones factory and its expansive gardens, crossing the highway and heading into an ordinary-looking neighbourhood. The factory was long closed and had become a second-hand market, but its beautiful gardens were still a local focal point. Families had laid out picnic blankets on the well-kept lawns and children chased each other in the late afternoon sun. A group of twenty-somethings had set up a game of croquet at one end of the garden. At the other end, a mother and daughter fed ducks in a pond. Bec was intrigued by the giant silver ball standing on three huge red legs some fifty metres in the air, towering over the scene.

'A *War of the Worlds* leftover,' said Clay.

'A what?'

'I'm kidding. It's the old water storage for the factory's sprinkler system.'

'They never took it away?'

'Built to last, I guess. Bit of a Warrnambool icon now. God forbid anyone ever tries to pull it down – the locals would go ballistic.'

Past the gardens and they were into a hodgepodge suburbia. None of the houses looked the same and every front yard had a different expression. Kids gathered with their bicycles outside a milk bar. Old men in terry towel hats watered their gardens. Mums in Activewear jogged along with all-terrain prams.

Bec was enamoured with the scene. As she directed her car along the residential street she found herself feeling a warm familial sensation that she'd experienced only a handful of times over the past two decades. It was a sense of belonging, of relaxing into a place and succumbing to its charms.

They drove on, under a rail bridge dotted with graffiti, past a carefully maintained cemetery and on towards the river. As they pulled into a car park near a timber building with a red tin roof, Bec gazed across the dark blue waters of the Hopkins River. Beyond the slow-moving current, large expensive-looking houses gazed out across the vista from atop a short limestone cliff.

They parked and Bec followed Clay into the timber building past a sign marked Proudfoots Boathouse.

'Looks nice here,' said Bec.

'Break your arm for a table on the weekend.'

Winding their way down some stairs to only a metre or so above water level, she found herself in a cosy little room with a bar on one side and tables set up for dinner service. A sheltered deck ran around the outside of the building, where dozens of people sat at small tables, drinking and laughing in the afternoon sun.

Clay snagged the last available table and lit a cigarette as he sat, gesturing for Bec to take the seat opposite him, which had the best views of the river. She marvelled at the scenery as she gazed up the water. A cruise boat sat next to a pier further along, while several small tinnies held docile fishermen in the centre of the calm blue waterway. The scene was peaceful.

'This is magnificent,' she said.

Clay exhaled. 'Yeah, it's not bad.' It was typical Australian understatement.

A waiter approached and Bec judged him to be of Middle Eastern extraction. One thing she'd noticed about Warrnambool was a distinct lack of ethnic diversity, which made the handsome dark-haired waiter stand out to her.

'Clay. What's happening, bro?' said the waiter, shaking hands with the journo as soon as he was within reach.

'Not much, JT. JT, this is Bec. She works with me.'

'Nice to meet you, Bec.' JT shook her hand too. 'What can I get yas?' His voice gave no hint of accent other than the drawling Australian one common in Warrnambool.

They both ordered beers and JT sauntered off to get them.

'Where in the Middle East is he from?' said Bec once JT had left.

'Who? JT?' Clay proceeded to laugh. 'He's from Geelong.'

'No, I mean what's his heritage?'

'Welsh.'

'Really?'

Clay continued to laugh. 'Yeah. He gets the Middle Eastern thing a lot. It's great – he goes into bars and gets people to guess his heritage. Bets they can't get it in ten guesses. If they can't, they buy him a beer. No one ever guesses Wales. He gets a lot of free beers. It's always funny to watch.'

Clay finished off his cigarette and Bec looked past him out across the water.

'I appreciate you bringing me here,' said Bec. 'I mean, this view is something else. But I can't help but feel you didn't have me drive you here so I could admire the river.'

Before Clay could answer, JT returned with the beers.

'You got a sec?' said Clay to the waiter.

'Sure, man,' said JT. 'What's up?' Bec watched as JT looked around at the other two waiters to see they weren't being run off their feet before pulling up a spare seat.

'Did you know that girl, Kerry Collins?' asked Clay.

'The one that washed up at the Bay of Martyrs? Not real well, but yeah. That was real sad.'

'Had she been working here long?'

'Six months, eight months, maybe. Got the hang of it real quick. Smart kid.'

'What was she like?'

'She was a real sweetie. Got along with everyone here. Seemed to have a lot of friends. She'd just finished school and was keen for a lot of shifts over summer. Things have been a little bit hectic here since she died. We had to cover her shifts, plus it hit a few of the other girls here pretty hard and they took some time off, too.'

'So she was close to some of the other girls?'

'Oh, yeah, for sure.'

'Did any of them know where she was working the night she went missing? We heard she was supposed to be working at a private function.'

'I dunno. I could ask them for ya.'

'That would be great, JT. Sorry to be a pain. I'm sure they've already had to go through all this with the cops.'

'What? Nah, man. The cops just talked to the boss. They didn't interview the staff or nothing.' JT rose and pushed his chair back in. 'I better get back to work, but I'll keep you posted. I'll text ya.' With that he headed off across the deck.

Bec gazed at Clay and sipped her beer. 'I can practically see the cogs in your mind turning, Clay,' she said.

He lit another cigarette. 'The cops didn't even interview her co-workers. What does that tell you?'

'They did a bad job?'

'Maybe. The cynic in me says they didn't want to dig too hard, for some reason.'

'Oh, come on,' said Bec, exasperation creeping into her voice. 'Please don't tell me you're seeing a conspiracy here. I don't want to be the Scully to your Mulder. I mean, it's Warrnambool, for Chrissake. We're in the middle of rural, quiet, country Australia. Look at this place. This is not the city. This is a sleepy town, not some hotbed of dodgy deals. Don't you think it's more likely the cops were just lazy or over-worked rather than up to their eyeballs in a cover-up?'

'Let's wait and see what Kerry's co-workers say and we might have an answer to that question.'

Chapter 13

Ordinarily Clay had no time for blues music.

At home in his little apartment, he was likely to listen to the classics of his teenage years. Nirvana. Soundgarden. Pearl Jam. Blur. Radiohead. Lately he'd been revisiting his Aussie favourites. You Am I. Custard. Regurgitator. Spiderbait. But there was not a single blues CD in his collection.

Despite this, Clay was at The Loft, listening to a blues band. The sound of the music had wafted across the street and into his lounge room window, beckoning him out into the night. 'Wouldn't you rather be out, lost in a crowd,' the music seemed to ask, 'rather than stuck in your apartment, not sleeping, yet again?'

It was an invitation he couldn't pass up and his Thursday night was improving because of it. The Loft was a small upstairs music venue furnished in polished timber, stark metal, and rock'n'roll memorabilia. The place was buzzing to the sounds of the local musicians churning through a list of blues standards. The crowd was enthusiastic and joyful, grateful for the weekend warm-up. The beer was also flowing, which helped Clay let go of some of the anger he had for Fullerton's arrogance and the police inaction that JT had pointed out in Proudfoots. Nothing was going to wash away the growing sense of injustice he carried in him, though. A young girl had died, and nobody seemed to care; least of all those who should care the most.

A song came to a clamorous end and punters cheered. Clay took the opportunity of a break in the music to head downstairs and onto the street for a smoke. There were plenty of familiar faces puffing on their rollies and tailories, standing in small groups a short distance from the doorway. Usually he would have joined them, but tonight he moved beyond the fringe and leaned on the doorway of a neighbouring restaurant with a closed sign hanging in the window. Away from the music and buzz of the bar, Clay felt tired all over again. A sleepless night here and there had started to roll into an insomniac streak. His muscles ached, a dull and heavy listlessness that felt far worse than any exercise-induced fatigue.

The low notes of the next song crept out the door of The Loft and into the warm night air, mingling with the din of conversation, and Clay closed his eyes for a minute as he exhaled his cigarette smoke. There, in the darkness of his eyelids, he could see Kerry Collins' face again, at once real and living as it had been in the portraits on the walls of her family home. At the same time, it was also the face he'd seen tangled in the decaying seaweed at the Bay of Martyrs.

Clay opened his eyes again, grabbed a deep gulp of air. He was startled to see Senior Constable Eddie Boulton standing before him, dressed in a gaudy Hawaiian shirt that was louder than the blues band inside.

'Catching up on your beauty sleep, Clay?' said the cop.

'Yeah, it's not working... Does Weird Al know you can access his wardrobe?'

'Ha. Good one. And you're right, the beauty sleep isn't working.' Eddie laughed and gestured to a man standing next to him; he had short brown hair and the tanned complexion of those who work outdoors. 'This is Dave, a mate of mine. Used to go to school together. Dave, this is Clay. He works at the paper, but don't hold that against him.'

Clay ignored the jibe and shook Dave's hand. 'Pleased to meet you. You still live around here?'

'Nah, just down visiting the folks with the missus,' said Dave. 'Although you never know, I might have to move back in with my parents the way things are going.' He gave Eddie a knowing look.

'Why's that?' said Clay.

'I just lost my job. Got the arse. Pack of wankers.'

'Bummer. What happened?'

'I was working on construction up on the Gold Coast. Was

good coin, especially 'cos I'd made it to foreman, so there was a bit of responsibility and a bit of extra money.'

Clay sipped his beer. 'How did you get sacked, if you don't mind me asking?'

'Because I was working for a pack of dodgy bastards. Fullerton Industries can go and eat a bag of dicks, if you ask me.'

The mention of Lachlan Fullerton's company grabbed Clay's attention. 'Dodgy, how?'

Eddie laughed, leaned in. 'Careful, Dave, you'll see this in print tomorrow.'

Clay gave Eddie a glare. 'Off the record, of course.' He waved his lit cigarette around, taking in the night with his gesture. 'Do I look like I'm on duty?'

'Hard to tell with you,' said Eddie.

'What do I care?' said Dave. 'I'm happy to tell whoever's listening about what a bunch of lying mongrels they are.'

'Is this to do with the Gold Coast hospital deal?' said Clay.

'Nah, that's only in the early stages just now. But I did a bunch of other big jobs for them, they've no shortage of them up around there. My face didn't fit, though, I've never been able to keep my trap shut and they don't like answering too many questions from the workforce.' Dave gestured to Clay's cigarette pack. 'You mind if I bum one of those?'

'Sure, go ahead.'

Dave took a cigarette and lit it before continuing. He seemed to find some release in slagging off his former employers. 'See, when I started with 'em ten year ago down here, everything was sound. Good company to work for. Then they start bringing in overseas workers on those 457 visas. Supposed to be for skilled workers, but Fullerton's just bringing in a bunch of young Chinese fellas who don't know a hammer from a hard hat. Pays 'em peanuts and slowly kicks all the local construction workers off the job – once they've trained up the Chinese fellas, of course, who can't speak a word of English, mind you.'

'Surely the union would have something to say about that, wouldn't they?' said Clay.

He almost spat at the suggestion. 'Yeah, you'd bloody think so, wouldn't you. The union blokes are turning up less and less at the Fullerton sites. A few guys I know who worked for a bunch of other construction companies said the union reps were still turning up at their jobs, but they weren't showing up at the Fullerton ones for some reason. I don't know what the score is.'

'You any idea why the union's bailed?'

'I can only guess. But whatever the reason, I'll bet it ain't legit.'

Clay watched Dave knock the ash from his cigarette; he was not a happy man. 'And you say that you started asking questions?' said Clay.

'Yeah. Silly me. Apparently I was supposed to shut up as my mates got the flick one by one and replaced with a bunch of blokes getting paid half as much. Or less than half, more than likely.'

'Would you go on the record about this stuff?'

'You mean for the newspaper?' He shrugged. 'Sure. I got nothing to lose.'

'Bloody brilliant.' Clay exhaled the last of his cigarette and stomped the butt of it out on the footpath with a sense of triumph. Dave's story wouldn't bring Fullerton down, but it was a start.

Dave pointed upstairs. 'You coming up for a beer? It's my shout.'

Clay looked at Eddie; he nodded back. 'Sure,' said the journalist. 'I'll join you fellas for a round.'

The trio headed up the stairs of The Loft. Dave tottered off towards the bar and Clay and Eddie went for a quiet corner away from the stage. 'Seems like a nice guy,' said Clay.

'Yeah, he's a good bloke,' said Eddie. 'Shame about the job. He and his wife have a baby on the way, too, so it's bad timing.'

'I'm sure he'll bounce back.'

'Speaking of bouncing back, I don't suppose I could ask a small favour of you.'

'I'm pretty sure I owe you a couple of favours, Eddie, so fire away.'

'That photographer you were with the other night, the Irish one – is she seeing anyone?'

Clay was blindsided, not only by the question, but by a surprising and sudden rush of emotions brought on by it. It hadn't occurred to him until right at that moment that he could be protective of Bec. He told himself that's all it was, though. She was intelligent, easy on the eye, and the accent was kind of attractive, but that's where it ended. They were colleagues. And the fact she took no crap, least of all from him, saw to that.

'Nah, I don't think so,' muttered Clay, unable to lie quickly enough.

'Great. I don't suppose I could get her number off ya, could I? I mean, do you think she'd mind if I give her a call?'

Clay paused. His mind was racing through a bunch of bad ways to brush off Eddie's enquiry, but none of them rang true. In the end he relented, saying nothing as he dug his old Nokia from his pocket and read Bec's number to Eddie, who saved it into his shiny new iPhone, with a grin.

'I thought you were stuck all the way out in Port Campbell. Would be a bit of a trek every time you wanted to catch up with Bec, wouldn't it?' Clay tried to make his attempt at dissuasion as subtle as possible.

'Aww, nah, haven't you heard? I just got reassigned back to Warrnambool, effective immediately. A spot opened up back here. What great timing, hey?'

Clay smiled, but was less than pleased. He was jealous and that bothered him. It was such a petty emotion, and Clay had long prided himself on his complete lack of envy. Envy meant giving a crap about what others had or what they were doing, and in turn it meant looking down on your own situation, which meant wallowing in self-pity. Clay had no time for that. But Eddie's interest in Bec had riled up some long dead emotions within Clay, and that made him angry. Not at Bec or Eddie, but at himself for bothering with such cheap feelings.

Chapter 14

The claims of Dave the construction worker had run in Saturday's edition.

It was a heavily expurgated version of the one Clay had handed to Tudor at first. The editor had sent the copy up the line to the lawyers, who had sent it back with a bunch of metaphorical red lines through many of the accusations. Clay had also called Fullerton's people for a comment. The PR woman in Fullerton Industries' Sydney office had spoken to Clay with the usual over-the-top enthusiasm of those who had sold their soul to work in the corporate sector, but as the conversation wore on, she ditched the meet-and-greet girl for bad-mouthed bag lady. By the time the phone call had ended, Clay was confident he would be getting nothing more than a 'no comment'. At 5 p.m. on Friday, he was proven right.

Clay glanced through the Saturday paper in the café below his apartment over a late breakfast of eggs, bacon, avocado, and hash browns, with an extra-strong heart-starter of a coffee to perk him up a little. Sleep had passed him by yet again, despite a few more joints and whiskies than usual in his lounge room the previous night. Upping the intake didn't worry him when the only option was a restless night, and the increase always washed away bad dreams.

Clay scanned his article, checking to see if it had been softened even further than the lawyer's cautious handling of the matter. He wasn't aiming to get sued and had written a version he thought was legally beyond reproach, but admitted to himself he'd been trying too hard to rile up Fullerton and Swanson. The more Clay thought about it all, the more he was convinced the pair were in cahoots over the Warrnambool Airport deal. So what if he didn't have the proof? He had something almost as good: a story in his sights, and his journalistic instincts told him it was a big one.

After breakfast and a half-hearted attempt at the sudoku, Clay decided to take a chance and wandered a couple of blocks to the Victoria Hotel. He was yet to hear from JT, but had a feeling he'd find the waiter hunched over a form guide in the Vic, watching the horses do their thing on the racing channel.

The Vic was one of the last real pubs in Warrnambool. Almost every other venue had been modernised, gentrified, demolished, or re-purposed, but the Vic was a remaining bastion of what pub life was once like. There was a tote in the corner for placing bets, a few TVs to watch the sport of the day, a chalkboard menu offering a few basic bar meals, and a hardy crew of regulars sinking ale. All that was missing from the glory days was the stratocumulus of tobacco smoke hovering over the beer taps.

As Clay's eyes adjusted to the dim light of the room, he spotted JT, propped up on a bar stool next to a near-empty pint of Guinness, his gaze transfixed by the Test Match cricket on one of the big screens. Clay had little time for Aussie Rules football these days – the rabid fans put him off – but he enjoyed cricket. This was a gentlemen's sport, particularly the drawn-out Test Match variety, where the game became as much about the ball-by-ball happenings as it did the grand plan spread across five days. It took patience, stamina, and intelligence, unlike the mile-a-minute thuggery and chaos of the AFL.

Clay positioned himself on the stool next to JT. 'I had a feeling I'd find you here on a Saturday.'

'It's pretty much my office lately,' said JT.

'That your lunch?' Clay nodded at the pint glass.

'You know what they say – there's a meal in every Guinness.'

Clay laughed. 'Have you got any news for me?'

'Oh, yeah,' he said, smacking his forehead with the heel of his hand. 'Sorry. I meant to call you. I spoke to the girls at work and none of them know where exactly Kerry was working on the night she disappeared, but one of them remembers her getting the job.'

'What do you mean?'

'A girl called Sally, who was one of Kerry's closest buds at work… she said she remembers this suit coming in, slick as goose shit, dark hair, briefcase, Rolex, the works. Sally reckons the suit took a shine to Kerry. Talking to her the whole time he was there. After he goes – and he pays with some gold credit card or some shit – Kerry tells Sally she's got a gig. Good paying. One night's work, first Sunday after Christmas. On a private yacht.'

Clay came close to spitting out his coffee. 'You're kidding me? Whose yacht? Where?'

'Here's the bad news, man – that's all I got.'

'What?'

'I asked every question I could think of, but that was all she knew.'

'Did she recognise him? Had she seen him around town before?'

'Never laid eyes on him before. Could have been an out-of-towner.'

'Damn.' Clay turned his gaze towards the bar, was about to Frisbee the beer mat. 'Wait a minute… he paid with a credit card. Is there a record still? If we matched the date and time?'

'Already thought of that. Those receipts are long gone. And the boss isn't going to let me just start browsing through the restaurant's bank details.'

'What about CCTV? Could we go back through the tapes and see if we can ID this guy in the suit?'

JT laughed. 'Mate, the cameras in the restaurant aren't plugged into anything. They're just for show.'

Clay sensed desperation sinking into him; he stared at the cricket on the TV screen without really looking at it. 'Do the cops know any of this?'

'Don't think so. Like I said the other day, they only spoke to the boss. And I'm pretty sure he doesn't know any of this stuff.' JT sipped on his pint. 'You want me to tell them?'

Clay shook his head. 'Nah. I'll pass it on to the right people, through the appropriate channels. I know a cop who might do the right thing with this information, on the off-chance the detectives are deliberately doing a dodgy job.'

'Are you for real? You think there's a cover-up?'

'Maybe.'

JT shot a questioning glance at Clay. 'Jeez, man, I smoke a fair bit of weed, but even I'm not that paranoid. Cops around here can be fools, definitely. Cops around here can be a little bit lazy, maybe even look the other way every now and then on some minor things. But I highly doubt cops around here are covering up something as big as a murder. This is Warrnambool, mate. It's not bloody Chinatown.'

'People keep saying that. You're probably right, though, I just need a good night's sleep, more than likely.' He glanced at JT's pint glass, which was well on its way to empty. 'You want another one? My shout.'

'Sure. I don't have to work for another couple of hours. You having one?'

'Sure, why not? The sun's over the yardarm, after all.'

Chapter 15

'Is this Clay Moloney?'

It was Monday morning and Clay had barely turned his computer on when his phone rang. The voice on the other end was all business. It was not what he wanted to hear after another weekend of too much drinking and not enough sleeping.

'Yeah, Clay speaking,' he managed.

'Clay, this is Mark Webster from the *Sydney Morning Herald*. I read your article about Fullerton Industries on your paper's website over the weekend. Great stuff.'

'Thanks, Mark.' Clay's brain caught up at last and connected the dots to the name; he'd read Webster's stories on Fullerton in the metros on the day he and Bec had driven out to the airport. Webster had broken the story about the investigation into Fullerton and Wayne Swanson over the Gold Coast Hospital.

'I was wondering if you can help me out with a couple of things,' said Webster.

'Shoot.'

'First, I hope you don't mind if I use some of your words in my next update on the Fullerton matter. I'll give you a joint byline, of course.'

'No worries.'

'Great,' said Webster. 'Now the second thing is part-favour, part-tip-off. I want you to keep your ears on the ground for me down there. Obviously you're on Fullerton and Swanson's home turf, so you might be privy to some contacts and conversations I can't be.'

Clay was intrigued and leant forward without even realising it. His pen was poised on his notepad. It was all atavistic, senses readying to greet something that might help make a story.

'This Warrnambool Airport deal... something's not right about it,' said Webster.

'You're telling me,' said Clay. 'It doesn't make sense.'

'Have you spoken to Fullerton and Swanson about it?'

'Sure did.' Clay detailed his conversations with both men.

'Right,' said Webster, as if Clay's chats had gone exactly as expected. 'At first I figured it was just Swanson grandstanding, starved of attention while Parliament's not sitting. Or maybe he got rattled by the last lot of polls – he was listed as one of the frontbenchers in the most trouble if a snap election was called. And that's even before I started digging up this Gold Coast Hospital stuff. But that's not the reason for the airport announcement. There's more to it. Fullerton has something over Swanson.'

Clay's pen stopped moving. 'What do you mean?'

'I don't know what it is exactly, but Fullerton knows something about Swanson, and Swanson doesn't want it to get out.'

'Fullerton's extorting Swanson? Are you serious?' Clay struggled with the enormity of what Webster was saying, this changed everything. 'I figured the airport deal was just a jobs-for-the-boys type of situation, with some kickbacks thrown in for good measure.'

'I think that's what the Gold Coast Hospital deal was,' said Webster. 'But there's been some kind of falling-out between Fullerton and Swanson since then, and as a result, Fullerton forced Swanson's hand on the Warrnambool Airport.'

'How do you know this?' Clay snapped like a clapperboard, his enthusiasm was spilling over.

'This is the thing, I can't get it confirmed. One of my sources reckons Fullerton's blackmailing Swanson, but I can't get that on the record. At this stage it's just rumour, albeit one I'm hearing from a couple of places now, but that doesn't prove anything. I can't publish it, not without getting sued. But I might be able to leak it to one of my cop buddies. I need more info, though. I need another source. Or to find out what Fullerton's got on Swanson, if that is indeed the case.'

'You don't fully trust your source?'

'He's a union guy, could be making it up as payback on all the lay-offs Fullerton's been making to bring in overseas workers on 457 visas. Plus there's another source of mine, a government guy, who says the extortion angle's a lie.'

'What's his spin?'

'He says Swanson's getting kickbacks from Fullerton. Which is still bad and highly illegal, but nowhere near as exciting a story as the blackmail one. Plus, if I say he's getting kickbacks and it's something worse, I'll get sued and the story dies before I can get to the bottom of it.'

'So what do you want from me?'

'I want you to keep your ear on the ground. Maybe talk to Dave the construction worker again. He might know a guy who knows a guy, you know what I'm saying? Now that you're armed with the right information, you might be able to ask the right questions.'

Clay nodded to himself. 'Sounds good to me. But why are you so hell-bent on taking down Fullerton and Swanson?'

There was a gentle laugh down the phone line. ''Cos they're corrupt. You never let it get personal, Clay. It's always just about keeping the bastards honest.'

Proudfoots Restaurant was packed, despite it being a Tuesday night. Bec conceded the dining room was on the smallish side, but there were still plenty of people crammed in for the evening meal. The fact it was a public holiday – Australia Day, Bec had realised belatedly – might have had something to do with the restaurant's busyness. But the waiting staff were well-trained, they carried an air of calmness in the face of the obvious pressure that came from both the customers and the kitchen.

Bec spotted JT whizzing back and forth between the tables and the bar, pouring and serving drinks without showing the pressure. She waved at him as she entered; he smiled back, but he didn't have time to chat. Bec caught herself wondering if he'd passed any information onto Clay about Kerry Collins. There hadn't been time to find out for herself. Her shifts had been filled with photography assignments, and any time she'd seen Clay in the office, he'd been on the phone and managed little more than a casual wave.

'Do you know that guy?' said Eddie, gesturing at JT.

'Yeah... no... I only met him once. He's a friend of Clay's. Like you.'

Bec wasn't sure why she'd said all that or why she suddenly felt so flustered. Senior Constable Eddie Boulton had asked her out on what could only be described as a date, and from the moment she'd seen him pull up in the car park beside her, she'd felt like a tongue-tied teenager. Sure, Eddie was handsome, with his short-cropped blonde hair, tanned complexion, and solid frame. She thought of him as a modern update of the clean-cut Californian surfers she'd seen in those old Elvis Presley movies. But that wasn't what was making her lose her cool. Was it just the idea of going on a date? Of a man being obviously interested in her? How long had it been? Six months? A year? She thought back to the last time she'd been with someone. It was a beach in Laos and—

'Are you OK?' said Eddie. A silence had arisen while she'd been lost in her thoughts, but before Bec could respond, a young waitress arrived. Her name tag said 'Sally' and she asked them if they would like to order drinks.

They both ordered light beers – it was a work night, after all – and set about perusing the menus. Sally had returned with the drinks and taken their meal orders.

'You know, I've never actually eaten here,' said Eddie as he gazed out at the river, which shimmered in the late afternoon sun. 'Lots of coffees and beers here, but never a meal.'

'If it's any consolation, me neither. I only picked it because it's one of the few places I've been to since I came to the area.'

'You live in Koroit, yeah?'

'Yes.'

'I hear there are some good restaurants out there, too. Maybe next time...' Eddie trailed off and the silence rose again.

Bec sipped her light beer before trying again. 'What about

Port Campbell? I'm sure it's another nice spot on the Shipwreck Coast.'

'Oh, yeah, sure is. Although I just moved back to Warrnambool. Reassigned.'

'Really? Is that a good thing or a bad thing?'

'Good thing. I was getting a bit over the whole small town cop thing.'

'Sounds like a TV series.'

Eddie laughed. Bec was warming to him, feeling more at ease. The pressure had been taken down a notch with one laugh. 'Yeah, it's not as glamorous as a TV show. You do lots of miles and deal with the same drunks every Saturday night. And on weeknights, it's the same fighting couples.'

The words tipped Bec's mind back in time, to Dublin, to an angry mother, to her cowering father, trying to protect young Bec but too afraid to stand up to the vicious woman he'd married, to the police arriving and going again, solving nothing. Bec quickly squashed it all back down again and took a large swig of her light beer. Ireland was a long way away, and home was Koroit now. The two places didn't have to co-exist in her mind, unless she let them.

'Surely it's not always that bad,' she said, trying to keep the conversation flowing. 'Policing a place like Port Campbell must have its upside.'

'It's a nice town. I got to do a lot of surfing on my days off. But usually you're not doing the type of police work that made me want to be a cop in the first place.'

'Not catching enough bad guys?'

'Something like that.' Eddie sipped his light beer and gestured out to the decking where she had sat with Clay over a week ago. 'I have to admit, what Clay was talking about the other day, about the cops not fully investigating that drowned girl, that kinda stuck in my craw a bit.'

'Why's that?'

'Well, for starters, that's exactly the kind of case I'm talking about, that's the stuff that made me become a cop. And that's why I think he's wrong, with his little hints about there being a cover-up. Every police officer down here is busting for a case like that. Why would they sweep it under the rug?' His face turned to a frown, little creases lined his forehead, as he thought about what he'd just said. 'You'd have to be a pretty bad person to do that. I guess I don't want to think the worst of my colleagues.'

'Do you think Clay might be onto something?' The conversation interested Bec now, the Kerry Collins case had a hold of her because she'd seen another family in pain and felt for them.

'I hope not. I don't think so. I don't know. I just know that I was the first at the scene when that girl washed up and if I knew it was a murder, and if it was my case, I'd move heaven and earth to find out who did it.'

'You're a good cop,' Bec reassured him. 'I hope they're all good cops.'

Eddie shook his head, and the lines on his forehead receded. 'I'm not that good a cop. Do you know what I did today? All day I dealt with domestics, husbands and boyfriends going off at their wives and girlfriends, and vice versa. It gives you a pretty dim view of people after a while. I had some dark thoughts today that don't make a good person, let alone a good cop.'

Bec's mind again drifted back to her childhood. The screaming, the hiding. The funeral. She hadn't thought about that stuff for a long time. She didn't want to think about it now, but it was always there.

She sipped on her light beer and screwed up her face. 'This tastes like horse piss, let's get a bottle of wine,' she said.

'A bottle?'

'Yeah, you only live once, after all.'

'OK, looks like we're making a night of it.'

Eddie hailed the waiter.

Chapter 16

After two days of testing phone calls, one after another, Clay decided Mark Webster's tip-off about Fullerton blackmailing Swanson was likely to remain an unrealised fantasy. It was an interesting theory, but it relied on facts that remained elusively hidden. No matter how hard he tried, every phone call only retold him what he already knew.

No one would talk on the record and anything off the record wasn't worth knowing. He'd started with Dave the construction worker, who'd given him the names of some aggrieved co-workers. It was enough to build a solid follow-up to his article from Saturday, but nobody had worked high enough up the ladder to have any real dirt. They were all just construction workers, and the occasional site foreman – not exactly the kind of Fullerton Industries players that would be privy to the corporate politicking Clay was looking for.

After spending almost two whole work days exhausting Dave's contacts and Dave's contacts' contacts, Clay decided to take another tack. He called Liz Fitzgerald.

Liz was Wayne Swanson's former communications manager, a position she'd held for twenty years until she'd quit a couple of elections ago. She insisted on meeting in person and Clay had happily agreed. He liked Liz, she was a fast-talking, heavy-smoking, hard-drinking dynamo, and the pair had shared a few encounters of varying kinds a decade ago, back when Clay was tipping thirty and Liz was closer to forty. Naturally, she wanted to meet at the Hotel Warrnambool in the smokers' lounge. Clay paid for her usual, a gin and tonic, with a slice of lime, not lemon, and placed it in front of her, alongside a pint of beer for himself. They both pulled out a smoke and Clay lit Liz's for her before lighting his own.

'Thanks, sweetie,' said Liz, her voice husky from her pack-a-day habit. 'Happy Australia Day!' Clay noticed she was on a lower milligram cigarette than she'd smoked ten years ago. For what little that'll help, he thought, probably as effective as drinking diet Coke instead of real Coke if you're trying to lose weight.

Liz was finally starting to look old, Clay realised. Her dye-job was more obvious, the crow's feet longer. She was still attractive for her age, and in reasonably good shape, but her habits were catching up with her. Her skin had the smoker's tawny tinge and Clay could make out the subtle glow of broken capillaries beneath her foundation. He gazed past her shoulder and assessed his reflection in the polished glass wall behind her. The lack of sleep didn't help, but he didn't appear to be faring much better than Liz with his own habits, he discovered.

'So what did you wanna talk about, darl?' she said, sipping her G & T. 'Something juicy, I hope.'

Clay smiled. 'The juiciest. I wanna talk about your old boss, Wayne Swanson.'

'That old prick!' She let out a raucous cackle, followed by a hearty cough. 'What do you wanna talk about Wayne the Wanker for?'

''Cos I think he's up to some dodgy business.'

'That's nothing new, darl. Wayne Swanson was the minister for transport, infrastructure, and dodgy business when I worked for him. That bastard couldn't lie straight in bed. You name it, he probably did it.'

'Anything he could get blackmailed over?'

'Why? You wanna make a quick million?' Liz chortled again, followed once more by another practised cough.

'Not me. Someone else.'

Liz's demeanour changed. 'Are you serious?'

Clay nodded and took another drag, watching the expressions wash one by one over the ex-staffer's face.

'I'm not surprised,' she said finally.

'That he's being blackmailed?'

'Absolutely. That's if it's true, of course.'

'So you don't know if what I'm hearing is true?'

'Like I said, it wouldn't surprise me. But how would I know if he's being blackmailed? I haven't worked for him these last six years.' She puffed on her cigarette and her eyes narrowed. 'What's this all about, anyway?'

Clay told her what Mark Webster from the *Sydney Morning Herald* had told him the day before, about the airport deal, the strange timing of it, the rumours. Liz listened in silence, sipping her G & T and inhaling and exhaling her Peter Stuyvesant Classic with steady regularity.

When Clay had finished, Liz shook her head. 'I can't help you, sweetie. On the record, off the record – I don't know anything. And anyone who does ain't gonna say.'

'If you had to guess?' Clay knew he was reaching.

'That's the problem… there's too many things.' Liz threw her hands up. 'He took kickbacks of one kind or another from the minute he walked into Parliament, but no one will speak against him because he used to share the rewards around. His colleagues, his staffers, we all benefitted from his ill-gotten largesse from time to time. Hell, even I got taken to dinner once in a while, or got some pricey gifts the odd occasion. He's a generous man. Everyone knew he was getting it from somewhere that wasn't exactly legit, but no one had the balls to say "no". I mean, this is politics we're talking about. That's how politics works.'

'What about sex?'

'That's a little forward – you could at least buy me another drink!' Liz was lost in a storm of laughter and coughing. Clay felt his cheeks flush, but concentrated on taking a long sip of his beer to hide his embarrassment.

'Funny, ha ha,' he said as Liz's sputtering died down. 'I meant Swanson. Could he be blackmailed over sex stuff?'

Liz took a lengthy drag on her Stuyvesant and her expression became sterner. 'I don't know, darl. Doubtful. He used to be a bit grabby at times, back in the day. God knows I had my arse slapped on a couple of occasions. So did a few of the other girls in the office. But it never went any further, at least not around here. That was a long time ago, though. He cleaned up his act as the times changed and the term "sexual harassment" entered the office vernacular. He went from being a slapper to a leerer. If you wore a short skirt or a low-cut top around the office, you could feel his gaze on you. You'd catch him staring at times, but that was it. It wasn't anything worthy of blackmail.'

'He's married, right?'

'Yeah, for what it's worth. Lesley Swanson is her name. Silly cow. I couldn't stand her. I don't think Wayne can, either. Doubt they've even slept in the same bed in the past twenty years.'

'If he's not getting laid at home, is it likely he's getting laid elsewhere?'

A sly smile walked across Liz's face. 'Something on your mind, soldier? You sure this is just a business call?'

Clay glanced at his watch. 'It is after 6 p.m., so technically I'm off the clock,' he said. 'But let's stay focused here, Liz. Is Swanson the type to have an affair?'

Liz took a long drag and exhaled. The smoke wafted slowly across Clay's face. 'I sure wouldn't put it past him,' she said finally. 'But now that you mention it, you've reminded me of something – prostitutes.'

'Really?' he said, unable to keep the excitement out of his voice.

'Calm your farm, sweetie. It wasn't confirmed. They were just rumours. There used to be talk that Swanson was partial to the occasional hooker, especially when he was up in Canberra, but that's all it was – talk. Either he was really careful or it was just scuttlebutt. No one knew then, and I don't think anyone will now. A good prostitute's not gonna rat out a well-paying John. And he's too clever to get caught, believe it or not.'

Clay deflated again. He tried not to show it, but he knew Liz had clicked on.

'Oh, don't be so disheartened, darl,' she said. 'These guys are good at what they do. They lie, they cheat, they do their little deals, and at the end of the day, they dance and dodge and say the right things so nothing sticks to them and people re-elect them. And Wayne Swanson is one of the best dancers and dodgers there is. I'll be taking a very long sleep in the Warrnambool cemetery before he gets caught out, I can tell you that.'

Chapter 17

Clay and Liz had dinner in the bar and a couple more drinks together before Liz said goodnight.

'I can't handle as much midweek drinking these days,' she said by way of an excuse, and gave Clay a peck on the cheek as she departed.

Clay checked his watch. It was 10 p.m. Food service was long finished and those that remained were the seasoned drinkers still celebrating Australia Day. A large group of musicians and artists Clay knew were hanging around in the smoker's lounge. Some itinerant workers clustered around the pool table. The bar was lined with familiar-looking suits and less familiar-looking professional types. A couple of the tables were full – a group of twenty-somethings yelling over the top of each other when not looking at their phones, an increasingly drunk collection of middle-aged women squawking louder and louder, some randoms in casual attire minding their own business and chatting quietly over large glasses of wine.

He thought about calling Bec to see what she was up to, but decided to leave her alone. Maybe he should call Eddie and tell him what JT had said about Kerry Collins getting hired to work on a boat the night she went missing. Nah, that can wait, he thought. Maybe he could call Gabby... nah, probably best to let that wait a bit, too. Maybe you should just go home, said a little voice inside his head. Don't have another pint. Just walk home. Go to bed.

Clay took a deep breath and headed out the door. The night air was cool, with a gentle sea breeze, enough to make him wish he'd thought ahead to bring a jacket, even though his apartment wasn't far. He moved a few steps down the street from the pub door and pulled his nearly empty cigarette packet out of his shirt pocket.

He heard the door open behind him as he popped a smoke between his teeth and took the lighter from his pocket. The streetlights gave everything an orange glow as he flicked the flint wheel. The flame grabbed at the end of his cigarette and another orange glow emerged.

'Can I borrow a light?' An abrupt voice, full of confidence but lacking charm, came from behind him.

Clay turned and saw two men, neatly dressed, coming toward him; they'd just exited the pub, the door still swinging on its hinges behind them. One of the men had a shaved round head to match his roundish body, the other man was a slightly taller rectangle of solid mass, but with slicked-back black hair. The one with hair had a cigarette partway to his lips. Clay handed him the lighter. 'Sure thing, mate,' he said. Deep in his guts, he didn't like the look of these guys. There was no humour in their eyes, which seemed odd for two guys leaving a pub at 10 p.m. on a Tuesday. And on Australia Day, no less.

Slicked-hair guy took the lighter and lit his smoke. The round guy watched him. Not a word was spoken, which made Clay feel uncomfortable enough, but what really got to him was the fact that Slick looked Clay right in the eye as he pocketed Clay's lighter.

Clay forced a grin, a pained one, and let a small exasperated laugh sneak out. 'That's fine, keep the lighter.' He turned to head for home.

'Mr Moloney.' There was that charmless yet cocksure voice again. And dammit, they know my name, this cannot end well.

Clay turned back around. 'Yeah?'

'We have a message for you.' It appeared to be the round guy with the brusque voice after all, not the smoker.

'Couldn't text it? Email, maybe?'

'Whatever you're digging for, you ain't gonna find it, so maybe save yourself some pain and grief and give it a rest, hey?'

Something at the back of Clay's brain told him to run, but four pints said otherwise. He dragged on his cigarette in a way he thought might pass for nonchalance, and exhaled the smoke into the cool night air. 'What the hell are you talking about?'

'If you're too dumb to understand this is a warning, then perhaps we can beat it into you. Would that make things a little clearer?'

'Oh, my God,' said Clay, hamming up the fake exuberance. 'Are you guys... hired goons?' He let his face light up like a kid's at Christmas. 'What a great day! I've always wanted to meet hired goons!'

It was a split-second move and Clay was doubled over. Too focused on the round guy, Clay hadn't seen the dark-haired rectangle step forward and land a quick jab in his stomach.

Clay attempted to suck in air, his smoke falling from his fingers and onto the asphalt footpath. 'You son of a bitch,' he squeezed out between gasps.

'Is the message clear?'

Clay made himself stand up straight, panting. 'So,' he managed. 'Let me get this right. You want me to stop digging for information.' His breathing was becoming easier, air flowing back into his lungs like the false bravado he could feel filling up his brain. 'And even though I'm apparently not gonna find this information, someone deemed it worthwhile to send you two handsome chaps along to warn me about looking for said information. Which I'm apparently not going to find. Now, doesn't that seem a tad redundant to you two? I mean, if I wasn't going to find the information anyway, then—'

The next punch hit him square in the left eye socket. It came from the round guy and it was a quick, boxer-like jab. Clay felt nothing at first, yet staggered back from the heavy force. There was no sound. Then, as one, the pain and noise showed up, forcing Clay to stagger again. A high-pitched ringing in his ears matched the raw throb pulsing through his head. Clay stood up straight again, blinking like he was in a spotlight, trying to shake off the ache.

A third punch dropped him to the ground. It came from the slick guy and struck him in the jaw. Already in pain, Clay barely felt it but knew it was a good one as it had forced him to his knees, his forehead scraping the footpath following his collapse. He could taste blood. He felt a flicked cigarette bounce off him.

'Screw you guys,' he offered between gritted teeth, but could say no more as a swift boot to the stomach took the last gasp of air from his lungs.

That self-assured voice was close to his ear. 'We found you once, we'll find you again if we have to,' it said.

Clay rolled onto his back on the footpath, his eyes pinched closed as he struggled for oxygen. Over the high-pitched whine he could hear the two men walking away.

The pain escalated as his breath returned, one aching inhalation at a time. He turned to his side and tried to stand, but couldn't. Clay coughed. More blood. He spat. He wished for unconsciousness, but it didn't come.

For nearly ten minutes he lay there. Not a single person passed him on the street. The violence, he realised, had moved him away from the windows of the Hotel Warrnambool and into the alleyway between the pub and the cinema next door. I must have been backing down the alley without even noticing, he thought. What a tough guy I am. But if a situation like this arises again, he warned himself, I better keep my mouth shut.

Chapter 18

'Jesus Christ, what happened to you?'

It was Wednesday morning, the day after the beating, yet Clay had been determined to go to work. His left eye was almost fully closed due to the swelling and his right cheek was a purplish colour. A gash on his forehead completed the picture, while a dull headache and a pulsing throb across his entire face added a tactile quality that made him feel as bad as he looked. He was also starting to suspect he had a broken rib.

It was Bec who had blasphemed and asked the obvious question, rushing up to him. Everyone else had watched him pass in gaping silence.

Clay knew he looked like shit, but what surprised him was that Bec didn't look the greatest either. He could smell alcohol, her clothes were the same ones she had worn the day before, and her eyes indicated a hangover or a lack of sleep or both.

'I'm fine. What happened to you?' said Clay. 'You look like you slept on my couch again, except I know you didn't because I did.'

Clay could have sworn Bec blushed slightly, but it was hard to tell as she was standing on the side of his bad eye.

'Seriously, Clay, what the hell happened?' she said.

His co-workers were slowly gathering around him, offering a mixture of expletives and variations on the question, 'Are you OK?'

'Moloney, my office, now!' The bellow came from the editor. Bradley Tudor had poked his head out his door long enough to yell, but Clay could tell it wasn't long enough to notice anything more, like the fact everyone in the office was now crowding around him or the fact his face looked as though it had been used as a punching bag.

The circle of co-workers parted and Clay shuffled to the

door of Tudor's glass-walled office. Tudor didn't look up as Clay entered; he was staring at his phone, reading a text.

'Clay, what's this I hear about you harassing every Fullerton Industries employee this side of the— What the hell happened to your face?' said Tudor, who had made the mistake of looking up from his phone mid-sentence.

'Do you want the real story or the believable one?'

Tudor's eye's narrowed. 'Spit it out.'

'I got beaten up by two hired goons outside the Hotel Warrnambool last night. They told me they were delivering a message.'

'*Hired goons?*'

'Believe it or not, but I actually made the mistake of calling them that, right before one of them punched me the first time.'

'What was the message they were delivering?'

'I believe it was the same one you were just about to deliver.'

Tudor shook his head, his hands came level with his shoulders then fell limply. 'Why do I get the feeling this is the unbelievable bit of the story?'

'Believe what you want, but I'm fairly confident Fullerton sent those guys to get me to lay off the story.'

'Did they say they were sent by Fullerton?'

'Of course not. They weren't so stupid.'

'Then how do you know it was about the Fullerton story?'

'What else would it be about? They told me to stop digging for information.'

'That could refer to anything.'

Clay felt the anger rising inside him. A throbbing in his head became a persistent pounding. 'Are you serious, Brad? I was beaten up last night and you're questioning my story. Weren't you just about to tell me to lay off the Fullerton story?'

'I got a text from Lachlan Fullerton himself, asking me why you have been harassing his staff. That hardly sounds like the kind of follow-up one makes to sending in the hired goons.'

Clay slapped the table; it stung his palms where they'd been scuffed on the asphalt. 'You are unbelievable!' he yelled at

Tudor. 'Why the hell did I get beaten up, then?'

Tudor looked confused, the edges of his mouth drooping. 'How should I know?' he said. 'You probably said the wrong thing to someone at the pub while you were drunk again and concocted this whole story for all I know. It was Australia Day yesterday, after all, a day renowned for its drunken violence.'

Clay stood and pointed a crooked finger at Tudor. 'You piece of shit. You filthy, arrogant son of a bitch. I'm on to something – a real story, not some prissy regurgitated PR crap that you think counts as news. You wouldn't know journalism if it bit you on the arse and crapped in your shoes, you dickless arse-hat.'

Clay glared at Tudor. He could feel himself breathing heavily, and the pounding in his head was almost unbearable now. A wave of dizziness washed over him and he fell back into his seat. All the while Tudor's face remained emotionless, not even a twitch to give away some hint of a reaction; Clay was disappointed, his pride hurt because he knew his wordy attack bordered on eloquence.

When Tudor finally spoke it was in a measured tone, slow and solid. 'Go home. Consider this your final official warning. I would dearly love to fire you, and trust me, I could after that barrage of abuse, but believe it or not, I actually feel sorry for you. You're not in your right mind, Moloney. Now, you've obviously had a rough night, whatever the reason, but you've been doing some good work of late. The obit on Kerry Collins was outstanding. However, I think you need a break. Take the rest of the week off. Heal up. Sober up. Get your head together, for Chrissake. I don't want to fire you, despite what you may think. But one more meltdown like that and you're out the door for good.'

'What are you saying? Are you suspending me or something?'

Tudor rose, stepped away from his desk and headed to the door. He held it open for Clay as he spoke again. 'Go. Out. We'll call it annual leave.'

This was a new assertiveness from Tudor that Clay had never seen before. He wondered what was at the back of it, because Tudor didn't do cocksure. He was acting like a bullied schoolboy who'd been learning tae kwon do on the fly.

'OK. I hear you.' Clay dragged himself to the door, eyeing Tudor. 'I'll take a few days off.'

There was a moment's stilled silence as the pair faced each other. Nothing was said, words had no place between them now. Everything that needed to be said had been said.

As Clay walked away he felt alone and defeated. He felt like he had nowhere to go. Until now losing his job had seemed highly unlikely, and he didn't need it anyway, the job didn't define him. But somehow the thought of not having the paper behind him to bring justice to Kerry Collins' killers looked like a real prospect.

Tudor spoke as Clay trudged out the door: 'Don't test me again, I'm warning you.'

'Duly noted.'

Clay left Tudor's office feeling even more punch-drunk than the night before. He saw Bec watching him from across the office, moving towards him, but he waved her off and headed towards the exit.

Chapter 19

It was raining heavily for the first time since New Year's Day. The weather had turned cold and a biting sou'wester roared through Warrnambool. Summer was on temporary shutdown.

Bec cowered from the weather at Clay's door, but it did no good. There was no hiding from it – the door faced south-west, looking out over a large empty car park from one storey up. The unseasonable wind and rain had trapped her. It was bracing.

Bec banged on the door again and waited. It had been a long day. She'd gotten minimal sleep the night before after deciding it would be a good idea to (a) get drunk, (b) go back to Eddie's place, and (c) sleep with him. *I regret nothing except for this hangover*, she had told herself in the morning, and nothing had changed over the course of the day, aside from the hangover being downgraded to a dull roar by the afternoon.

Bec knocked again, but still nothing. The day was always going to be a long one thanks to the hangover and lack of sleep, but it got longer when Clay was sent home after looking like he'd been in a fight and then getting in an argument with the editor. *What the hell is going on with him?* Her concern was genuine. *And where the hell is he? Why did he text me and invite me here if he wasn't going to be home?*

The wind kicked up a notch, sending the rain horizontal. *Bugger it*, she thought, *I'm trying the doorknob*. To her surprise, it opened.

Clay's apartment was dark. It was just after 5 p.m. Still plenty of daylight left, in theory, but the heavy dark grey rainclouds outside seemed to suck all the light out of his home. No lights were on. 'Hello?' she called. 'It's Bec.' She paused. 'From work,' she added, to be on the safe side.

She took a couple of steps down the hall and heard the low pulse of bass guitar and kick drum, mingling with the smell of burning marijuana. As she moved through the hall and into the dining room, the sensations increased. She followed her nose and ears to the lounge room, pushing open the door to reveal the louder sounds of a stereo playing. The pungent aroma of joint smoke wafted before her, solid as a wall.

Clay was lying on the couch she'd slept on just over a week ago with what appeared to be the joint between his lips. His left eye was practically closed from the swelling. Close to hand on a glass coffee table was a bottle of Black Douglas whisky and a glass filled with ice, an ashtray, a pack of cigarettes, a lighter, and a small amount of marijuana, finely chopped in a bowl.

'So what the hell happened to you?' she yelled over the music.

Clay gestured at the stereo and Bec reached over and turned it down.

'So what happened to you?' She tried again as she moved to the other side of the room and sat in a chair next to the stereo.

'Which bit?'

'All of it – the bruises, the argument with Tudor...'

Clay toked heavily on the joint before resting it on the edge of the ashtray, exhaling more of the acrid smoke into the air. The lounge room window was open a crack, but it did little to hide the smell. 'I don't want to have to go through all this twice, so wait up...' he checked his watch, 'five minutes. How was your day?'

'My day? What? What is wrong with you, Clay? I've been worried sick about you all day and you invite me around here and then you tell me to wait five minutes!'

'Alright, alright, calm your farm. All will be revealed. But seriously, wait five.' There was a bang on the door. 'Aha,' said Clay, 'that will be our guest. Would you do me a favour and answer the door, please? I'd do it myself but, y'know, I have some aches and pains... Thank you.'

Bec glared at Clay. She was in no mood for his games, but she rose and walked back to the door. Opening it with a huff, she was shocked to see Eddie Boulton standing on the other side, his coat pulled up against the wind and rain.

'Ah, hi,' she managed.

'Hi, yourself. What are you doing here?' said Eddie.

'Probably the same thing as you.'

'Right. Can I come in, or do I have to stay out in this stupid weather?'

'Oh, sorry.' Bec backed out of the way and Eddie moved inside with an exaggerated shiver. She closed the door behind him; it was very quiet in the dim hallway and they were standing a little too close together. Unsure of what to do, Bec reached up on her toes and gave Eddie a peck on the cheek, feeling silly the second she did so. 'Clay's down here,' she said, moving past Eddie and toward the lounge room, putting her back to Eddie so he couldn't see the slideshow of expressions crossing her face.

As she entered the lounge room, Bec immediately noticed the mixbowl was gone, along with the half-smoked joint. The window was open wider, a stick of incense was burning, and Clay was sitting up with a lit cigarette in his mouth and the glass of whisky in his hand.

'Eddie, how goes it?' he said without taking the smoke from his lips.

'Jesus H Christ, Clay, you look like a dog's breakfast,' said Eddie.

'Ah, well, we can't all be as handsome as you, Eddie, now can we?' Clay's voice was chipper and upbeat, not the tone Bec expected from someone who appeared to have been at the wrong end of a beating. 'Now,' he continued, 'why don't you two lovebirds take a seat and let ol' Uncle Clay tell you a story?'

Bec looked at Eddie, who offered her a smirk. He seemed as comfortable as she was with Clay's teasing.

'Oh, come on now, children,' said Clay. 'Your little rendezvous might have stayed secret a bit longer if you hadn't had it at the restaurant where one of my best contacts works.'

Eddie laughed; it sounded forced. Bec wasn't sure what to make of the situation so opted to say nothing.

Clay chuckled as he went for another sip of his whisky. 'Can I get you guys anything? Coffee? Beer? Whisky?'

'You can hurry up and tell us your damned story,' said Eddie.

'Alright, keep your pants on,' said Clay, punctuating his remark with an obscene wink in Bec's direction.

Before Bec could rebuke him, Clay launched into his story. He started with a tip-off he'd received from a *Sydney Morning Herald* journalist, and worked his way through two days of phone calls, a boozy dinner with one of Wayne Swanson's old staffers, and capped it off with a climactic bashing outside the Hotel Warrnambool last night. As a footnote he recounted a 'disturbing conversation', as he put it, with an unusually bullish Bradley Tudor early that morning.

Bec and Eddie sat speechless at the end of Clay's account of the past two and a bit days. The music was still playing and seemed to get louder as no one spoke.

'Good album, this,' said Eddie.

Bec glared at him. 'That's all you've got to say? Our friend just got bashed by a couple of thugs who work for Lachlan Fullerton and all you can say is "good album, this"?'

'He's right, though,' grinned Clay. 'You Am I's *Hourly Daily*. Classic.'

'How can you both?' said Bec, but Eddie was already moving on.

'What proof do you have they worked for Fullerton?' said the cop.

'That's the problem – I have none. They never said anything about him, except to tell me to "stop digging". And Fullerton Industries is where I've been digging.'

'CCTV?' asked Eddie.

'Not of the assault. I walked home from work this morning past the Warrny and scoped it out. No cameras pointed at where I had my arse handed to me. They couldn't have picked a better spot. But there's probably footage of them inside the pub.'

'Could you ID your assailants if I got the footage?'

'Absolutely. But I'd bet my possibly broken rib they're out-of-towners.'

Eddie leaned back in his chair with a look of contemplation on his face. Clay puffed on his cigarette. Bec switched her gaze between each of them.

'Seems like a pretty dumb move,' she said.

'How's that?' said Clay.

'Assaulting a journalist? That's asking for trouble. And besides, you weren't even getting anywhere with the story. I don't see how you were worth going to the trouble of importing a couple of thugs for.'

'Thanks,' said Clay, with mock indignation.

'You know what I mean,' she said. 'Why bother? You've got nothing on Fullerton.'

'Maybe they're scared,' said Clay. 'Maybe I'm getting close, or there's more at stake than we imagine. Like you say, we don't know enough at this stage, but that's not to say there isn't a whole lot more to find out. People get jumpy under pressure, that makes me think we're really onto something big.' No one said anything for a while and Clay lit another smoke.

'You wanna press charges?' asked Eddie.

'If you can catch them. I get the feeling these guys might not be easy to find. I'm really only telling you this in case I go missing... it might be a good place to start looking. Not that I think it will come to that, not yet, anyway.'

Bec frowned. 'I don't think it will come to that.'

'Well, I'm glad we agree about that for now,' said Clay. 'I've got something else that might interest you both as well.' He proceeded to tell them about what JT had uncovered from his work colleagues about the job offer Kerry Collins had received before she was killed.

Bec could see the anger rising in Eddie; he'd started to become irritated, leaning forward and planting firm elbows on his thighs. 'Are you saying no one interviewed her workmates?' he asked.

'No one.'

'I find that hard to believe.'

'Me, too. Got any explanation for that one?'

'What are you insinuating?' Eddie's volume was increasing; his hands got jittery and looked ready to throttle someone.

'Easy, mate. I'm not insinuating anything. I'm genuinely asking. Why would the officers investigating the death of a young woman not talk to the victim's workmates?'

Bec watched as Eddie appeared to deflate. 'Sorry,' he said. 'There's only two possible answers to that question. And I don't like either of them.'

'Sloppy or deliberate. Which would you bet on?'

Eddie looked out the window, watching the rain. Bec wanted to reach over and touch his arm, be reassuring, but it didn't seem right. They'd connected last night and Eddie was nice, but he wasn't really her type so she didn't want him to get the wrong idea about her. The night before had been good for her, a confidence raiser, but somewhere in her mind a voice was saying 'You just used him to get laid!' She didn't like the voice because she was still trying to figure out whether it was right or not.

Eddie turned back to Clay, snapping Bec from her thoughts. 'Whichever one it is, I have to be very careful with what you've told me. Someone is likely to be in deep shit one way or another.'

'Will you keep me in the loop?' said Clay. 'I mean, as far as you can.'

'No worries.' Eddie rose from his chair. 'You've done some good work, mate, but you might want to be careful about that Fullerton stuff. The kinda bloke who sends thugs after someone is not the kinda bloke you wanna mess with.'

'Obviously.'

'No. I mean it. Until we fully know what we're dealing with here, keep your nose out of trouble.'

Eddie headed towards the door, then stopped and turned to Bec. 'What are you up to?'

Bec was caught off guard. 'Ahh… I'm going to hang here for a little bit. OK?'

'Fine. Hey, do what you want.' He looked across at Clay and back to Bec. 'Although maybe lay off whatever it was he was smoking in here before I arrived.' Eddie winked at Bec, waved at Clay, and was gone.

The sound of the front door closing coincided with Clay tapping the side of his hexagonal coffee table. Bec had noticed its weird shape when she stayed over, and had assumed the table was solid, but at Clay's tap a secret little drawer slid open, from which he pulled out the mixbowl and the ashtray with the half-smoked joint resting on the edge.

'Nice table,' said Bec.

'Thanks. I bought it at a garage sale. I think a bikie owned it originally.'

'Maybe you should give that stuff a rest.'

'Hey,' said Clay as he relit the joint, 'I just had my face bashed in. Gimme a break.'

'Then maybe you should lay off the Fullerton story.'

Clay inhaled deeply and eyed Bec in a way that she didn't like. 'Why would you say that?' he said, as he exhaled.

'Because I'm worried about you. A beating like the one you took... you could've been killed.'

'I may have embellished the story a little in the retelling.'

'I'm not joking around. One punch is all it takes.'

Clay toked again and exhaled. The smoke sat in a thick cloud between them and Bec could barely see his face.

'I'll be careful,' he said finally. 'But to be honest, this whole incident is only going to make me chase harder.'

'I know,' said Bec. 'I mean, I've only known you a bit, but I knew you were going to say that.'

Chapter 20

Clay usually relished a few extra days off work, but they passed at such a languid pace he wished he was back at his desk. He was reluctant to leave the house while his face still resembled a dropped pie, not out of vanity, but because he couldn't be bothered dealing with the funny looks and accompanying questions.

He read books, tidied his apartment, and almost turned the television on, but knew it would just burn up his blood. Clay couldn't even remember the last time he'd turned the damned thing on, but it had probably ended in a close call between hurling it out the second-storey window and switching it off again.

With so much time on his hands, it was difficult not to start drinking or smoking weed early in the day, but he resisted for as long as he could. In the end, Clay told himself it took the edge off and distracted him; stopped him running the incomplete stories of Fullerton Industries and Kerry Collins through his head again and again. That was the real reason he wanted to be back at work, he realised: unfinished business.

By Saturday morning, the swelling around his left eye was gone, in its place a purple smear like someone had attacked him with a packet of blueberries. Feeling like he could face the world again, Clay opened his door to a warm sunny day and stood on an envelope that must have been slid partway under the door.

For reasons he couldn't fathom, a feeling of dread started rising in his chest and up to his throat as he tore the envelope open. It turned out to be well-founded.

'Dear Mr Moloney, we regret to inform you that you are required to vacate your premises within 28 days... orders of the building owner... due to refurbishment... to repurpose the premises... thank you for your tenancy... valued customer...

hope you consider Willis Real Estate for your future rental requirements… apologise for inconvenience…'

Clay screwed the letter into a ball, threw it into the hallway, and yanked the door shut. The wood hit the jamb with a thud, releasing a cloud of dust. What more could go wrong? Stories still in the trap. Face used as a football. And now a bloody eviction.

'Bugger this, I'm going to the pub!'

Ordinarily, Clay's feet would have propelled him straight to the Hotel Warrnambool, with no effort of deliberation needed. But today he stalled. The violence of a few nights ago replayed in his mind and for the first time ever the thought of going near the Warrny caused a ball of anxiety to start bouncing in his gut. What if the goons returned? What if they were waiting for him?

Heat rose in his chest; it was anger splashing against dread, like the ocean meeting a breakwater. Those bastards had not only physically injured him, they had him fearful of going to one of his favourite places, of doing something he wouldn't have thought twice about normally. He was starting to feel sorry for himself, and he resented that the most. Self-pity wasn't worth spit to Clay.

The sun shone. The previous day's rain had evaporated, but it felt like more was on the way. I can't let them win, he thought. But still he couldn't stand the idea of facing the scene of his bashing. He didn't want to see his blood on the asphalt. He didn't want to be reminded of the night because he didn't know how he'd react. What if he flipped out?

He lashed out at the world: 'If I can't go to the Warrny, I'll go to every other bloody pub in town.' A pub crawl is an act of defiance, he thought. He wanted to believe he was right, but was hit with a twinge of disdain. He was just looking for an excuse to get fall-down drunk and he knew it. But as far as lame justification went, an eviction and an assault were pretty good excuses.

The morning and early afternoon passed in a steady progression of bars and beers – the Vic, the Cally, the Whalers,

The Last Coach. Early in the proceedings Clay had bumped into Al Smithson, a co-worker responsible for the arts and music pages at the paper. Al was in his sixties, from England originally, vaguely eccentric, long-haired and bearded, and a good bloke. He was also one of the guys Clay occasionally bought marijuana from. They sat on opposite sides of the office and didn't mingle much at work, but Clay was a big fan of Al's. He always had interesting stories to tell about the good old days of punk rock in England or his early days of journalism in Australia or the time he took acid with such-and-such at some exotic location. And he was more than keen to join an impromptu pub crawl.

'Is that the Irish lass, the photographer, over there?' said Al. They were seated at one end of the bar at The Last Coach, half a dozen pints into the day, and Al was nodding to the far end.

Clay glanced along the run of timber and beer taps to where Bec and Eddie stood, ordering from the girl in black next to the till, before eyeing Al, who had a cheeky grin on his face.

'Yep.'

'Who's that fella she's with?'

'Copper named Eddie. Mate of mine.'

'Ah.'

'What? What do you mean by "ah"?' Clay suddenly felt really drunk. He realised it, like a wave crashing in and taking him out at the knees. He was trying to get his thoughts in order and they wouldn't line up. That was when he knew that he was truly intoxicated – that lost at sea, pummelled from all sides, can't keep your feet, feeling. It hit him all of a sudden. Belligerence started to build.

'What I mean, Clay my friend,' said Al, a slightly drunken wobble creeping into his London accent, 'is that you have set a fine woman up with a fine friend, probably. That is what I mean by "ah".'

'Whatever. It won't last.'

'And then she'll come crawling back to you?'

Clay glared at Al, but didn't say anything.

'I've seen you around the office, mate, and the way you talk to her,' said Al. 'I have worked in newsrooms from here to Istanbul to Seattle and back again. I have seen this a million times over. You like her.'

'Piss off.'

'What? Why is that such an antagonising thing to say?'

Clay continued to glare at Al. The silence dragged out. 'You got any weed?' Clay said eventually.

'Of course. But this ain't over.'

The pair downed the last of their pints and exited the pub into the orange glow of late afternoon. Bec and Eddie didn't appear to have seen them and Clay didn't attempt to catch their attention on the way out.

Clay followed as Al crossed the street and sat on a park bench out the front of the Gallery, a nightclub that Clay avoided at all costs, not least because its signage spelt the word 'niteclub'. It was yet to open for the night and fill to the brim with fake-tanned girls in too-short skirts and the throng of tight-shirted males that followed in their wake. The street corner was quiet and peaceful. Aside from The Last Coach on the opposite side of the intersection, no pedestrians were bothering with this part of the CBD at this hour of the afternoon.

Al pulled a small pre-rolled joint from his tobacco pouch and lit it after a short glance up and down the street. He inhaled and passed it to Clay.

Just below the surface, Clay was fuming about Al's insinuations, but refused to bring it up lest it be revealed that Clay was fuming.

Al flicked his gaze to Clay as Clay handed the marijuana cigarette back. 'It's OK, man,' said Al. 'Bec seems like a lovely bird. But you might want to let her know you fancy her. Before it's too late and that.'

'I don't *fancy* her,' said Clay.

'Yeah, ya do.'

Clay glared at Al again but Al didn't reciprocate, too focused on the plume of smoke rolling out of his pursed lips. 'I got evicted today,' Clay said eventually.

'Bummer, man. What are you going to do about it?'

'I don't know. I was thinking maybe I'd call...' Clay stopped dead mid-sentence. He'd been on the verge of saying Bec and he knew it, and he knew Al knew it, but he hoped otherwise. Clay looked at Al, trying to figure out what to say next.

'Bec,' said Al. 'You were thinking maybe you'd call Bec. Or me. I'm your next best friend at work, right? I won't be offended. Who's it going to be?'

Clay realised he'd backed himself into a corner and sat without speaking for a while. The Englishman passed the joint to the Australian, who accepted it gratefully, happy for the distraction.

Clay sucked on the joint and exhaled. He was already starting to feel more relaxed and even a bit more sober, or at least, the joint gave him the illusion of sobriety. 'So what do I do, Al?' he said. 'I can't very well walk back into The Last Coach while Eddie's here and say to Bec, "Hey, I like you."'

'So you admit it then?'

Clay looked at Al, who had a gleeful look in his eye. 'Screw you,' said Clay.

'Oh, come on!' said Al. 'Why is it so bad and terrible to admit you like someone? I mean, what are you, twelve?'

Clay dragged on the joint again and passed it to Al, and from that moment on Clay kept his mouth shut. Al murmured a few platitudes but Clay wasn't listening. When the joint was finished they walked east towards the main street. There were only two bars left in the CBD – aside from the Hotel Warrnambool – that Clay hadn't been to on his spontaneous pub crawl and they both lay across the road from his apartment.

'Seanchai or Loft?' asked Al as they approached Liebig Street. The sun was kissing the horizon and the main drag was starting to get a vibe about it.

'Loft.'

The pair headed through the haze of smokers arced around the door, and up the stairs. The night's bands were still a couple of hours away from starting and there were only a few handfuls of patrons present.

Al ducked into the toilets and Clay headed for the bar. As he waited for his order he looked around, wondering if Bec and Eddie had changed venues, despite knowing they were probably still at The Last Coach. He could feel his chest tightening as he gazed around the pub.

The barman returned with his two pints of beer, distracting Clay, who fumbled with his wallet, showering a random assortment of notes onto the beer-soaked mat covering the hardwood countertop. 'Sorry, Jarrod,' he mumbled to the barman.

Jarrod picked out the right note without a word and Clay stuffed the rest of the money back in his wallet before continuing his scan of the bar.

'You look a lot cuter without coffee poured all over you,' said a familiar voice behind him.

Clay turned and there was Gabby. She was wearing a lot of eye make-up, her lips matched the colour of her hair, and the ring in her left nostril was now a stud with a small blue gem in it. Clay unconsciously inhaled – she smelt amazing. Gabby was wearing the perfume she knew he liked.

'If you order a coffee, I'm out the door,' he said.

'I'm sorry about that,' Gabby said. 'I got a bit jealous.' She was suddenly taken aback – she'd just gotten a good look at Clay's bruised face. 'What the hell happened to you?'

'Nothing major. It's fine. And that woman on the couch – she's a co-worker. And that couch is where she slept, for the record.'

'I don't care. I did care, but I don't. I don't own you. You're not my boyfriend. You can sleep with whoever you want.'

'Like I said, I didn't sleep with her.'

'Like I said, I don't care.'

'Well, I'm glad we sorted that out.'

'Me too. Wanna get drunk?'

'I've got a six-pint head start on you.'

'Maybe I better get a couple of shots then. No one likes to be the sober one at the party. But are you sure your face is OK?'

'It's fine. You should see the other guy.'

Gabby snorted a raucous laugh. 'I don't believe that for a second. Even I could take you in a fight, old man!'

'Rubbish. You want a shot at the crown, little lady?'

'I sure do.' She grinned. 'The match is set for later this evening. Your place.'

Chapter 21

Under the light of a full moon, Jacinta Porter watched the waves roll in towards Thunder Point. From her seat behind the wheel of her rusty Ford Laser, she couldn't quite see the swells reach their destination against the rocks below, but she could hear them. It was a windless night, odd for Warrnambool, and the sound of water crashing on limestone rang up through her open window with surprising clarity.

Jacinta flicked her cigarette butt out onto the asphalt of the empty car park and checked the time on her phone again. This guy isn't usually late, she thought. Arrogant, yes, slightly scary, yes, and filthy rich, yes, but never late.

A set of headlights appeared in her rear-view mirror and Jacinta took a deep breath, bracing herself. Tonight is the night, she thought. Tonight you ask for more money. Right after you finish having sex with him, as he's going through that overflowing billfold of his, you ask him for more money. He can't say no, she told herself. You know too much.

'I know too much,' she said out loud to herself, practising a confident tone. 'I could go to the police.' Jacinta cleared her throat and tried again. 'I could go to the police,' she said, in a more strident voice this time. 'I know too much. Pay up, hotshot.'

Jacinta giggled a little at that last bit. She was still kinda high. She probably shouldn't have been driving, but she hadn't expected to get the call. Saturdays were her one night off, so Jacinta had thought she would be fine to have a couple of drinks and do a few lines of MDMA.

The car rolled around the roundabout slowly, its headlights caressing Jacinta's car, before accelerating and disappearing off into the night. She was alone at Thunder Point again, and Jacinta realised she'd been holding her breath. She wished she had some more MDMA to snort, but it was back at June's house. Instead, she pulled out a Choice filtered and lit up.

Ten minutes passed before another car arrived. From the shape and halogen glow of the headlights, Jacinta was certain this was the rich guy's car. She took a deep breath, flicked on the interior light, and checked herself in the mirror. Hair good, no lipstick on teeth, top adjusted for maximum cleavage. She flicked the light off again. Her pulse – already running pretty fast from the amphetamine in her system – bumped up another notch. She hated this part of the night. So far there had been nothing untoward happen, but the rich guy's insistence on her not bringing a minder made her feel far from safe. The small handgun in her handbag did little to allay the fears, but Jacinta told herself everything had been fine so far. Nothing bad was going to happen.

The car pulled up a short distance away from hers and turned its lights off. She peered into the moonlit night, but couldn't make out anything inside the car. The light of the night reflected off the roof of the car and its tinted windows.

Jacinta waited for the signal, staring at her phone, willing it to come through, wishing for this job to be over. 'Just think of the money,' she told herself. 'Just think of the money.'

A loud *ting* and the bright flash of her phone's screen indicated a text had arrived – it made Jacinta jump. There it was: the signal. A simple text from a blocked number. No words, just a thumbs up emoji. Jacinta swallowed nervously. She'd noticed her body producing an involuntary shiver whenever she saw that emoticon now, even if it was being sent by friends in a harmless conversation.

Jacinta dropped her phone into her handbag and heard it clink against something hard and metallic in there. That was probably the gun, she thought. Although it could have been a vibrator. Or the handcuffs. It will be just my luck, she thought, that when I dig in there for the gun, when I need it most, I'll end up pulling out a dildo.

She laughed to herself at the thought and felt her body relax.

She grabbed her bag and stepped out of the car into the night. The evening was still warm; for once her short skirt and skimpy top matched the weather.

Jacinta locked the car, dropped the keys into her enormous handbag and began tottering towards the rich guy's BMW on shiny six-inch heels. Her new boots – a purchase made thanks to the recent pay she'd earnt from her new wealthy client – had almost made her forget the horrible incident that had led her to this place. Don't think about that now, she reminded herself, just do the job, and then get more money out of this scumbag.

As per routine, she walked around the car and climbed into the passenger seat. The door closed behind her. 'So what's it gonna be this time, handsome?' she said, searching her bag for lubricant and a condom.

The internal locking mechanism of the doors made a click that startled her. Jacinta looked across to the driver's seat; the rich guy wasn't there. In his place was a thuggish, ugly man, with a round bald head.

She was suddenly aware of a presence in the seat behind her and turned her head. In the dull moonlight coming through the sunroof and the windows, she could make out the figure of a broad-shouldered man, with slick dark hair and a hawkish nose. The smell of cigarette smoke filled the car.

'Who are—' Jacinta began, but she never finished. Hands were around her throat and beginning to squeeze. She tried to scream, but nothing came out. The man with the round bald head stared at Jacinta, watching her with a curious look on his face as the man behind her clenched his hands tighter around her neck.

Jacinta's own hands scrabbled at the strangler's, but she realised that was a lost cause. He was too strong.

The gun. Her eyes widened at the realisation and she fumbled in her bag, searching for the unfamiliar shape of the weapon. Deeper her hands dove, seeking with desperation.

The grip on her neck grew tighter. Oxygen had long stopped getting through – she could feel things cracking inside her neck.

Tears ran down her face. The pain was unlike anything she'd felt before and she could feel the world slipping from her grasp.

With a burst of recognition her fingers fell upon the cold steel of the pistol and she pulled it out with a wild sweep of her hand, squeezing down on the trigger at the same time. The resulting gunshot was deafening inside the confines of the car. It almost drowned out the shattering of the driver's side window and replaced the sound of rushing blood in Jacinta's ears with a high-pitched whine that eradicated all other noise.

'Jesus Christ!' She could make out the muffled yell of one of the men over the tinnitus frequency, and suddenly another set of hands were upon her, this time grappling with her own hands in an effort to extricate the gun from her control.

The gunshot had made the hands around her neck release their grasp and she gasped, sucking air into her lungs like a drowning woman. Incredible burning pain racked her throat as the priceless oxygen slid down her damaged windpipe.

As she breathed that precious air, and tried to ignore the blazing ache in her oesophagus and numbing scream in her ears, Jacinta lost her grip on the gun. The weapon was now in the hands of the bald man sitting next to her.

'No, no, no, no—' she screamed, her broken voice racked by sobs and heaving breaths.

There was one more gunshot and Thunder Point was silent once more, but for the sound of the waves crashing against the limestone cliff below.

Chapter 22

Clay dared to open one eye. He could see wall. Painted wall, light green bordering on grey, like you might see in a hospital. His bedroom wall. He was in his own apartment, in his own bed. That's a good start, he thought. He tried to recall how he'd ended up back there, but drew a blank. Let's see… Clay rolled his mind back through the previous day's events. The pub crawl, that's right. Drinking with Al. Joints with Al. The Loft. Gabby. Oh, yeah.

Clay rolled over and there she was, a sleeping mess of snores, her dyed-red hair splayed across her face and the pillow. The doona was somewhere at the foot of the bed. It must have been a warm night and Clay noticed there was no morning chill in the air. Was it still morning?

Gabby was naked. That sight triggered a bunch of memories, vague, hazy grabs of recollection, but recollections nonetheless. Clay was naked, too. He sat up in bed and reached for his watch: 9.30 a.m. I could really use more sleep, he thought. But the heat of the day was already starting to increase the temperature in his room to a level he realised would make sleeping impossible. That, and the sure-and-steady rise of a hangover. More slumber was not an option.

There was a low buzz from his bedside table and Clay remembered something had awoken him. His phone, vibrating away like a dying blowfly. Who the hell would call me at such an undignified hour on a Sunday?

He grabbed the mobile. 'BEC – WORK' said the screen. He pushed the answer button.

'Surely you know better than to call me at this hour of—'

'Don't start, Clay,' said Bec, all business. 'We need you to come into the office.'

'I'm not rostered on today.'

'I know. But Tudor told me to call you. The Sunday reporter's called in sick and we've got some serious stuff going down.'

Clay tried to rub the hangover out of his eyes as Gabby stirred in her sleep. This was more punishment from Tudor. He could have asked Bec to call any other journo on a Sunday morning. 'This better be good.'

'Oh, it's good. And by good, I mean bad. We've got a burnt-out car with a body inside. Somewhere called Thunder Point.'

A switch flicked in his mind. 'OK, OK, give me fifteen minutes.'

'I'll be there to pick you up in ten.'

Clay rolled out of bed and stood up in a cautious manner. The hangover wasn't as bad as he expected, which either meant he was still a little bit drunk or he had dodged a bullet. He had definitely imbibed enough to warrant queasiness and a killer headache. Maybe I'm a little too match-fit at the moment, he thought.

Clay was in and out of the shower in record time. He pulled on last night's jeans, picked up from the corner of the bedroom floor, and found a clean shirt in the drawer. He was lacing up a pair of Converse when he heard the knock at the door.

Throwing open the door revealed a level of sunlight Clay didn't feel equipped to handle, and Bec holding two coffees.

'Holy crap,' said Clay. 'Gimme a sec to find some sunnies.'

'You've got thirty seconds,' said Bec.

Clay walked back to the bedroom, where Gabby was now sitting up in bed, the doona wrapped around her naked body. He spotted his sunglasses on a desk in one corner of the room and grabbed them.

'Where are you off to?' said Gabby.

'Work. Dead body in a burnt-out car at Thunder Point.'

'And I suppose you'll be hitting me up for a leaked autopsy report in the near future?'

'You are so much more than just a pretty face,' Clay said, laying on the charm. He leant over and kissed her quickly. 'Make yourself at home and just pull the door closed when you go. I'll call ya.'

'Oh, you better, mister.'

Clay was back at the door, sunglasses in position and pulling it closed behind him, in less than thirty seconds. He went to grab one of the coffees from Bec, but she moved her hand away at the last moment, teasing him.

'Who were you talking to in there?' she asked, a mischievous grin on her face.

'My priest. I was taking confession.' He reached for the coffee again, but Bec pulled it away again.

'Uh-uh. That was a woman's voice I heard.'

'The Vatican made some changes recently.' In trying to take the coffee from her, Clay was now well inside Bec's personal space. He could smell her perfume, a subtle flowery number that made him think of a long lost summer spent in Queensland. He was even close enough to see two rogue grey hairs snaking amid the brunette strands over her ear and flowing down to her shoulder. For some reason, that sight intrigued him.

'Funnily enough, I don't believe you,' she said.

'I thought you were in a hurry.'

Bec narrowed her eyes. She handed Clay the coffee. 'Sadly, you're right.' She headed down the wooden stairs into the car park below where the office Subaru waited.

'For the record, it was Gabby,' he said, as he climbed into the passenger seat.

'The coffee thrower?'

'Yes, the coffee thrower.'

'Ha!' Bec slapped the steering wheel. She started the car and slapped the steering wheel again, letting out another chuckle. 'You're a sucker for punishment, aren't you?'

Clay didn't respond as Bec backed out of the car park and sped off towards the street. 'Take it easy on the corners there, Bec, I'm not exactly feeling a million dollars today.'

'Are you hungover again?'

'What's with all the questions?'

'Clay, I think you might have a problem.'

'Oh, I've plenty of those.'

'I mean one you haven't considered – a drink problem.'

Clay heard a serious edge to her tone that he had no time for. 'Bec, I'm not an alcoholic. I'm Australian.' He sipped on his coffee. It was blood-warm and strong, with half a sugar. Just how he liked it. 'And besides, you've caught me on my day off. And it's Sunday morning. I'm allowed to be hungover. And I'm pretty sure you were out at the pub last night with a certain senior constable, so don't pretend you're all Little Miss Innocent.'

'How did you know that?'

'I have spies everywhere,' Clay said with a sly smile. 'It pays to remember that Warrnambool is a very, very small town. It may look like a city, and technically it is a city, but at its heart it's a country town dressed up in city clothes. And in country towns, everyone knows everything about everyone.'

'I'll keep that in mind.'

The jovial mood and warm coffee lifted Clay's spirits. His hangover lost some of its edge, but the sight awaiting them at Thunder Point brought new grief.

The police had blocked off an area of the car park with their cars, angling them around the centrepiece of the scene – a Ford Laser reduced to ash and warped metal.

Bec stopped the car a short distance away from the police blockade and the pair stepped out. Clay smelt the carbon in the air and a faint hint of burnt rubber, merged with the salty sea air of the coastal reserve. The car park, located as it was at the edge of a short cliff and the start of a number of walking trails, would usually be full of tourists seeing the sights and locals walking their dogs. That had been replaced by half a dozen police cars.

Clay and Bec were still fifty metres from the husk of the Laser. At least ten cops stood between them and the remains of the car. Clay knew right away they weren't going to get very close. He'd also noticed another problem: standing next to the ashen hatchback was the corpulent shape of Detective Sergeant

Frank Anderson. He had his back to Clay as he motioned to uniformed officers that scampered around him like trained dogs. When he turned and caught sight of Clay, his eyes were as black as the burnt-out car.

Clay nodded at Bec to start snapping and turned his attention to the nearest cop. He was an older officer, well into his fifties, with a sweep of thick white hair and the features of a kindly grandfather. Clay recognised him and breathed a sigh of relief that it was an officer he knew well enough and who was one of the older brigade who was more likely to talk to a journo rather than follow the new protocols of the police media department.

'Senior Constable Hawker – long time, no see,' said Clay.

'Hello, Clay,' said the officer, offering a small smile. 'Nice morning.'

'Except for that.' Clay gestured at the burnt-out car with his notepad, before tapping it with his pen and giving the policeman a nod. 'What do you know?'

'Nineties model Ford Laser, discovered by a couple of joggers,' said Hawker. 'Called in about half an hour ago. One deceased female on board.' He wiped a bead of sweat from his brow and shooed away a blowfly. 'What a way to go.'

'Tell me about it,' said Clay without looking up from his notes. 'Know who she is?'

'We have our suspicions.'

'I'm not after a name.'

'Female. Caucasian. Twenty-eight years of age. From Warrnambool.'

'What the hell was she doing up here?'

'She was known to police, let's put it that way.'

Clay thought for a second. 'Drugs?'

'Bit of that. But mostly we brought her in for doing things in public one should probably do in the privacy of one's own home. Or in her case, a hotel room.' He offered Clay a quaint wink that made Clay wince in recognition.

'A lady of the night, eh?'

'That's one way of putting it.'

Clay looked at Hawker; he was staring at Detective Sergeant Anderson, who was leaning over the wreckage. 'He doesn't look too happy,' said Clay.

'Bloody oath. Been like a bear with a sore head for weeks.'

'Why's that?'

Hawker returned Clay's gaze, changed tone. 'Ah, just busy, y'know how it is.'

The remark rankled with Clay. Anderson certainly wasn't busy on the Kerry Collins case, which had already been shoved in the back of a drawer. And with hired goons walking the streets, dispensing their own brand of justice, the place didn't seem like the peaceful coastal idyll it once was.

'Is that a line, mate? Is there something going down I should know about?'

Hawker's expression tamed, his jaw looked set in steel. 'No, Clay. It isn't. The city's expanding and with it our workload, that's all I'm saying.'

'What about Frank's…?'

The senior constable cut the air with his hand. 'You've got all you're getting. Now bugger off before you're in my bad books, too.'

Chapter 23

'So what do you want to hear about first? The dead hooker, the hired goons, or the girl who washed up at the Bay of Martyrs?'

It was Monday afternoon, the day after the burnt-out car had been found at Thunder Point, and Senior Constable Eddie Boulton had asked Bec and Clay to meet him at Fishtails Café after work. The colourful restaurant, located only a few shops down from the one Clay lived above, seemed to be in the midst of a post-5 p.m. coffee blitz, which meant every table inside was full. This suited Clay just fine – they would have to sit in the small courtyard out the back, where smoking was allowed.

Clay had noticed the light peck on the lips Eddie and Bec had exchanged on arrival and it irked him more than he cared to admit, but he played it cool, or at least he hoped he gave the appearance of playing it cool. He sipped on a Corona that helped to take the heat out of the late afternoon. The brickwork that fenced in the narrow courtyard was retaining a fair bit of heat, but large umbrellas at each table were taking the edge out of the sun and mid-twenties air.

'Tell me about the escort first,' said Clay, as he lit a cigarette.

Eddie pulled out a notepad. 'Jacinta Porter, twenty-eight, of Warrnambool. She's got priors, a nice mix of stuff. Bit of possession, used cannabis and speed, some driving infringements, a few charges that I can only presume relate to getting busted in the middle of servicing a client. Certainly nothing major on her rap sheet.'

'And why did she burst into flames?' asked Clay.

'The prevailing theory is she fell asleep with a cigarette and accidentally caught fire.'

Clay looked at Bec, who was sipping on a cider. 'What do you think?'

Bec shrugged. 'Seems like a reasonable hypothesis. Is there

any reason to suspect foul play?'

'Not at this stage,' said Eddie. 'Can't say the boys at the station are looking real hard at this one.'

'What about the other cases they're not looking real hard at? Like Kerry Collins?' Clay hadn't meant for the edge to creep into his voice, but he knew it was there and he couldn't hide it.

'They're still not looking at that one,' said Eddie, the reluctant sound of defeat sneaking into his own tone, 'and I think you may have been right about it.'

'Which bit?'

'The bit about them deliberately avoiding the case. Like they're covering something up. I spoke to some of my friends in the criminal investigation unit, low-level fellas, and told them what you told me about Kerry getting a private job off a rich-looking dude in a suit. They went off and came back real sheepish. Warned off it, they said. Dismissed. One of them said to me he was told the matter was under control. I hate to say it, but someone's hiding something about that one.'

Clay dragged hard on his cigarette and stared up at the clear blue sky. Ordinarily he would have enjoyed being right, but not this time. He said nothing, but he could feel Eddie and Bec watching him.

A long moment passed. 'And what about my hired goons?' said Clay.

'I pulled some footage off the Hotel Warrnambool's CCTV system. They've got cameras pointed all around the bar.' Eddie fished his phone out of his pocket and tapped the screen a couple of times. 'Are these the guys that prettied up your face for ya?'

Clay leant forward and squinted at the screen. Despite the pixelation and distortion of the image, he recognised the bald-headed man and his accomplice with the slicked-back hair. 'That's them.'

Eddie nodded. 'I thought as much. I've already run them through our system, sent it up to the Melbourne stations. No bites so far. But something will land.'

There was another moment of quiet. Finally, Bec piped up. 'So we've got a dead escort nobody cares about, a dead teenager the police are sweeping under the rug, and a couple of thugs roaming around bashing journalists. This must be a veritable crimewave for Warrnambool.'

'Sad but true,' said Clay.

Chapter 24

A week passed. January had given way to February. The weather turned sour. The bruising on Clay's face disappeared with the sunshine and he slipped into a kind of holding pattern. There was no news on his three big stories. His hopes of finding out what Lachlan Fullerton was blackmailing Wayne Swanson over vanished like his black eye. Kerry Collins was still listed as an accidental drowning; a death at the hands of 'misadventure'. And the matter of the incinerated prostitute had run only briefly, grabbing everyone's interest instantly, and then disappearing just as quickly.

All three stories were yesterday's news, and Clay found his days filling up with the same petty rubbish they had consisted of at the start of the summer. Inconsequential stories about car parks. Back to school stories. Previews of fundraising events. In between he read the real estate section of the paper, searching for a new apartment. Nothing promising was available. The university students had begun rolling back into town before Australia Day, sucking up every available flat, apartment, unit, spare room, share house, bungalow, and affordably priced home for rent. Warrnambool was full, and it had no space left for Clayton Moloney.

In the wake of Jacinta Porter's death at Thunder Point, Clay kept in touch with Gabby. He called her every couple of days just to say hi, waiting for her to let him know when Jacinta's preliminary autopsy report came in, having dropped a hint about it early on. They caught up over the weekend. Clay stayed at her house – his apartment had become infested with a growing pile of brown cardboard boxes.

Finally, ten days after Jacinta's death, Clay received a text from Gabby: *I've got something for you. It's going to cost you dinner and a box of cookies.*

Clay almost jogged from his desk to the photographers' department, where Bec was processing photos from what looked like a school swimming sports day. 'You busy?' he asked.

Bec looked up from her screen, eyes wide and hopeful. 'Are you kidding? I'm so bored I could watch cricket.'

'Wanna come and read an autopsy report?'

Bec tipped back her head, laughed a little. 'Is it worrying that I really, truly do?'

Clay grabbed a set of car keys and told the deputy editor he needed Bec to come with him to follow up a lead. Clay didn't specify what the story was and didn't give Terry Kenna's usually slow-responding brain time to kick in – he and Bec were already out the door and on their way to the police prosecutor's office, by way of the bakery.

As they had before they took the report to Cannon Hill, where the beauty of the view, even in the inclement weather, was in direct opposition to the gruesomeness contained in the photocopied words and pictures in their hands. Sitting in the work car, with a light drizzle falling on the windscreen, Clay read each page and passed it to Bec, who devoured it just as quickly. He waited in silence as she finished with the last page, watching her read and willing her to hurry up.

'Holy crap,' said Bec finally. 'The fire didn't kill her.'

'Nope,' said Clay. 'The .38 calibre bullet in her head did.'

'What the hell is going on here?' She turned in her seat to face Clay.

'I have no idea.'

'What do we do with this information?'

'We print it.'

Bec frowned, forcing down the corners of her mouth. 'Can we do that? Won't the police come looking for you and ask how you got hold of an autopsy report? They're going to want to know who leaked it to you.'

'So? A journalist doesn't have to give up his sources. There are laws about that. And besides, you heard what Eddie said the other week, the cops aren't looking real hard at this case.

What if it's another Kerry Collins? What if they're deliberately not looking? If we go to print with this, it makes it a lot harder for the cops to do nothing.'

Bec broke off from his gaze and Clay watched her as she stared out the window. 'Why didn't you do the same for Kerry Collins?' she said eventually.

'I wanted to,' he said. 'I thought about it. I could have run a story about the mysterious man in the suit seen talking to Kerry, offering her a job just prior to her disappearance. But it all feels so much like gossip, like Chinese whispers. And I couldn't do that to her family. But this,' Clay pointed at the autopsy report, 'this is official. This is documented. We can run this and the cops have nowhere to hide.'

'The cops were probably waiting for this report before they did anything, Clay. No offence, but you're starting to sound a bit paranoid.'

'Can you blame me?' he said, his voice getting elevated in tone and volume. 'I got beat up a couple of weeks ago. I've got a cop telling me his colleagues are covering up a case. Every big story I touch hits a brick wall. And I've just been evicted. Who's to say that's not wrapped up in all this? Who's to say all of this isn't linked together?'

'Whoa, I think you're drawing a longbow on that one.'

'Says who? If someone had told me last year about all this crap happening, I wouldn't have believed them. This is Warrnambool, the nice, quiet, peaceful city by the sea. The tourist hotspot. Sure, it has its occasional slips, but all this stuff: cover-ups, murders, beatings… I don't know what to think any more, Bec. This is all just nuts, y'know, but I sometimes get this feeling like I'm being watched. Like someone's going to jump out of an alleyway and beat the crap out of me. Now, you may say that sounds far-fetched, but did I mention it has already happened once before?'

Clay was looking out to sea; he could feel Bec staring at him. She didn't say anything, though, and that only made him wonder what was going on inside her head. Waves crashed on the coast, white rollers followed further out, threatening and menacing and never-ending, like the thoughts in Clay's mind. All of a sudden he felt drained, like he needed to sleep, probably for an entire day.

'This is a personal question, I know,' said Bec. Her voice was pitched low, laced with concern. 'But how much marijuana are you smoking these days?'

'It's got nothing to do with it,' said Clay, unable to stop himself snapping. 'I'm just not sleeping very well and it helps me sleep. And I think I have every right to be paranoid. It's got nothing to do with smoking weed and everything to do with being set upon by a couple of no-neck thugs, just because I'm trying to do my goddamn job!'

Clay slammed his fist on the dashboard to emphasise his sentence. It caused the glovebox to spring open. Clay stared at the emptiness of the drawer for a moment before closing it again. It had completely derailed his train of thought. Unable to help himself, he burst into laughter. He heard Bec start giggling beside him.

'Well, that ruined your big dramatic moment,' she said, laughing.

'Sorry, I got carried away there.'

'But seriously, lay off the weed.'

'OK. I hear you. But if I can't sleep, I'm calling you at stupid o'clock in the morning to let you know.'

'Fine.' Bec handed the autopsy report back to Clay, who stared at it for a few seconds, focusing on the words *.38 calibre bullet*. Shootings in Warrnambool were a rarity. It almost seems surreal, he thought. 'Who would want to shoot an escort?' he said.

'I don't know. You could make a list: angry wife, disgruntled boyfriend, ripped-off customer? But, hypothetically speaking, how would you find out the answer to that question?'

Clay's brain ticked over and a thin smile arose on his face. He felt more awake all of a sudden. He turned away from the crashing waves. 'I might have a couple of ideas,' he said.

Chapter 25

The hotel room was small and in dire need of a makeover. It was clean, Bec decided, or at least as clean as it was going to get, but there was something in the air… not so much a smell, but more of a taste somehow, that explained why this was the kind of room you rented by the hour, not by the day.

A small fridge stammered mechanically in the corner. It sat below a bench that ran the length of one wall. Bec had chosen to sit on the bench rather than the bed. While its floral bedspread had the smell of fresh laundry, she had visions of a UV light revealing something akin to a Jackson Pollock painting. The more she thought about it she realised the bench probably looked like a painter's drop sheet under a UV light as well, but she convinced herself it was the lesser of two evils.

Bec leaned back against the wall and could hear the murmur of the TV in the next room. Aside from the fridge, it was the only sound. Clay sat in a chair in another corner, silently smoking his foul-smelling cigarettes in direct contravention of the no smoking sign plastered above Bec's head. He had cracked open a window in deference to Bec's protestations, but all that had done was let in a cool sou'wester to blow the smoke further into the room.

Bec watched Clay as he smoked and stared out the window into the hotel car park. She hated to admit it, but she was becoming increasingly worried about him. His moods wavered between paranoia and apathy, between bubbling anger and childlike over-enthusiasm. She wasn't sure if it was the lack of sleep, or his reliance on booze and weed, or a lingering after-effect of his beating. Either way, he was not quite the same charming rogue she'd met over a month ago.

'Show time,' he said in a low voice, stubbing out his cigarette on the windowsill and dropping the butt into a nearby bucket that had been pressed into service as a bin.

Thirty seconds later, the door opened and a woman entered wearing a dress that Bec reckoned was at least two sizes too small. It barely covered her underwear or her bulging breasts, and combined with her black high heels, peroxide-blonde hair, and dangerously long fingernails, Bec was in no doubt this was the woman who advertised in the paper as Candy. Candy, which Bec figured was undoubtedly not her real name, appeared to be roughly Bec's age, but Bec noticed with a pang of guilt that time had been less kind to Candy. She's a damn sight better at applying make-up than I am though, Bec thought.

'Hello, darl, I wasn't expecting a sheila,' said Candy, through chews of her gum. At that moment she spotted Clay sitting in the corner. 'Ah, right, a couple is it? Just so's ya knows, that's gonna cost a bit extra.'

Candy closed the door and crossed to the bed, where she began pulling an array of objects out of her bag, the kind Bec had euphemistically heard described as 'marital aids'. Bec watched in a kind of perverse awe at Candy's arsenal before suddenly realising she was gaping, mouth open, at what Candy was producing, and that Clay was staring at her and trying to keep a smirk under wraps.

'So, how you wanna do this?' said Candy. 'Do one of yas wanna go first and the other watch, or do we all just go at it and see what happens?'

As Candy said this, she held up a large black phallus and Bec could feel herself blush, much to her own annoyance. She'd been around the world a couple of times, including prolonged stints in Amsterdam and some less savoury parts of Bangkok, but for some reason Candy's paraphernalia, coupled with Clay smirking in the corner of the room, was making her cheeks heat up to a deep shade of red.

To her relief, Clay finally broke the awkward silence. 'It's OK, ma'am, we just want to talk. And no, we're not cops. We're journalists.'

Candy looked from Clay, to Bec, and back to Clay, and then

to Bec again. 'That's a shame,' she said, and began packing her tools away.

'We'll still pay you for the hour, so as not to waste your time,' said Clay. 'I'm sure you're a very busy woman.' There was not a single hint of sarcasm or irony that Bec could detect in his voice.

'Good,' said Candy. 'So, what is this? Some big exposé on being a prossie? You wanna know what it's like suckin' dick for a living?'

The accent is so ocker, so twangy, so *Strine* that Clay almost sounds British by comparison, thought Bec.

'No, Candy, we want to talk to you about Jacinta Porter,' said Clay.

Candy had finished repacking her bag and at the sound of Jacinta's name, she froze for a moment. Her expression glazed and her jaw stopped its constant work on the chewing gum in her mouth. Candy turned and sat on the bed, her movements almost mechanical.

'The poor darl,' she said. Her oversized handbag was now on her lap and she held it like she was cuddling a small child. 'The poor little darlin'.'

'How well did you know her?' asked Clay.

'Well enough. Her and me are some of the only girls based in town. Most of the ones doing this area come down from Ballarat or Geelong, maybe Melbourne, but you get to know the local girls real well. So's ya don't cut each other's lunch, ya know? And ya kinda keep an eye out for each other a bit. Plus, we share a booker.'

'A booker?'

'The guy that books the work. He's like a pimp. He's waiting out in the car.'

Clay nodded. 'You obviously heard about what happened to Jacinta.'

'Yeah. Burned alive. What a way to go.'

Bec watched as Clay's gaze flicked from Candy to her, and she found herself watching in eager anticipation to see how the next few moments would play out.

'Candy, the fire didn't kill Jacinta,' said Clay in a soothing low tone. 'She was shot.'

Candy's hand went up to her mouth and her eyes grew wide and watery. 'Oh, my God,' she said. 'Oh, my God.'

Bec could see the tears welling up in the escort's eyes. Clay stood and took the couple of steps between them. At first Bec thought he was going to sit next to Candy and console her, but instead he offered her a tissue, which Candy accepted. Clay then offered Candy a cigarette, which she waved off before pulling her own pack out of her bag and lighting one.

Clay sat back down and lit up as well. The room slowly filled with smoke again as Bec looked on, not daring to say anything.

'Candy—'

'Please, it's June. Don't call me by my work name. Not now. Not while we're talking about all this horrible stuff.'

'Sorry. June. Have the cops spoken to you about Jacinta?'

'Nuh. That was weeks ago and I haven't had a single bit of nothin' from 'em. Not that I really wanna talk to the pigs, though.'

Bec frowned. Jacinta died three weeks ago and it had taken Clay a week to arrange this meeting. She was puzzled – if a journalist could talk to people like June, why couldn't the police?

'Did they talk to your booker?'

'Yeah, but I don't think he would have said much. He keeps us all at arm's length, ya know what I'm sayin'?'

Clay nodded. 'June, this might be a tricky question, but do you know anyone who would have wanted to harm Jacinta? Or could have shot Jacinta?'

June nodded straight away. 'Lerner.'

'Who's Lerner?'

'That's her ex. He's dodgy as. Real aggro, real loose. She ditched him a year ago, but he's the jealous type. Which isn't ideal for someone dating an escort, ha.' Her laugh was nervous and she was puffing on her cigarette almost between every sentence. 'She had to go get an intervention order and all that, for what it's worth. Yeah, Lerner's dodgy as, all right, probably got guns and that. He's on the ice, too, so ya never know what he's gonna do. He's sketchy. She said he'd been hasslin' her a bit lately, too.'

'What do you mean?'

June took a long drag and exhaled a large drift of smoke, causing Bec to stifle a cough. 'Jacinta's been doin' real good of late, like work-wise. About a month ago, she fell in with a client, a regular one, who was loaded. She'd see him a couple of times a week. Paid her real well, she said. Like, *real* well. She cleared her debts and started splashing a bit around. Bought a few new dresses. Stopped buyin' cheap pingas and started buyin' good MDMA. Even bought some coke one night. Man, that was a helluva night. But I think word got back to Lerner, probably through her dealer, I reckon. He's a real stooge.'

'Does Lerner have a first name?'

'Nuh, never bothered to know it. He's not worth learnin' his first name, ha!'

'What's her dealer's name?'

June looked at Clay like she was sizing him up and Bec wondered if Clay had pushed her trust too far. 'I dunno his real name,' said June eventually. 'He's got a nickname, but I can't remember what it is. Something flashy.'

Clay smiled. 'Vegas?'

June's face lit up. 'Yeah, that's it.'

Clay nodded. 'I know Vegas.' He dragged on his smoke and leant forward as he reached into his back pocket, pulling out his wallet. 'You've been very helpful, June. How much do we owe you for the hour?'

Bec half expected June to dismiss Clay's offer, but the escort stuck out her hand and took the cash. Clay thanked June again and then the woman was gone, tugging her dress down over her butt with one hand as she tottered out the door.

Bec watched Clay as he finished his cigarette. 'Now what?' she said.

Clay offered a look she was beginning to associate with one of his cheekier moods. 'We're goin' to Vegas, baby,' he said, in a bad American accent.

Chapter 26

Clay wasn't proud of the fact that he claimed the man known as Vegas as an acquaintance, but he wasn't too stuck up to deny it. They'd met at a party close to ten years ago and had hit it off in the way typical of 1 a.m. introductions. Clay had been the really drunk guy looking to get high and Vegas had been the really high guy who had the drugs. They'd bonded over lines of speed, the remainder of a bottle of butterscotch schnapps, and a love of *South Park* and stoner rock.

Clay was also not proud of his drug use, but again, he wasn't too stuck up to deny it. Aside from his recent increased usage of marijuana, he was a party dabbler. He never touched heroin or ice, but if pretty much anything else got offered his way at a gathering, he rarely said 'no'. Clay understood drugs could be bad, but as far as he was concerned, the bad things only happened to the stupid and careless people. He was neither.

As a result, he'd kept in contact with Vegas. Clay would be the first to admit most of their contact centred around Clay buying the occasional bit of pot from him, usually when he couldn't get any from Al at the office. But Clay and Vegas had a few friends in common and had enjoyed a few drinks together at the Hotel Warrnambool or The Loft or some other bar in town.

'I'm pretty sure he still lives here,' said Clay. He and Bec were parked outside what he presumed was Vegas' house. It was situated in Wanstead Street, an address regarded around town as the worst in Warrnambool. The street name was known to make police officers shake their heads, journalists give a wry smile, and real estate agents cringe.

'First a prostitute and now a drug dealer,' said Bec. 'You sure know how to treat a girl to a fun Saturday. I have to say that while I have really enjoyed tagging along with you for all of this, even when I didn't need to, maybe I should have sat this one out.'

'Why is that?'

'Look at this neighbourhood. I feel like I'm going to get knifed for just being here. It's so....' She searched for the word.

'Mish?' offered Clay.

'"Mish"? What's *mish*?'

'It's a Warrnambool word, local slang,' he said. 'It's short for "commission", which is short for "housing commission". But basically it means this is a government housing area. So "mish" has become slang for the lowest of the lower class, with all the horrid connotations that come with it.'

Clay watched her look around, taking in the unmown lawns, the rusted out cars, the busted toys, the weeds, the fallen-down wire fences, drab brown-brick houses, the torn curtains, the broken security doors.

'Mish,' she said, as if she was tasting the syllable. 'It's a good word.'

Clay nodded and looked over at Vegas' house. 'I'm glad you came along, Bec. I like having you around. It makes me feel less crazy, or less like I'm completely in over my head. And it makes me feel like someone's got my back.'

He could feel Bec looking at him but he didn't turn his gaze. Instead he opened the car door and went to step out. He felt a hand on his arm and finally turned back to face Bec.

'Wait – what are we doing?' she said, with more than a hint of concern in her voice.

'We're just going in to have a talk to my mate Vegas.'

'You're about to go into a drug dealer's house in *the mish*.'

'You've already got the hang of the word. I'm impressed.'

Bec scowled at him. 'This is no time for jokes, Clay. I'm not going in there with you. You shouldn't go in there, either.'

'Bec, I've been in there before. I've bought drugs here before. Hell, I've been to a party here once before. And to be honest, you're probably safer in there than sitting out here by yourself.'

'It's the middle of the day, I suppose. What's the worst that could happen?'

'Probably nothing,' said Clay. 'But before I leave you here, you should probably know a few things.' He pointed a little way down the street. 'A woman was murdered in that house in 2003. They never found the killer.' He turned and pointed back down the other way. 'That house on the corner was set alight by a bunch of punk kids about ten years ago. Or rather, that house was built on the site of the one the punk kids burnt to the ground.' He pointed at another house nearby. 'Someone put two bullets through the door of that house last year—'

'OK. OK. You've made your point. Y'know, Warrnambool seems less and less charming, the more time I spend with you.'

'Every town has its dark side. This is Warrnambool's. The other ninety-nine per cent of it is brilliant. The dregs tend to get concentrated into the mish.' Clay still had his car door open and began to step out of the vehicle. 'So are you coming or not?' He finished the sentence by closing the door behind him.

Clay didn't look back as he began walking across Vegas' front yard, but he heard Bec's door open and close, followed by the sound of feet speed-walking to catch up to him.

Like all the houses in the neighbourhood, Vegas' place had a metal security door in front of its regular wooden door. Clay rapped on the security door, making a harsh clatter. As the last rattles died away, Clay heard the music within the house get turned down.

The door opened and there was Vegas – a skinny, pale guy in a basketball singlet, with a baseball cap over his bleached-blond hair.

'Oh, hey Clay,' Vegas said. He seemed confused.

'Hey, Vegas.'

'Did you text me?'

'Nah, man, I just dropped by for a chat.'

Vegas relaxed. 'Oh, cool, I thought I'd just gotten all forgetful and stuff. Come on in.' He unsnibbed the lock on the security door.

'Who's the chick?' asked Vegas, as Clay and Bec entered the lounge room. It was just as Clay remembered it. The room was dominated by a huge TV and sound system, situated in front of a pair of curtains that never opened. The TV lorded over a coffee table covered in the detritus of a hundred late-night video game sessions – a hubcap used as an ashtray, empty cans of beer and energy drinks, junk food bags, a bong – and two impressive armchair recliners.

'This is Bec. We work together. Bec, this is Vegas.'

'Cool,' said Vegas. 'So, ahh, what's goin' on, man? You chasin'?'

'Nah, man. Like I said, I wanna talk to you about something.'

'You ain't gonna put me in the paper or nothing?'

'No. It's all off the record.'

'Sweet.' Vegas plonked into one of the armchairs and grabbed the bong. He didn't offer Bec or Clay the other armchair.

'Vegas, did you know Jacinta Porter?'

'Oh, yeah. Misty. That was her hooker name... *sorry*... working name. Yeah, she was a cool chick. I heard she died or something.'

Clay watched Vegas as he packed the cone-piece with a mixture of marijuana and tobacco. 'You didn't hear how she died?'

Vegas shook his head, hardly breaking concentration.

'She was shot,' said Clay.

Vegas stopped packing his bong for a second, looked up. 'Whoa. For reals?'

'Yep. Do you know who did it?'

'How would I know, man?' He picked up a lighter and was about to light his bong, but seemed to be carried off by a rapid stream of thoughts.

'Do you know a guy called Lerner?'

Vegas stopped again, but this time his whole body froze. He was already a pale-skinned person, but Clay could have sworn Vegas went another two shades paler at the mention of Lerner's name.

'No.'

'No?'

'No… just… *no*… Tell me Lerner didn't shoot Jacinta.'

'So you do know him. I don't know that Lerner killed Jacinta for certain, but that's the best guess at this stage.'

Vegas sat the bong and the lighter on the coffee table, his interest vanished. He stood up, putting his hands to his face as he looked at Clay. 'No way,' said Vegas. He began walking around the lounge room, turning this way and that in a state of agitation. 'No way,' he repeated.

'What's wrong, mate?' said Clay.

Vegas paced a bit more, grabbing his singlet in his hands, looking for comfort in the action. He was distressed, uneasy in his skin. He sat back down again and grabbed the bong, lit the cone-piece and inhaled the resulting smoke with one quick, well-practised move. Clay pulled out a cigarette and lit it as Vegas exhaled, the journalist watching the smoke rise to the ceiling, which was stained a light-brown tinge above Vegas' reclining armchair.

'Lerner came round here, like three weeks ago,' said Vegas, as he sat the bong back on the table. 'He was coming down, edgy as. Been on a week-long ice binge and was flippin' out so he wanted some weed.' He had been talking to Clay but he turned his attention to Bec for a second. 'I don't sell ice, that stuff's messed up,' he said, before turning back to Clay. 'So I sell Lerner a stick, but he doesn't leave, wants to use my bong and hang out. We pull a few cones and chill for a bit, he calms down, it's all cool. But he still won't leave. I mean, I don't like the guy, but he scares me so I don't wanna tell him to get out or nothin'. Anyways, we kinda talk and play some *Grand Theft Auto* for a bit and have a few more cones and he starts bangin' on about Jacinta Porter. And I'm like, hey, I know that chick. And he starts gettin' a bit edgy like "how do you know that chick?" like he thinks I'm sleepin' with her or somethin', which I would never do. I mean, I don't need to pay for it, ya know what I'm sayin', and the idea of bangin' a hooker outside of her work hours…'. Vegas screwed up his face by way of illustration. Clay felt Bec's angry glare boring into the side of his face as

Vegas continued.

'Anyways, so I says, "Nah, man, she just comes around here and buys some weed occasionally." And then, and I don't know why, but then I says, "Actually, she's been buyin' all kinds a shit lately." Lerner's real interested and I can't shut up. Probably 'cos I'm stoned. So I tell him how I got her some real primo MDMA, like a big bag of the powdered shit, and then how another time I got her a big bag of coke. Hardly anyone buys coke around here, it's way too dear, like you can get twice as much speed for the same amount, ya know what I'm sayin'? And Lerner's all like, "Where'd she get so much money?" And I'm just flappin' my lips like an idiot and I tell him how she told me she hooked up with this real rich suit who drives a top-notch BMW, and how he was paying her top dollar, like well above her goin' rate. She's got it made. Sees him a couple of times a week.'

'How did Lerner take that information?' said Clay, quietly adding to the collection of smoke in the room.

'Not well, dude. Not well. He started getting angry again. I made him have another bong or two to chill, but it did nothing. He starts goin' on about how "that bitch owes me money" and how she ruined his life, and I'm just like, whoa, how the hell do I get this guy out of my house? Eventually he just took off. Like real abrupt.'

Vegas had grown increasingly animated during the telling of his story, racing out his words, but he went quiet for a moment, like a vacuum cleaner getting turned off, leaving a strange silence in the room.

'Jacinta was dead two days later. I didn't piece it together until now, but yeah, Lerner was here two days before Jacinta died. That dude's mental. Someone said they saw Lerner out at one of the pubs recently and he was off his head on ice and he just went nuts, takin' on the bouncers and shit. He's a freakin' psycho. He's… oh, shit… I shouldn't have told him all that stuff about Jacinta buyin' coke and havin' money, should I? Oh man, I did bad, didn't I?'

Vegas looked up at Clay then looked back down at his own shoes, but it was enough for Clay to see the genuine sadness and remorse in Vegas' eyes.

'It's not your fault, Vegas,' said Clay. 'You're not to blame for the actions of a psychopath like Lerner.'

'Yeah, but if I hadn't…'

'Not your fault. Don't beat yourself up about it. If it's any consolation, Lerner will be found sooner or later and brought to justice.' Clay could feel Bec bristle beside him and out the corner of his eye he could see the confused look she was throwing him.

Clay finished his cigarette and thanked Vegas for his time, promising to come round soon for a beer under better circumstances. With that, he and Bec made their goodbyes and headed back out into the sunshine, which seemed brighter than usual after the dark air of Vegas' lounge room.

'He's going to be caught and brought to justice?' said Bec, as they walked back to the car. 'What are you on about?'

'Yeah, well, I had to say something.'

'Eh, my point remains the same – we've seen precious little justice for anyone so far. And the way things are going we're far more likely to see more trouble, especially with this Lerner nutcase on the loose.'

Clay shrugged as they climbed into the office Subaru. 'I wanted to put his mind at ease. Poor guy went and blabbed the wrong thing to the wrong guy and he feels bad about it. I felt sorry for him. That could have happened to anyone.'

'No,' said Bec, as she started the car and pulled away from the kerb. 'Telling meth-heads about what drugs their prostitute exes have been buying and how they made their money screwing rich guys in BMWs does not happen to anyone. You have to have made some bad life choices to have ended up in that situation.'

'Come on. Vegas is a nice enough guy. He means no harm, and he's going to be shaken up for a bit. I just tried to tell him something to make him feel better.'

'Yeah, but the hell do we do now?' said Bec. 'We've got two people pointing the finger at Lerner, but you can't print any of it, and you can't go to the cops with it. If they don't care about this case, they're certainly not going to care about what a hooker and a pothead told you about it.'

Clay nodded. 'True, but we do have one cop on our side. We need to talk to your boyfriend.'

'He's not my boyfriend,' snapped Bec.

'Whoa, sorry. I didn't mean to hit a nerve. What's the matter? Did you guys have a fight or something?'

Bec swerved to the side of the road with a savage twist of the wheel and slammed on the brakes. Clay had to put his hands out to stop his head hitting the dashboard.

'Why do you keep doing that?' she said.

'Doing what?'

'Having subtle little digs at me and Eddie. Like high school crap.' Her voice changed, switching to a tone dripping with exaggerated sarcasm and teenage fakeness. 'Ooh, he's your boyfriend, ooh, you love him, ooh, you had a fight.' Her expression returned to normal, albeit an agitated version. 'What are you? Fifteen? Do you have a problem with me sleeping with Eddie? He's your mate, you introduced us, but I'm not allowed to shag him? Is that it? Women aren't supposed to have sex with men unless they're our boyfriends. Is that it?'

Clay felt ambushed. Something had been brewing he wasn't aware of, but he conceded maybe his own feelings had been manifesting in a way he hadn't intended.

'Hey, I'm sorry,' he said, hands raised in a *don't shoot* gesture. 'I was just trying to make a joke.'

'Well, cut it out. Do I go around saying Gabby is your girlfriend just because you two are doing it?'

Clay shook his head. 'No, but to be fair, you have made jokes at her expense before, and passed a vaguely snide judgement on me and my choices in relation to her.'

There was silence in the car. Clay wanted to say something. Deep inside, a feeling was struggling to get free, but he couldn't even bring himself to put it into words in his own head, let alone say it out loud. The emotion died before it even reached his lips, and the moment passed.

Bec put the car into gear and they drove back towards the centre of town in silence.

Chapter 27

'Are you OK?'

Bec realised with a start she was miles away. She should have been in the present – Saturday night with Eddie at the Pickled Pig, which he had assured her was Warrnambool's classiest restaurant – but her mind was stuck several hours in the past, playing through the day's events. Talking with June, visiting Vegas, the weird and uncomfortable fight she'd had with Clay after leaving Vegas' house.

Bec had dropped Clay off at his apartment and Clay had said something about telling Eddie what they'd learnt from June and Vegas. She'd muttered a 'yeah, yeah, yeah' and driven off in a mood. Why had they fought? She wasn't even sure why she'd snapped at him. There was tension between them, she knew that, but frankly she was getting tired of it. She was tired of Clay's juvenile asides about her relationship with Eddie, yet she knew she was edging dangerously close to doing the same thing to Clay in regards to Gabby. What the hell did that mean?

'I'm fine,' said Bec. 'Sorry, long day. Weird day. Really weird.'

'Wanna talk about it?'

Bec looked around the restaurant. It was full but it didn't have a sense of bustle or busyness to it. The lighting was low, the music was quiet and the conversations were low-key. The waiting staff glided between the tables as if on hoverboards. All in all, it hardly seemed the place to discuss prostitutes, drug dealers, and potential murderers.

'I dunno... I spent the day following Clay to some odd places.'

Bec caught a flicker of something in Eddie's expression at the mention of Clay's name, but it was gone before she could pin it down. 'Oh, you definitely have to tell me now,' he said, the interest spiking in his voice.

Bec sipped on her Sauvignon Blanc and began detailing the occurrences of the day. It took all of five minutes and she laid it out in a low, rushed voice, wary of the next table hearing. She talked about Clay's chats with June and Vegas, and about how they both pointed to the ex-boyfriend, Lerner, as prime suspect number one in Jacinta Porter's murder. Bec had just finished recounting the day's events when the first course arrived.

Bec thanked the waitress and stared at Eddie, waiting for a reaction. Deep thought lines dug their way across his forehead. He paused, seemed to be considering his words for a moment. 'I think you guys need to back off a bit,' he said eventually.

Bec had been thinking the same thing, but hearing the words come out of Eddie's mouth made her feel slightly defensive. 'Why?'

'Why? Because you're not cops. Clay's running around like he's Dick Tracy or something, and no good can come of that.'

'No offence, Eddie, but the cops haven't exactly been on the ball of late. You said so yourself. The Kerry Collins case, now the Jacinta Porter case. It's starting to look like you can kill a woman in Warrnambool and the authorities look the other way.'

Eddie exhaled and frowned. 'I know,' he said.

He didn't follow up on his comment. Instead both started tucking into their first course, a succulent piece of pork belly, sided with the unexpected combination of pumpkin, pomegranate, and radish. My God, this is amazing, thought Bec, and for a couple of minutes there was nothing but the sound of eating and the murmur of the restaurant. When they had finished their starter, Eddie looked Bec in the eyes and leant forward.

'You and Clay need to leave this story alone,' he said, in a quiet but firm voice.

'Which one? The dead teenage girl or the dead hooker?'

'Both. I'm trying to do all I can with the information you guys have dug up, but there are some serious blockages above me. I've spoken to some fellow officers and some union guys to try and unplug some of those blockages, but in the meantime you and Clay need to sit tight.'

'Why?'

'Why?' he said, his voice rising enough to get a sideways look from the woman seated at the next table. 'Because you're one degree of separation from a meth-head who just might be a murderer.'

Bec noticed the volume level in the restaurant drop off, like an abrupt gap between songs on the radio. Eddie, who was on his second glass of red, had been a fraction too loud. She waited a moment for the conversations to pick up around them again, flashing a couple of forced smiles to the nearby diners.

'I don't think Clay's going to stop,' she said, her voice edging close to a whisper.

'Then that's a real worry,' said Eddie, mimicking the low volume. 'Look, I've known Clay for a long time. He's a great guy. But, to be honest, I've never seen him like this. These cases… they've gotten under his skin. I've never seen him this intense. He used to be really flippant about his job, like he didn't care, it was all a big joke. But he's latched onto this stuff and, well, to be honest, he seems a little unhinged at the moment. He's a skilled journalist, but when you combine that with his recent beating, the fact he's smoking a lot of weed lately, and his past… it all points in the wrong direction. Have a think about it; what's his next port of call going to be?'

Bec thought for a second. Her mind had snagged on the bit where Eddie had said 'and his past' but she forced herself to consider the question. 'I don't know,' she said. 'I don't think I want to know.'

'I'll tell you where it goes, Bec,' said Eddie. 'His next stop is either talking to my superiors, who will make life very hard for him, or it's trying to deal with Lerner himself. Neither of those scenarios end well.'

Bec sipped on her wine and felt a wave of sadness wash over her. Eddie was right, as much as she didn't want to admit it.

For a moment, she wished Clay was Dick Tracy, like Eddie had said, and that he could solve all the cases by being smarter than everybody else and then they could just move on with their lives. But that wasn't how real life worked. Clay was just a journalist, she was just a photographer, and there was probably nothing they could do, especially if the local police force decided they weren't doing anything about it, either.

The next course arrived, but Bec didn't feel hungry any more.

Chapter 28

So this is what Sunday morning feels like without a hangover, thought Clay. He was perched on his windowsill looking out across the morning traffic on Liebig Street, enjoying his first coffee and cigarette of the day. Below his dangling feet was the roof of the café verandah, peppered with hundreds of cigarette butts, obviously having come out of Clay's window. He felt a momentary pang of guilt about this littering, but went back to soaking in the cool morning air and gentle rays of a new day's sun.

He'd begged off going out with Gabby for a typical Saturday night at the Hotel Warrnambool by using the legitimate excuse of needing to pack up his house. She'd offered to come and help, but he knew that would have ended with very little packing getting achieved. He was one week from eviction and had found nowhere to put the ever-growing pile of boxes that now filled every room in his apartment. All packed up, and no place to go, he thought with a sad smile.

But as much as Clay really needed to get his belongings organised, he had really needed time to digest the previous day's events – June, Vegas, the weird argument with Bec. What the hell was all that about? Bec had flipped out, from out of nowhere. But, more importantly, what was he going to do about Lerner?

Clay finished his cigarette and added the butt to those scattered below just as there was a heavy knock on the door. He felt a chill pass through him. It's 9 a.m. on a Sunday morning – anyone who knows me wouldn't come knocking at that hour... unless they were in trouble or needed something badly.

He swung his feet back inside the lounge room, careful not to spill his coffee, and made his way around the maze of brown cardboard boxes and through the small apartment to the door at the rear. 'No good can come of this,' he muttered.

Clay pulled open the door and there stood the rotund frame of Detective Sergeant Frank Anderson. Barely visible around the sides of his bloated form were two younger men, whom Clay assumed to be fellow detectives, judging by their suit jackets and single-coloured ties, that looked like Kmart buys.

Beneath Anderson's overgrown moustache, his mouth was contorted into a smile that made Clay's stomach lurch a little. 'Good morning, Mr Moloney,' the detective said, with a snide mixture of sarcasm and false bonhomie. 'I do hope we're not intruding.'

Thoughts raced through Clay's mind. What does he want? That was the first one discernible over the din in his head. The second one was something along the lines of, I hope I put all my drug paraphernalia in the coffee table drawer.

'How can I help you, Frank?' said Clay. He leant against the wall just inside the door and sipped his coffee, hoping to give off an air of calm, despite being anything but. He's either here to bust me or warn me off, he thought.

'Aren't you going to invite us in?' said Anderson.

'Sorry, but no, the place is a mess. I'm in the middle of moving out—'

Anderson turned to his colleagues, who stood a couple of steps below him. 'Hear that boys? He's invited us in. That means we don't need a warrant.' With a violent surge of energy, Anderson pushed past Clay and headed up the hallway into the apartment, leaving Clay covered in his coffee.

'Hey! What the hell do you think you're doing?' Clay yelled at Anderson, before turning to the other two detectives. They avoided eye contact and followed their superior into the flat.

Clay trailed them into the lounge room, where Anderson was opening boxes and rifling through the contents. His fellow detectives started to do likewise, making an exaggerated show of ripping the cardboard and spilling whatever was inside onto the floor. Whilst the cops were occupied, Clay quickly scanned the room: no sign of any marijuana. At least that was one plus.

'I said, what the hell are you doing?'

Anderson didn't look up from the box he was searching, he merely shoved it aside aggressively, tipping it out like he was emptying a bin, before moving on to another one. Clay heard the sound of breaking glass.

'I think the more pertinent question, Mr Moloney, is what the hell have you been doing?' said Anderson. The younger detectives were also searching; one was digging through boxes, the other was pulling up the couch cushions, skimming them across the room.

'I don't know what you're talking about.' Clay abruptly felt a calming breeze blow over him. Whatever it is Anderson thinks he's looking for, Clay was confident he wouldn't find it. But more than that, this was obviously an exercise in intimidation, and Clay resolved not to let Anderson get to him. The simple rule he had to abide by was: stay calm.

Clay walked out of the lounge and into his bedroom. He changed his shirt, exchanging the coffee-drenched one for a clean one bearing the Rolling Stones tongue on the front before heading into the kitchen to make another cup of coffee. The kettle was still warm, and the kitchen was only equipped for coffee, so it didn't take long. He then returned to the lounge room, walked to the window, and perched up on the sill. Clay sat half in and half out of the apartment in a look of practised nonchalance. He lit a cigarette and blew the smoke at Anderson's back. The detective was digging in yet another box and Clay could tell Anderson's agitation was growing as quickly as the damp streak was descending down his back.

'This would go a lot quicker, Frank, if you told me what you were looking for,' said Clay. 'Also, you'll see I've labelled the boxes using a texta to make it easier to figure out what's in them, so you could try reading the side of the box first. Might make this illegal police search move a lot more quickly. See, I'd hate to waste your time. I'm helpful that way.'

Anderson wheeled around as fast as his weight allowed – his girth meant the movement was something more akin to a semitrailer attempting a three-point turn. 'I know where you've been, Moloney,' he said with menace in his voice. 'I know what you've been up to.'

'And what's that?'

'You were at the home of a known drug dealer yesterday. You and that tart of yours. So where are the drugs?'

'I didn't buy any. I went around there to have a chat with him. He's an old friend. And calling my co-worker a tart doesn't do you any favours, Frank. You're better than that.' Clay was dialling up the cockiness. If Anderson wanted a battle of wits, so be it.

'Oh, really. And what were you talking about?'

'I thought you said you knew what I'd been up to. Or were you just making that up, Frank?'

Anderson's moustache rippled as a scowl crossed his damp face. 'I know you've been sticking your nose where it doesn't belong.'

'I'm a journalist. I can stick my nose wherever the bloody hell I feel like it.' He sipped his coffee and flicked the cylinder of ash from his cigarette onto the verandah roof below. 'And I'm especially going to stick it wherever I smell a police cover-up.'

Out of the periphery of his vision, Clay could see the other two detectives stop what they were doing and look at Anderson, a mixture of confusion and fear in their eyes. But Clay didn't take his gaze off Anderson, who was lumbering toward him in the surreal manner of a stampeding pig.

With one fat-fingered hand, Anderson grabbed the front of Clay's Rolling Stones T-shirt and hefted him off the windowsill. More coffee went flying, this time over the carpet and Anderson's trouser leg, and Clay's lit cigarette flew out the window.

'I'm going to say this clearly so you can get it through your thick head,' said Anderson. 'You're conducting an illegal investigation that is disrupting a *legal* police investigation. If you don't stay out of the way and cease what you're doing, I'm going to throw you in a cell down at the station, preferably with a couple of meth-heads. Then I'm going to tell the meth-heads that you work at the newspaper that wrote up their last court appearances. And then I'm going to walk away. Do you understand?'

'I understand you're a corrupt piece of shit.'

The punch wasn't powerful, but it was well placed. Clay dropped to his knees fighting for breath.

'If you're thinking about reporting this, I'd like to remind you there are three of us and one of you. We're officers of the law. You're a grubby low-life journalist who spent most of yesterday hanging out with a prostitute and a drug dealer. How do you think that's going to fly?'

Clay gulped for air but couldn't respond.

'Now, one more time, for dramatic emphasis,' said Anderson. 'Stay away from my cases. Your interference isn't appreciated and won't be tolerated any longer.'

Clay finally managed to suck in enough air to squeeze out a sentence. He had a thought that it would be wise to keep his trap shut, but it was immediately cancelled out by a second thought that said he had never been wise. 'If you did your job properly, I wouldn't have to do this.'

'And if you did yours properly, I wouldn't have to do this.' With alarming speed, Anderson hoisted Clay up by the shirtfront and sank a fist into his stomach again, before throwing the journalist to the floor. Clay landed heavily, curled over, and gulped like a fresh-landed perch. He could feel his face turning red, his eyes bulging, as he sought out the other two detectives, who looked uncomfortable and embarrassed.

'Sir,' said one of them, 'I think he's got the picture.'

'He's got the picture when I say he's got the picture!' roared Anderson.

Clay croaked in an attempt to form words. Anderson turned back to him.

'Got another wisecrack, smart-arse?' said Anderson. 'Something defiant? Or an apology, maybe?'

Clay sucked in enough oxygen to stop himself blacking out.

He rolled onto his back and closed his eyes, before whispering something he knew Anderson couldn't hear.

'What did you say? I can't hear you, maggot,' the detective said, leaning closer.

With as much energy as he could muster, Clay got his whisper to an audible level. 'I hope Kerry Collins haunts you for the rest of your life, you fat bastard.'

Anderson drew back his foot as if to kick Clay, who flinched, but the cop seemed to think better of it. 'Come on, boys,' he said and stormed out of the apartment.

Clay lay staring at the ceiling waiting for his breathing to return to normal. Another day, another beating, he thought.

Chapter 29

'I don't believe you,' said Bec. 'There isn't a scratch on you.'

Clay was taken aback. They were in the smoking section at the Hotel Warrnambool and he'd just finished telling Bec and Eddie what had transpired that morning in his apartment. He had not received the level of sympathy and outrage he had expected. Maybe she's still mad at me, thought Clay. Or maybe this latest turn of events did sound a little far-fetched, even for those who had been keeping pace from the start.

'He was careful to avoid my face,' said Clay, and immediately felt like he was being too defensive.

'I'm with Bec,' said Eddie. 'Detective Sergeant Frank Anderson coming into your house and performing an illegal search before assaulting you? Look, I know he's not the nicest of guys, but—'

'Why is this so hard to fathom?' asked Clay. 'We've been discussing the likely possibility of a cover-up for weeks, and now that I've got proof Anderson's behind it, all of a sudden it becomes too much to take in? *Really?*'

'You don't have proof,' said Bec in a low voice.

'What?' snapped Clay.

'You don't have proof,' she said, louder this time. 'You have your word against Anderson's. And two other cops, apparently. Did you think to film it or record it on your phone? That would have been proof. You telling stories in a bar is not proof.'

'Why would I make this up?'

Eddie looked away. 'Cops don't go around Warrnambool beating people up. It doesn't happen, not in my fairly extensive experience, anyway.'

Clay scoffed. 'Cops don't go around Warrnambool covering up murders, but we're fairly sure that's happening. But you didn't answer my question, Eddie – *why* would I make this up?'

'How the hell should I know?' said Eddie. 'Because you're paranoid? Because you're not sleeping? Because you're smoking too much weed? Because you think you're bloody Robocop or something, running around trying to solve crimes that you don't have the training or authority to solve?'

'You think I've finally gone crazy – is that it?'

Eddie shrugged. He averted his gaze from Clay's.

Clay looked to Bec. 'And what's your theory?'

'All of the above.'

Clay shook his head. 'I don't get it, guys. You were happy to believe it's possible a cop is covering up a murder, but for some reason you can't believe it's possible a cop could beat me up in my own home. Isn't it obvious? Frank Anderson is the one doing the covering up. Someone bigger and more powerful is in the mix here and he's doing their dirty work. It means we're getting close to the truth, guys.'

'The truth?' said Eddie. 'I thought you said some meth-head called Lerner killed the prostitute.'

'So why isn't that being investigated?'

There was silence around the table. Clay sipped on his pint. His ribs and stomach were still sore from the punches. He could handle the pain because it hurt his pride more to know that Anderson had been clever and left no discernible marks.

'Look,' said Clay, 'you don't believe me – that's fine. I understand my behaviour has been a little erratic, and yes, I'm not sleeping well and whatever. But do me a favour, Eddie. The two cops who were with Anderson today at my place, I'm pretty sure their names are Cooper and Crowe. I've seen 'em around on jobs before. You know 'em?'

Eddie nodded, grudgingly. He still couldn't bring himself to look in Clay's direction, the allegations against a fellow officer seemed to be taken almost personally. 'Yeah, they're in Anderson's division.'

'Good,' continued Clay. 'I want you to ask them if they were at my place this morning. If they deny it, you'll know they're lying, because if they weren't there, then I've magically guessed the names of two cops who work with Anderson. If they admit to being at my house, then ask them what went down. You're a good cop. You'll know whether they're telling the truth or not.'

'Yeah, I can do that,' he said casually, following it with a sigh. Eddie stood and grabbed his jacket from the back of his chair. 'I have to start work in an hour. I'll let you know how I go, but I'm not going to pretend I feel happy about any of this.'

'No, I can't pretend I'm happy either,' said Clay. 'But thanks, Eddie. I know this is chewing you up.' Clay watched as Eddie gave Bec a peck on the cheek and headed out through the glass doors leading back into the bar.

A heavy silence pulled up a seat as Clay watched Bec stare through the window and into the bar until Eddie was gone from sight. She stirred a gin and tonic with a straw. She'd had just one sip from it, but it was taking up all her attention.

'I'm sorry I upset you the other day,' said Clay in a croaky voice, as he pulled a cigarette from his pack and lit it. 'I'll stop calling Eddie your boyfriend.'

'It's not that,' she said, weariness weighing on her tone. 'I'm sorry I snapped. It's just this whole situation… it's so, y'know, intense.'

'Which bit?'

'What are we doing, Clay?' said Bec, her voice wringing with exasperation. 'Eddie's right. We're not cops. We're not private investigators. I'm a bloody photographer. You're a journalist. Last week we did a job together about a bloody Rotary club holding a game of cow pat lotto to raise money for the local hospital. And yet in between such riveting stories as that, here I am, following you around when I really don't need to while you interview drug dealers and prostitutes who you think might be connected to a murder. What the hell are we doing?'

Clay took a drag on his cigarette and sighed as he exhaled the smoke. 'Beats me, Bec.'

'I mean, I understand some of this was for the paper, but it's not any more. You haven't written anything about this stuff for weeks. The Kerry Collins case, the airport stuff, now Jacinta

Porter… you're flailing in the dark, Clay, hoping you can land a punch with one of these stories.'

'My only hope is to put things right… a young woman was murdered, two young women, and it's happened right under our noses. Is it wrong to care about that?'

Bec shook her head. 'Of course it's not. But you're missing the point. Where will this end? You seem to be getting beaten up an awful lot. Once I can believe, but twice? And by a cop? I like you, Clay, I like you a lot. But I'm worried about you and some of the choices you've been making lately.'

'Is this, by a chance, a drugs lecture?'

'Clay, I remember what you said about Kerry Collins being the same age as your daughter, and honestly, I think that's triggered a whole wave of mental issues you weren't prepared for and aren't dealing with. Kerry Collins' death got to you; I know this, you told me this. But it's unlocked some misguided notion that you have to prove yourself to a daughter you've never known. Is this your mid-life crisis? Most guys just hook up with a twenty-two-year-old with perky tits, and buy a convertible, but you've decided to play cop or vigilante or something. It's not healthy. It's bloody dangerous.'

Clay waited for Bec to finish. He felt tired and sore, and didn't have the energy to fight. Besides, he thought, she's probably right about most of that – the thing is whether I concede that fact or not. He puffed on his cigarette and let her monologue sink in.

'If I admit you're right about a lot of that,' he said, 'will you believe me about Anderson coming to my apartment and assaulting me today? Because it's true. And I need you on my side.'

Bec inclined her head. 'Why? Why do you need me? You've known me for three minutes.'

'I don't know why. But I feel like we…' He trailed off. The end of his sentence would sound like a corny line from a bad movie and he couldn't bear to say it. 'Look, I need someone in my corner, if for no other reason than to keep me in line. Like you're doing. But I also need you to trust me. And believe me. Can you do that?'

She paused, then nodded. 'OK. I can do that. I can even say *I believe you* if that really helps. But will you please give these murder investigations a rest for a bit? Will you please stay away from the cops and promise me you won't go chasing after this Lerner character?'

Clay took a long drag on his cigarette. He didn't want to back away from the Porter story, or the Collins case, despite it having gone cold. And he certainly didn't want to let Anderson off the hook. But he knew it wasn't his place and he knew Bec was right. He exhaled.

'I promise,' he said.

Chapter 30

Monday morning was a beautiful one. Warrnambool was burnished by a golden sunshine that made everything look crisp and clear. It was the perfect February day. The temperature was mild and the wind was a zephyr, instead of the usual gusty sea breezes and flaming northerlies of the summer so far. In times like this nothing could touch the town, nothing bad. Only good things happened beneath the sun's rays, and even in the shade, dappled bursts chased away any threat of shadows.

Clay met the day with a frown, however. His life was in a holding pattern, he was a pilot circling the runway waiting for ground control to say a slot had appeared. But it hadn't... would it ever? A level of depressed angst that he hadn't felt in months started to grip him.

The morning news conference dragged, and afterwards Clay slumped at his desk unable to muster the effort to do anything beyond read and delete the emails that had amassed over the weekend. He didn't want to blame Bec, but telling her he was going to back off from the Porter story had deflated him. His motivation was gone, replaced by a state of depressed nihilism, and it was all because he had given in to Bec and her concerns. Had that really been the right thing to do?

His desk phone rang, trilled loudly beside him, but Clay could barely be bothered to answer it.

'Hello?' he said flatly, not even finding the enthusiasm to give his name or the name of the paper.

'Ah... hello? Is this Clayton Moloney?' said a woman's voice.

'Yeah, it is. How can I help you?'

'Liz Fitzgerald gave me your name and number. She said you were doing some digging around about Wayne Swanson.'

The mention of Swanson was unexpected, it hit him like a shot of adrenalin. 'Yes. Yes I am.' Clay sat upright in his chair and pulled his notepad closer.

'I may have something for you. I…' She hesitated. 'Can we meet in person? It feels weird talking about this over the phone.'

'Are you in Warrnambool?'

'No. I'm in Port Fairy. Can you come and meet me over here?'

Clay nodded with the phone in his hand. 'Absolutely. I can be there in half an hour.'

'That would be fine…'

Thirty minutes later, Clay sat at a table outside Charlie's, a little coffee and lunch café run out of the Port Fairy Surf Life Saving Club overlooking East Beach. The perfect day in Warrnambool extended as far as Port Fairy. The temperature was rising in the stillness of the day, but the clear skies meant Clay could see all the way across the bay to Warrnambool. For a second he realised he wasn't far from Lachlan Fullerton's palatial beach house, but his thoughts were disrupted by a stunning woman who had stopped at his table. She wore a white and yellow sundress that stuck to sensuous curves. Dark sunglasses rested on a strong Greek nose, perched above full lips that were painted a shimmering red. Her long dark hair, tied in a glossy ponytail, reached her shoulders and shone in the sun.

'Are you Clayton?' said the woman.

Clay stood and offered a hand. 'That's me.'

The woman shook his hand. 'I'm Theresa.'

'A pleasure.' Clay directed Theresa to the chair opposite him. A waitress arrived within seconds of them sitting down and coffees were ordered.

'So is this an off-the-record or on-the-record chat?' asked Clay.

'Sadly it has to be off-the-record.' Theresa removed her sunglasses, revealing bright hazel eyes with long lashes. 'Although I may change my mind once I've heard what you know.'

'What did Liz tell you?'

'She said you were digging for dirt on Wayne Swanson. We both worked for Wayne for a couple of years and Liz thought I might be able to help you. But first, tell me what you know.'

Clay eased himself forward, resting his elbows on the table, and told Theresa about the airport deal and the *Sydney Morning Herald* reporter's theory about Fullerton blackmailing Swanson. Clay watched Theresa, waiting for her to respond, as the coffees arrived, allowing her some time to pause.

'As far as I know, I'm not the reason he's being blackmailed, but I could be,' she said finally. 'This is still off the record, by the way.'

Clay nodded, but could feel the frustration mounting. Maybe Theresa sensed it. 'I'm sorry but I shouldn't even be talking to you,' she said. 'I'll explain. Do you mind if I smoke?'

Clay pulled out his own pack. They both lit up and Theresa began. 'When I started working for Swanson the other girls in the office, particularly Liz, bless her, told me to watch what I wore to work. She said Swanson could get a bit grabby. I didn't think too much of it. Or rather, I thought I could handle it. Figured it would be just a bit of friendly office fun. Harmless, you know? I soon learnt Liz wasn't kidding. One day I wore the shortest skirt I owned to work. Swanson didn't leave me alone all day. And by the end of the day he was practically dry-humping my leg, like a dog. At first I kind of laughed it off. He was like a randy teenager. But it just got worse, especially after Liz quit.'

She drew on her cigarette, leaving a red ring on the filter. 'I swear, one day I caught him just standing there in the office, staring at me, touching himself through his pants.'

'That's quite a picture,' said Clay.

Theresa shuddered. 'Eventually I made a complaint. Except I wasn't sure who to complain to. I talked to the other girls in the office, but they didn't seem bothered about it and they didn't want to rock the boat. I spoke to his press secretary in Canberra, who pretty much hung up on me. So I let it go. But then he got worse. He got really grabby. One day he bailed me up in the tearoom. He was pressing himself up against me and I could feel…' She broke off, shuddering again. Theresa stared out to sea, smoking her cigarette for a while, composing herself before she continued. 'If one of the other girls in the office hadn't come into the tearoom, I don't know what would have happened.'

'What did you do?' asked Clay.

'I called his press secretary again. I was in tears. I told him I was going to the press unless something was done. I wish I had gone to the press. Instead, they asked me to clean out my desk and not make a fuss. They reminded me about some clauses in the contract I'd signed about speaking with the media. I went home in tears and the next day some lawyers turned up at my door. They paid me well – really well – but part of the redundancy package was a non-disclosure agreement. Hence why I can't talk to you on the record about this. I still work in politics. If some others girls had come out with similar stories, maybe I would jump in, but I… I don't want to be the lone woman crying foul. You know what happens to women in the public service who do that – they get thought of as either a victim, a whistleblower, or some kind of psycho-feminist. And they don't get many job offers.'

'That's messed up,' said Clay. 'I thought we were past all that.'

Theresa shrugged. 'Apparently not.'

They both sipped their coffee and returned to their cigarettes, watching the waves roll in on East Beach. A few tourists wandered along the sand.

Clay rolled over Theresa's information, and how he might present it in the paper. It was a shocking case, but all it really amounted to was an anonymous story. Tudor would be nervous to print it at the best of times, but now it would give him heart palpitations. On top of all that, if she was the only girl Swanson had paid off they'd identify her easily, and that would make Theresa's life very difficult. She'd already been through enough.

'I appreciate you telling me your story,' said Clay. 'It's given me a lot to think about. And I'm very sorry to hear what happened to you.'

'Has it been any help to you?'

'A big help... Look, I doubt I can take this any further right now—'

Theresa cut in. 'That's fine. I mean, I didn't think I was going to tell you anything you hadn't heard already, there'll be a lot of similar stories out there. I just thought, with enough to go on, you might begin to get a picture of what kind of guy Wayne Swanson really is.'

'Oh, I'm getting the picture now. In neon lights, it has to be said.' Clay rose from the table, picked up his cigarettes. 'Thanks, Theresa.'

'No. Thank you for listening. I think, more than anything, I just wanted to tell someone about it all. A few people I tried to tell refused to believe me. They were like, "How could someone in such a position of power do that?" They dismissed me, called me a liar. Can you believe that?'

Clay gave Theresa a sympathetic smile. 'Believe it or not, I truly can.'

Chapter 31

Clay was still mulling over Theresa's story when he got back to the office. He was sorry for everything that she had been through, and more than a little angered at Swanson's behaviour, but he knew there was no chance of it getting into newsprint. He had one of the best stories of his career just waiting to be told, and he could do nothing with it. People deserved to know, they deserved better. Clay lost himself in the happy scenario of Swanson being publicly flogged and almost bumped into Al, the arts reporter, who was hurrying towards him.

'If I was you, I'd get the hell out of here,' said Al, rushing out the words. 'You're about to enter a shitstorm.'

'What? What's going on?'

Before Al could answer, the voice of Bradley Tudor bellowed from the editor's office. 'Moloney! In here! Now!'

Al gave Clay a look that Clay assumed was similar to the ones given to condemned men on the way to the gallows. This is going to suck, he thought. Clay drew in a deep breath, strapped on a fake smile and breezed into Tudor's office.

'Bradley,' said Clay with pre-heated enthusiasm. 'How's your day? How's the missus?'

'Sit.' Tudor had his back to the door and appeared to be looking out the window. Clay hated him with a sharpening vigour. The editor was posing – it was like something Tudor had probably seen in a movie; nothing too high-brow, though. *Kindergarten Cop* perhaps, that was about his level.

'Clay, can you tell me why I've had the police in my office for half the morning?'

Despite his better judgement, Clay couldn't help himself. 'Because they've finally arrested you as the Timboon horse rooter?' he said.

Tudor whipped around like Clay had shot him in the arse

with an air rifle. Clay continued smiling, but now it was genuine – he'd broken Tudor's big dramatic moment.

'*What*?' said Tudor. 'No…'

Clay was delighted. He'd really thrown Tudor off his game. 'Oh, that's right,' said Clay. 'They caught that guy, didn't they? How did he refer to himself in court? Oh yes, that's right – "Shetland pony enthusiast". That was a great story—'

'Focus, Clay. I had the police in here this morning. They were complaining about you.'

'Really? Was Detective Sergeant Frank Anderson complaining about the bruising my ribs caused his fist yesterday? Or maybe he left his nightstick behind when he was illegally searching my apartment?'

'What are you talking about?'

'I'm talking about Frank Anderson and two of his henchmen illegally ransacking my place yesterday and assaulting me. Did that come up in the conversation?'

'No, it did not.' Tudor was silent as he sat and stared intently at Clay. Clay knew what he was doing; he was doing the same thing Bec and Eddie had done, he was trying to figure out if Clay was lying or not.

'I'm not making this up,' said Clay. 'And I would very much like for you to believe me right now. I've had a rough few weeks.'

Tudor nodded in a small, minimal way. He still looked like he was sizing Clay up, but he was running some employee relations rules at the same time.

'Does this change what you wanted to ask me about?' said Clay.

'Not really,' said Tudor, finally averting his gaze. 'Anderson was here accusing you of… well, a whole bunch of stuff.'

'Let me guess; hampering a police investigation, maybe something to do with drugs. Am I close?'

'You left out interfering with witnesses, stealing police records, and harassing a couple of well-known local identities, namely Lachlan Fullerton and Wayne Swanson.'

'That's pretty funny, Tudor. I haven't seen Fullerton and

Swanson for over a month.'

'What about the rest of Anderson's accusations?'

'I've been doing my job. Interviewing people, chasing leads, investigating. You know – journalism.' The last point was a jab he didn't intend to deliver, but Clay was irritated. Anderson was really playing dirty. If the incident in Clay's apartment wasn't bad enough, it seemed like he was now trying to get Clay fired. Where this was going, Clay could only guess. But it didn't look good.

'Where are the results of this "journalism"?' said Tudor.

'What?' Clay was caught off guard.

'Where are the articles? What have these leads and interviews become? When do I get to print some of your so-called "journalism"? Or have you forgotten about the final stage of the process?'

Clay felt the temperature under his collar rise half a degree. Stay cool, he willed himself. Tudor's onside for now.

'I'm onto something big,' said Clay. He was thinking on his feet. 'Anderson's as crooked as they come, he's as bent as a boomerang. We've got two recent murders in Warrnambool that he's deliberately not investigating.'

'But you are?'

'Damn right. I've got solid leads on both of them. Nothing printable yet, but I'm close. Think about it. I'm on the brink of solving two murders before the police… imagine the headlines. Imagine the hits on our website. Imagine the circulation.' Clay was exaggerating, but he was trying to put it into terms Tudor would understand and get excited about. He needed Tudor behind him, but preferably far enough away so Clay could continue his investigation unhindered.

Tudor's eyes seemed to go out of focus. Clay pressed on. 'As for the Fullerton-Swanson stuff, I'm close to nailing something big there. I don't know how Anderson fits into that, but I do know that the Right Honourable Member for Warrnambool isn't quite so honourable.' Clay detailed the morning's conversation with Theresa in Port Fairy, leaving her name out of it. Tudor listened, but seemed to be growing increasingly agitated the longer Clay went on.

'How do you know she's telling the truth?' said Tudor when Clay had finished recounting Theresa's story.

'I don't, but we have a mutual friend—'

'She could be an opposition party mole for all you know. You'll end up getting us sued!'

Tudor's volume and tone had escalated and Clay was taken aback. 'Hang about,' said Clay. 'I'm not going to get us sued, I'm just saying that I'm digging into things and it's early days and I'm building towards a couple of big stories. I'm keeping you in the loop, Bradley.' The use of the first name is a bit of a suck-up, thought Clay, but desperate times, especially around Tudor, call for sucking-up.

'You give me migraines, Clay. From everything I've heard today, from either you or Detective Anderson, all I can foresee is you in jail or someone suing the paper for millions, which we don't have. The first option doesn't bother me so much, but the second one gives me night terrors.'

'And all I can keep thinking about is the quote: "News is what somebody somewhere wants to suppress, everything else is advertising."'

'Whoever said that never had you on their news team giving them migraines and night terrors.' Tudor ran a hand through his hair. 'I swear, if you cause so much as one lawsuit out of all this – in or out of print – I will fire you. I want you to think very carefully about what you do next, how you do it, and who you do it to. Because I do not want Frank Anderson in here again and I do not want to have to talk to the legal eagles or the press council or anyone else about some huge mistake you've made. Am I making myself clear?'

'Clear as can be, Bradley.'

Chapter 32

Bec had seen breakwaters back in Ireland, but none of those looked quite as sturdy – quite as fortress-like – as the one in Warrnambool. It stood as a towering reminder of man's ongoing and uneasy relationship with nature; a figurative and literal line in the sand, drawn in concrete and rock, between the sanctity of Lady Bay and the ferocity of the Southern Ocean.

Some of the sea walls she'd seen in the country of her birth were little more than a strategic row of boulders, while others featured smooth paved tops for pedestrians to wander along or fishermen to set up and cast a line. But the one laid out before her had cars parked on it, about a storey above the water on the beach side, while another storey and a half up, people walked along a barriered path like soldiers patrolling a parapet walk. But despite the height and size of the structure, Bec had seen photos in the office files where the ocean crashed over the top of the breakwater, as if nature didn't care for man's efforts to tame this part of the Shipwreck Coast.

There was no such battle taking place as Bec gazed across Lady Bay. The breakwater lined the right side of her view, and in front of her the expanse of the bay rippled and ebbed at a gentle pace. Beyond the water, a crescent moon of beach arced around for miles, and beyond that the city poked its head up sporadically on its way to the horizon.

Bec checked her watch again. She was unsure if she had the right place, because Eddie had said he would meet her here at 6 p.m. and it was now 6.10 p.m. Eddie had asked her to meet him at 'a picnic table near the breakwater at the end of the promenade', and she thought this was it. There were a few picnic tables scattered around and she assumed the path leading off around the bay was the promenade, but she'd found people assumed a lot when giving directions, which had led to some confusion at work.

There were worse places to sit and wait, she decided. Warrnambool was a nice place and she had met plenty of good people. That was why she'd left South East Asia, wasn't it? To meet nice new people in nice new places? She thought for a moment; she wasn't sure why exactly she'd decided to settle here.

She wasn't regretting it. Sometimes Clay made her think she regretted moving to south-west Victoria, but the feeling soon passed. He made her nervous and excited, like she was in her twenties again, but she wanted to live the quiet life of a more mature adult at the same time.

None of her misgivings really related to Clay. It was these stories, these cases – the death of Kerry Collins, the secret business dealings of Wayne Swanson, the shooting of Jacinta Porter. She disliked thinking of them as *cases*; as she'd told Clay, he wasn't a cop or private investigator. But more and more these things felt like cases for them to solve, to work out, to prove to people they'd been overlooked. And that also made her nervous and excited. She yearned for an uncomplicated existence, but something in her craved the same kind of justice Clay talked about.

Her life had been a constant balancing act between seeking peace and hunting adventure. Before her quiet little farmhouse in Koroit, she'd bounced between the bustle of big cities and quiet coastal villages of South East Asia, alternating from one to the other as her temperament required. Prior to that it was a similar story in India. A month in New Delhi or Kolkata or Mombai, then off to a retreat somewhere. She didn't know what she was searching for, or even if she was searching, it was just something she had to do. She'd know when she didn't need to search any longer.

Bec's train of thought was starting to roll further back through her memory, but was derailed by the arrival of Eddie. He sat down heavily opposite her and she could tell already that weighty thoughts rested on his mind. This didn't bode well.

'How are you?' he asked. No kiss in greeting, not even a smile.

'I'm fine,' she said. 'Are you OK?'

Before Eddie could respond, Clay arrived. He crashed onto the wooden seat beside her and immediately lit up one of his cigarettes. 'Lovely day for it,' he said, the smoke wedged between his lips as he used one hand to shield the wind from his lighter's flame. 'But couldn't we have met in a pub like normal people?'

'Some of us like to get outside once in a while,' said Eddie.

'Fine, fine,' said Clay, succeeding in lighting his cigarette and waving Eddie's dig away with a dismissive hand gesture. 'So why have you called this meeting of the Holy Trinity?'

Bec could see Clay's buoyant mood immediately grating on Eddie. 'More like The Three Stooges,' said Eddie. He looked flatter than a tack.

'What's going on?' asked Clay, glancing between Eddie and Bec.

Eddie appeared to repress a sigh as he gazed out across the water. 'I'm being transferred,' he said swiftly.

'What?' asked Bec. She had not seen that coming. 'You were only just transferred from Port Campbell.'

'I know.' He turned to Clay. 'I'd like to blame you for this, but I know it's not really your fault.'

'What do you mean?' said Clay.

'Well, first of all, I think you might be right.'

'About what?'

'About everything. I believe that Anderson came to your place and wrecked it up and assaulted you. I believe that Anderson is definitely covering up two murders. I believe you are on to something. I don't know who or what, but you're definitely on to something.'

Clay dragged on his smoke and Bec waited for him to crack a joke, if only to say I told you so. But he didn't.

'What happened?' he asked.

Eddie exhaled deeply and for a moment Bec thought he was

going to weep. He looked tired, beaten. Like a man at the end of his rope. 'I went to Cooper and Crowe, asked them about whether they were at your place on Sunday morning, like you said. Cooper denied it and I could tell he was lying. Crowe spilled his guts. Backed your story, one hundred per cent. In the meantime, Cooper went running to Anderson and the next thing I know, I'm getting hauled into Anderson's office. He starts blasting me, accusing me of leaking stuff to "that bastard, Moloney".'

'I told you he was a nice guy,' said Clay with a wry grin.

Eddie didn't respond to the comment. 'I tell Anderson I haven't leaked anything and he doesn't believe me. Says he's had officers tailing you. Seen us three meeting up. That's how he knew you'd been to see the drug dealer and the escort, too. I asked what authority or reason he had to put surveillance on a member of the press. He didn't like that. Started roaring at me. So I went for broke: I laid it all out on the table.'

Clay was wide-eyed now, like he sensed a threat. 'What the hell did you do?'

'I told him you're close to bringing him down. That you know he's been covering up the Collins and Porter murders. That you know who did both of them. And that in a couple of days you're going to blow the lid off the whole thing with a front page exclusive.'

Bec couldn't stop the gasp escaping her mouth. Clay swore, stood up with his hands on the sides of his head.

'I'm sorry,' said Eddie. 'It was the last roll of the dice. I was screwed one way or another. I'd been asking too many questions. He was either going to bust me back to constable or kick me off the force. So I thought I'd throw all that in his face and see how he reacted.'

Clay's cigarette was going unsmoked in his right hand. '*Jesus…* And?'

'He went real quiet and turned a lighter shade of his usual red. "I don't believe you," he said. I said, "I don't care if you believe me or not – you're screwed, you fat bastard."'

'Tell me you didn't say that.'

'I did.'

'Jesus, no way.'

'Fair dinkum. I've had enough of his crap. He's giving the police force a bad name and I'm sick of it. Officers die in the line of duty fighting against people like him. He thinks he can do whatever he wants? Well, screw him, I wanted him to know he can't, and that you're going to bring him down.'

Clay flicked the long collection of ash from his smoke and finally took a drag. He shook his head slowly. 'I admire your courage. And I appreciate your vote of confidence, but I don't have enough information to bring him down. I'm not even close.'

'I know that,' said Eddie. 'I just wanted to watch him squirm at the idea that you might be able to.'

Bec had been watching the back and forth without comment, but could hold her tongue no longer. 'Eddie, you're a bloody idiot,' she said. 'You've just put Clay in grave danger.'

'No, I haven't. I've just put the wind up Anderson.'

'He's already been round to Clay's place once to beat him up,' she said, her voice laden with exasperation. 'How do you know he won't go a step further? I wouldn't put anything past Anderson. And I've never even met the guy.'

There was a solemn silence at the table as Clay sat back down again. People wandered or jogged past, heading along the promenade or across to the breakwater. The ocean lapped quietly onto the sand nearby, shifting the seaweed inch by inch. A seagull cried. Aside from a cool sea breeze putting a chill in the air, it was a beautiful Tuesday afternoon.

'So, what do we do next?' said Bec finally.

'I don't know about you guys, but I have to relocate to Stanhope,' said Eddie. 'Thankfully I hadn't finished unpacking all my things from when I moved here.' For the first time since he'd sat down he gave Bec a smile, a forced and weary one.

'Anderson's relocating you to shut you up?' asked Clay.

'I think he's trying to divide and conquer. He's giving me

too much credit, he thinks by removing me it stops the flow of information to you.'

'You have done a lot. I appreciate it. I really do, mate.'

'Don't... seriously, it's the least I could do. In hindsight I should have done more. But it's too late now. I don't think I can help you from Stanhope.'

'I don't even know where that is.'

'It's near Shepparton and Echuca, I think. Middle of nowhere, by the sounds of it. A one-cop station – the ultimate punishment.'

Bec looked at Clay. 'And what are you going to do?'

Clay finished his smoke and stubbed it out. 'I don't know; but whatever it is, I get the feeling we've only got a couple of days to do it. Anderson's going to be rattled after what Eddie's told him we have on him. We just need to sit back and see what he does to either shut us up and stop the story, or cover his tracks and frustrate our efforts. He won't think doing nothing is an option now, that's for sure.'

Eddie stood. 'Look, I have to get going. A few of the guys at work got wind of my imminent relocation and have arranged for a get-together at the Warrny.'

'See?' said Clay, humour in his voice. 'We could have met at the pub!'

Eddie smirked and stood, extending a hand, which Clay shook. Bec watched the silent exchange and then realised Eddie was looking at her. She rose and Eddie stepped around the table to give her a hug, followed by an awkward, brief kiss. Bec couldn't tell if it was weird because of the way Clay was staring at them, or because it was a strange end to a short and strange, yet sweet, relationship.

Bec lowered herself onto the bench again and watched Eddie walk off towards the nearby car park. His movements seemed slower than she remembered, his shoulders perhaps a little rounder.

Chapter 33

After Eddie's departure, Clay and Bec sat in awkward silence for some time. As he looked out across the bay, Clay struggled to shake the feeling of being watched. It was a sensation that had been with him for a couple of weeks, but he'd been putting it down to the weed and a lack of sleep.

Eddie had confirmed it. Anderson had hinted at it in Clay's apartment, but Eddie had made it solid truth – someone *had* been following him, watching him. It was not idle paranoia. It was fact. And as Clay and Bec sat there at the table, he felt the sensation again.

'I've got that feeling too,' said Bec, and Clay feared he'd spoken his thoughts out loud for a moment. But he knew he hadn't. He turned to Bec and noticed an edgy look in her eye.

'I'm kind of glad it's not just me, then,' said Clay. 'Was I being that obvious?'

'I don't think so. We're both just being paranoid, I think.'

'And for good reason. Just because I'm paranoid, it doesn't mean they're not after me.'

'I think that's a Nirvana lyric.'

'Almost, although I'm pretty sure Kurt Cobain stole that off a toilet wall.'

Bec chuckled, and the sound of her laugh dialled the tension down a touch. Clay could feel himself relaxing. He stood. 'Let's walk,' he said, and headed towards the breakwater without looking to see if Bec followed. His eyes roamed the car park and promenade, studied the fishermen, families, and fitness fanatics. He was looking for undercover cops or goons and he couldn't stop himself.

'So how's your big move going?' asked Bec, right there beside him.

'Big move?' Clay was puzzled for a moment. 'Oh, the

eviction. I've got until the end of the week. I've moved most of my stuff into a storage shed in the industrial estate already, so all I've got to do now is decide which motel is the cheapest but not the crappiest. I'm basically balancing crapness with cost at the moment.'

'A motel?'

'Yeah. It's February, so the uni students are rolling back into town. Rents are up and decent places are in short supply. But there are a couple of motels that do weekly rates comparable to renting a one-bedroom apartment. They fill up with uni students too, eventually. Motels of last resort. Actually, one of them is the one where we met Candy... ah, June.'

'You can't stay in that motel,' said Bec. Clay tried to read her expression. It was a bizarre mix of outrage, concern, surprise, and fear. 'You shouldn't be staying in any motel.'

'Why not?'

'It's not safe.'

They had reached the flat cement wall of the breakwater. Clay led the way up a set of stairs and they began walking side by side along the rampart. 'If you're worried about Frank Anderson, I don't think anywhere is any safer than anywhere else at the moment,' he said eventually. 'If Anderson really wants to come and get me, there's not much that can stop him. And besides, I don't really have anywhere else to go.'

'You can stay with me.'

Clay hadn't expected that and, from the look that flashed across Bec's face for a split second, neither had she. He turned his gaze back to the ocean and waited.

'I mean, I owe you at least one couch sleepover,' she said. Clay turned to look at her again and she flashed a broad smile that gave Clay a funny feeling, forcing him to look away.

'You don't owe me anything,' he said.

'I know, but to be honest, I think it would be a lot safer if you were around the house.'

'I don't think they're going to come after you.'

'I meant for your sake.' Bec's smile was an out-and-out smirk now, and Clay could have sworn his heartbeat tripped out.

'Very funny,' he said in a flat tone, giving nothing away. 'And thank you. It's a very gracious offer.'

'And you accept?'

'I accept, thank you.'

'You can stay for a week.'

'You're too kind but—'

'A week.'

'OK, a week.'

'Starting tonight.'

'Starting in a couple of days. I've got a few more things I need to do in the apartment.'

'OK.'

'OK. That's one problem sorted.' He lowered his voice and was once again conscious of people nearby, though no one seemed to be paying him or Bec any attention. 'But what do we do about Anderson? If we don't print something in the next couple of days, we're going to let him off the hook. He'll know we've got nothing.'

'Eddie put us in a bit of a predicament.'

'I know, but I can't blame Eddie for doing what he did. I think telling Anderson we're on the brink of rolling him probably saved Eddie from getting kicked off the force. I'm just not sure what the next step is.'

'What do you need to go to print?'

'If I'm going to accuse Anderson of covering up an investigation I need something big.'

'What about the autopsy report? Can't you just run stuff from that?'

Clay shook his head. 'It's not enough. Anderson will just say they're still investigating. And then say our story has potentially disrupted his investigation.'

'What about the Collins case? What if you got Kerry Collins' workmates to go on the record about the guy in the suit hiring her?'

'Not enough. It raises doubts about the investigation, but

doesn't nail Anderson to the wall.'

They walked on in silence until they reached the end of the breakwater. Off in the distance, a skirt of high white clouds fringed the blue sky. Behind them, the sun was setting, casting long shadows out in front of them. Clay watched a pelican land on the water. 'There's only one thing I can think of that will bring Anderson down,' he said, 'but you're not going to like it.'

Clay felt Bec stiffen next to him. 'What?'

'We have to catch a killer.'

'No.'

'*No*? Just no?'

'No.'

'Listen, it's the only way. We go after Lerner. Get him to confess. That's the only thing that is going to make Anderson look bad. That's the only thing that's going to hit him where he hurts. We catch Lerner, make Anderson look bad, and potentially we can cast doubt on his other cases, such as the Kerry Collins case. It throws things wide open.'

'That's mental. You can't bring down a killer, especially one who's apparently a psychotic meth-head. You'll get yourself killed. There's got to be another... I've got it. You need a whistleblower. A cop close to the case who will go on the record to say Anderson's covering up the killings. And you already know the perfect cop for that.'

Bec's voice was creeping louder and Clay looked around. No one seemed to be paying attention to their conversation but he dropped the volume again, just to be sure. 'I already thought of that. But I can't ask Eddie to do that. For one, his career is more than likely hanging by a thread as it is. Secondly, they can make life really difficult for him. Cops don't like whistleblowers. He would be numbering his days in the force. And thirdly, it wouldn't take much to discredit him. He's a known associate of mine and he's been based at three stations in two months – that makes him sound like a bad apple already, and Anderson could make it sound as bad as possible. And even if I quoted Eddie anonymously, Anderson would know it was Eddie. Who else could it be, if not the cop who's been seen talking to us regularly for the past month? Anderson would ruin him. For now, he's just moving Eddie to try and cripple us, to take away what he thinks is our main source of information. Anderson figures he just has to do that and we'll just go away. The story will get old and the whole thing will blow over.'

Clay let a silence stand with them for a moment before turning around to walk back the way they had come along the sea wall.

'We have to catch a killer,' he said again.

Chapter 34

Gunshots rang out, but Vegas stayed cool. You've got this, he told himself. You know what to do. Just keep your head down and wait for your moment.

More gunshots. Footsteps and the sound of people arguing. They're close, thought Vegas. Where are they? He contemplated poking his head up to take a look, but decided against it. He could feel sweat starting to accumulate on his brow and his heart had gone up a few BPMs. Stay cool. Stay cool.

A loud knock at the door caused him to jump. He swore. Unannounced visitors were the worst, especially when he was right in the middle of a battle.

Vegas paused the video game and went to stand up. His muscles ached and resisted the movement. How long was I playing for? he thought. He could see daylight through the crack in the curtain. He looked at his watch – eight o'clock. 'Really?' said Vegas, to no one.

He stumbled to the door, attempting to open his eyes wider and get his body working and moving again. There was another knock, louder, more insistent this time. 'OK. OK. Hang on,' called Vegas.

He fumbled with the latch and as soon as he yanked open the heavy wooden door he regretted not peeking through the peephole. The security door beyond it wasn't locked, and there stood Lerner, grinning. Manic. Tweaking. His eyes were wild and a tic in his right cheek was spasming.

Vegas took it all in within a second, which was all it took for Lerner to push past him and into the house. Vegas tumbled to the floor, his small wiry frame easily jostled by the bigger ball of energy that was Lerner.

'Hey, man, what's up?' said Vegas, pulling himself up off the floor with the assistance of the doorknob. 'You need some weed?'

Lerner was already sitting in one of the recliners and was packing the cone-piece of a bong with marijuana and tobacco from Vegas' mixbowl.

'Help yourself, bro,' said Vegas, with more than a hint of reluctance. He watched as Lerner inhaled the bong's contents in one go, exhaled slowly, and then immediately started packing another cone.

Vegas didn't know what to do. It was a replay from a month ago. Lerner was more than likely going to hang around for a couple of hours and Vegas didn't relish the prospect. Just the sight of Lerner sitting there sent fear shooting inside him. He wanted him gone, but how? Lerner would stay as long as he liked and there was nothing Vegas could do about that.

Lerner polished off another bong before setting it back on the table. Vegas forced out a laugh. 'Hey, man, you feel better now?' he said. 'That take the edge off?'

Lerner didn't look at him. He was staring at the TV – no, through the TV, Vegas realised. He was looking very intently at something that wasn't in the room.

'So, you wanna buy some weed to take with you?' said Vegas. It was a desperate ploy. The sweat on his brow from the video game was nothing – he could feel damp patches pooling under his arms and in the centre of his back.

Lerner was still staring straight ahead. He looked like he hadn't slept for days, but was quite obviously wide awake. He didn't appear to have showered for a few days, either. Some of his black hair stood up in clumps, while thick patches were plastered to his head. The guy was a mess.

Vegas felt straighter than he'd felt in a long time. He hungered to rip another bong himself, but he dared not reach in front of Lerner to grab the water pipe. This is worse than last time, Vegas thought. 'You wanna play some *Grand Theft Auto*, man?' he offered. 'We can drive some fast cars and shoot some cops if you like?'

'I don't feel like playing some video game bullshit,' said

Lerner. His voice burst out in machine-gun rhythms – blazing and quiet, blazing and quiet. It was the most unnerving thing Vegas had heard in a long time. *Why?* Why was this happening under his roof?

Suddenly, Lerner was alive with movement. There was a loud crack, the TV went dead, and a strange smell wafted through the lounge room. It was the smell of burning, but it was different to the scent of burnt tobacco and marijuana already in the air. This was an acrid, ugly aroma.

It took a moment for Vegas to register what had happened. He took in the angry odour first, before his eyes started to make sense of the scene. The TV screen was shattered. Lerner was standing, his arm outstretched. He was holding a gun. He had fired it at the TV.

Vegas felt a warm sensation in his pants and somewhere in the back of his mind, buried beneath the mental shouting and terror, he realised he had just released his bladder. He found it harder to breathe, but he managed to form some words, which limped out of his mouth. 'What's going on, Lerner?' was all he could manage.

Lerner finally turned to face Vegas, the twitch working overtime beneath his left eye. 'I hear you've been talking about me,' said Lerner, through thin lips stretched over tightly gritted teeth. His chest rose and fell, his breathing deep and heavy. His arm was still extended in the dead TV screen's direction, but Vegas could see it shaking.

'What? No. No.' Vegas spat his words out; his voice sounded weak, shrill. 'Never. I dunno what you're talking about.'

Lerner rose to his full height and loomed over Vegas. His feet were planted, sure and firm beneath him. He seemed to be readying himself for blows or a strain of some sort, neither of which seemed likely in the shabby lounge room. Only Vegas was there, piss-smelling and limp beneath the bigger man, and he offered no threat at all.

'You're a lying bastard,' said Lerner. He took a step toward Vegas, whose gaze fell on the gun in the bigger man's hand.

'Just, take a minute… to think about this, man.'

'I've done all my thinking.'

'Then think again. You're wrong. I haven't done a bloody thing.'

'No, Vegas. The time's over for thinking. My thinking's all done, and guess what? It always leads back to the same place: you.'

The gun in Lerner's hand moved in a slow arc to point at Vegas. 'I'm only going to ask once, and if I don't like what I hear…' He pushed the gun in Vegas' face.

'Oh, please, dude, no, please,' Vegas blubbered.

'Who did you talk to, Vegas?'

Chapter 35

Clay felt exhausted already as he walked into the office on Wednesday morning. The list of reasons for his insomnia was growing. His well-founded paranoia, a restless plotting mind, the fact he was sleeping in a swag on the floor of his apartment because his bed was in storage, his aching ribs – these things conspired to keep sleep almost entirely out of reach. Only a few joints, more than he would usually smoke, were getting him to drift off, but it was becoming increasingly like passing out; it was not a restorative slumber. The weed erased most of his dreams, too, but the few he did have were the same recurring ones that flashed and crashed in his mind and often stung him awake, dripping with sweat.

There was the one where Kerry Collins' face from the portrait morphed into the face Clay had seen at the beach. That one had been getting a regular rerun in his head for well over a month now. But there were new ones, too. There was the one where Frank Anderson danced with glee around a flaming car at Thunder Point. Clay stood nearby with a fire extinguisher, but every time he got close to the car and tried to put out the blaze, Anderson jigged his way over and punched him in the face.

It didn't take a psychiatry degree to decipher that one, but what really unnerved Clay was the one he had about a woman standing on the cliffs at Thunder Point. It felt like it took place after the car had been extinguished, although he never saw that, and in his dream he didn't understand how the two events were connected, but he just knew they were.

He also knew the woman was his daughter. In his dream, he never saw her face – just her long hair, a long flowing dress, and bare feet. She faced the sea. He was running toward her. He was going to save her. But he never got there. She stepped off the cliff, and Clay woke up, sweating.

Bec was waiting at his desk for him to arrive. Clay collapsed into his office chair and took another swig of his large double shot espresso.

'You look like crap,' said Bec. 'Again.'

'And good morning to you, too,' he said, with as much enthusiasm as he could muster, which wasn't much.

'Did you stay up all night trying to figure out how to bring Anderson down? Or how to catch Lerner?'

'Not intentionally. But it's getting harder and harder to shut my brain off.'

Terry Kenna shambled up to their side. 'Would've thought it was harder to turn your brain on,' said the deputy editor, beaming.

'If you're just here to insult me, you'll have to take a number,' said Clay. 'I don't think Ms. O'Connor is quite finished yet.' He turned to look at Kenna and caught the dazzling smile. 'Jeez, it's a bit early for such unadulterated happiness, surely. Did someone spike your frappalatte or something?'

'It's always a good day when the front page is sorted by 9 a.m.'

'Oh, no,' said Clay. 'What's happened?'

'Shooting. At least one dead. In Wanstead Street.' Kenna's smile bordered on the delirious.

Clay scowled. He despised reporters taking delight in the misfortune and tragedy that befell others just because it was a good news story. He'd nearly come to blows with one journo who had started clapping after hearing about a fatal car accident. Gallows humour around the office was fine, he could handle that, it helped take the edge off the reality of the situation. But cheering and welcoming the horrific... that was ugly, disgusting, and all kinds of wrong in Clay's book.

'Wipe that goddamn smile off your face, you sadistic bastard,' he hissed at Kenna. 'Have you no self-respect?'

'Oh, come on.' Kenna waved a dismissive hand. 'It's Wanstead Street, it's full of ice addicts, welfare cheats, and women with four kids to three different fathers.'

'Last time I checked, they were still people.'

Kenna took a step back, hands raised in mock surrender. 'Alright, Mr Social Justice, take it easy. How about you and Bec and your bleeding heart get down to East Warrnambool and cover this story before you start taking a collection plate around for the family.' Kenna walked off, ignorant of the intention of Clay's remarks.

Clay lobbed invisible missiles at Kenna's back as the deputy editor walked away and into his office. 'What an absolute arsehole.'

'Easy, tiger,' said Bec. 'Come on, let's get down to the crime scene.'

Within minutes they were in the car, headed east on Raglan Parade. Clay stared out the windscreen with a glum expression, noting the brown grass beneath the huge Norfolk pines in the median strip. The summer had been longer and hotter than any he could remember. The front yards along the highway were a mix of the well-watered and those that had been left to wilt, and there were new cracks across the road caused by regular heat stress. The day outside the car was already in the low twenties. It had been that way for a couple of days, but Clay had heard the forecast – more heat was on its way.

Bec turned the office Subaru into Wanstead Street and Clay eased forward in his seat, gripping the dashboard. He heard Bec mutter 'oh, no' below her usual volume, but Clay couldn't even form an appropriate swear word, the speech function deserting him.

The street was clogged with police cars and they were all gathered around Vegas' house. Their lights flashed in warning, and the front yard was circled with crime scene tape that fluttered in the light morning breeze. Officers were everywhere. Some directed traffic away from the scene, others wandered the yard and surrounding area, looking for clues. The plain-clothes detectives gathered around Vegas' front door, talking and jotting things on clipboards. It wasn't the first time Clay had seen a crime scene like this, it just felt like it.

Bec pulled over a few houses down from Vegas' place and Clay got out of the car. He fingered the spiral of his notebook, but didn't open it. What was happening? There were people talking, voices imparting information that he couldn't process. He was in a trance, his mind racing in circles as he tried to comprehend what it all meant. Vegas shot and killed. We talked to Vegas. Vegas shot and killed. We talked to Vegas.

Without meaning to, Clay had walked up to one of the cops. He hadn't taken his eyes off the officers standing at the front door, which was wide open. He could almost see inside.

'It's a mess in there,' said the cop, as if reading Clay's mind.

The comment snapped Clay back to reality and he looked at the cop next to him. It was Senior Constable Hawker. The breeze ruffled his white hair and he had a ponderous look on his heavily-lined face. Clay had seen the same disposition on the older copper at Thunder Point when Jacinta Porter had been murdered. It was a rare policeman that could see so much over so many years and still keep his heart from hardening to the harshness of life.

'What happened?' said Clay.

'Kid shot dead. Bullet right through the face, probably from close range. Didn't stand a chance.'

'Jesus. *What…?* Who…?' Clay was struggling to control his thoughts. He was staring at the open door again. Christ, I was in that lounge room three days ago, he thought.

'No idea, but whoever did it wrecked up the place, that's for sure. Coffee table's smashed, TV destroyed… they did a real number on the joint.'

Clay heard the clicking of a digital camera nearby and turned to see Bec. She was right up at the police tape, snapping away, and it triggered something in Clay's mind. He blinked away his daze and raised his notepad.

Senior Constable Hawker shook his head. 'Don't quote me, Moloney,' he said. 'Everything goes through Detective Sergeant Anderson or the police media unit these days.'

Clay withheld the involuntary grimace that now appeared with every mention of Anderson's name. He offered Hawker the *help me* look he'd seen on beggars. 'I'll keep it anonymous, I'll call you "a police spokesperson". Come on, you know how useless the police media unit is...' He left a comment about Anderson unsaid, but Hawker smiled and bobbed his head in assent.

'We got the call shortly after 8 a.m.,' said Hawker. 'Neighbour called it in. Said she heard a gunshot, the sound of breaking glass and some banging, and then a car speeding off. She didn't see the car, but we've got officers going door to door at the moment looking for witnesses.'

Clay looked around the street. Pairs of blue uniforms were dotted among the front yards, on their way from one door to the next. Small crowds were gathering in pockets along the footpath as residents came together to ask questions of each other. Clay supposed they had a rough idea of what was going on. A gunshot at 8 a.m. around here would have gotten a bit of attention, but it was just as likely the locals had dismissed it as a car backfiring, he thought.

He looked back at Vegas' open front door. The three detectives standing on his porch had finished conferring and were walking back to their cars.

'And the deceased?' asked Clay.

'Male. In his twenties. Believed to be the guy that lives here.'

'Vegas.'

'Sorry?' said Hawker.

Clay turned to the old cop. 'They called him Vegas. I don't know his real name. Patrick something, I think. But everyone called him Vegas.'

'You knew him?'

'A little. He was a nice guy.'

'The other officers reckon he was a drug dealer.'

'So I've heard.' Clay looked back to the house, his face held firm, adding nothing to the debate. Hawker seemed to leave it at that.

A thought crept into Clay's mind and he scanned the crime scene. 'Where's Anderson?' he asked.

'In the house.' Hawker looked around before leaning a little closer to Clay. 'If I was you, Moloney, I'd get out of here before he sees you. Your name is akin to blasphemy around the station at the moment. Anderson's got it in for you like I've never seen before. Whatever you did to piss him off... it worked.'

'Just doin' my job,' said Clay. 'Thanks again, mate. I appreciate the help. It's nice to know there are good honest coppers still out there.'

It was a pointed comment, but Hawker took it as intended. 'There's still a few of us around.' He smiled.

Clay gave Hawker a gentle pat on the back and headed back to the car. Bec jogged across the street and intercepted Clay on the way.

'Are we going already?' she asked.

'Have you got a snap for the front page?'

'Yeah, I guess. I mean I think I've got something we could use.'

'Then let's go before Anderson gets here.'

Bec's gaze roved about as she quickened her step on the way toward the office Subaru. In a matter of seconds, Bec had executed a swift U-turn, turned a corner and the car was moving back towards the highway.

'Was it Vegas?' she asked within seconds of leaving the scene.

'Yep.'

'Oh, my God.'

'I know.'

She stopped the car at the traffic lights, waiting for a green to turn onto the highway. 'What does that mean?' she said. 'What the hell is going on?'

Clay searched for something to say. He could hear something close to panic in Bec's voice. 'I don't know.' It was all he could think to offer and it was worth less than nothing.

The light went green, but instead of turning right onto

Raglan Parade and back to the office, she went straight ahead. Clay didn't say a word. He watched as she drove up the hill, through a roundabout, and under a rail bridge. Clay could see the colour had gone from her knuckles – she was holding tight to the steering wheel.

Up ahead lay Proudfoots Restaurant, on their right was the cemetery, to their left, the Hopkins River. Bec veered wildly to the left, taking the entry to the river view car park a little too fast, before screeching to a halt at the river's edge.

The water was high and choppy in the rising breeze. It had breached the car park, as it did most days, and slopped against the Subaru's tyres. Seagulls sat on the guard rail that provided a laughable boundary between the car park and the river. The river cruise boat lay dormant, waiting for the night and the next party to arrive.

The car was quiet for a moment but the silence was shattered when Bec started pummelling the steering wheel with her hands. 'Ah!' she yelled. 'What the hell have you gotten me into?'

'I don't know,' he said again. Clay kept his voice as even as possible. He'd already had his minor freak-out back at the crime scene, but he knew Bec probably needed to have one of her own.

She looked at Clay with burning eyes. 'Vegas was murdered, yeah?'

'Yeah.'

Bec thumped the outer rim of the steering wheel again. 'Christ almighty. What are we doing?'

'I don't know.'

'What the hell is going on?'

'I don't know.'

'Stop saying that!'

'*Sorry.*'

'Do you know anything?'

Clay took a deep breath and looked out across the river. 'No. My mind's still reeling, much like yours is. All I know is someone shot and killed Vegas, before trashing his lounge room. That's it. That's all I've got.'

Clay's words, although they said little, seemed to calm Bec. He turned to look at her and she was gazing across the water. Her eyes looked like they were fixed on the houses on the other side of the river. Clay had heard people call the area Snob's Hill, as it contained some of Warrnambool's most expensive houses. He knew what Bec was thinking – the people who lived in those houses didn't have to deal with dead drug dealers and dead prostitutes and angry cops.

'I'm sorry I dragged you into this,' he offered.

Bec frowned. 'You know, I've lived in South East Asia, India, the Middle East… I've lived in some areas that a lot of people consider to be unsafe. I even spent six months in my idealistic twenties taking photos for Médecins Sans Frontières in some pretty bad parts of Africa. But I don't think I've ever felt as threatened or as in danger as I do *right now*. And I want to blame you for that.'

'That's probably fair enough,' he said, giving her a weak smile.

'Don't make jokes. I know it's not your fault, but I really, really want to blame you for dragging me into this. I want to blame you for taking me to crime scenes, for being followed by the police, for getting Eddie relocated, for introducing me to prostitutes and drug dealers and grieving fathers, for taking me to a house a matter of days before a murder was committed in it.'

'I also took you to Lachlan Fullerton's mansion.'

'Stop joking around – I'm warning you. Like I was saying, I want to blame you for all of that.' She sighed. 'But I can't. You were just doing your job, and you wanted me to come along for the ride. And I wanted to come along. And now, I don't know what's happening or why Vegas is dead or why it scares me so much, but I know I need you to stick by my side.'

Clay was momentarily silenced. He hadn't foreseen that turn in the conversation.

'I want you to stay at my place from tonight,' said Bec.

'Please. You're the only person I know and trust around here and I don't want to be alone.'

'OK,' said Clay. 'If it's any consolation, I need you by my side, too.'

Bec finally turned back to look at Clay. Clay smiled, but Bec didn't return the expression. The look on her face was unlike anything he'd seen before. He couldn't read her.

Chapter 36

Dusk settled across the paddocks on the outskirts of Koroit. It was about 8.30 p.m. and the last hints of orange grabbed at the sky from beyond the horizon. In the fading light Bec could barely see the yellow grass, left tinder dry by a long hot summer, extending across the flat plain to meet the night. The warmth of the day was hanging around, trapped in by the late clouds that had gathered. February was not far from finishing, but she could tell the heat would remain for a while longer. The sound of crickets buzzed in the air like white noise.

For the moment, Bec felt at peace. She had been trying to put the thought of Vegas' fate out of her mind all day. Work had helped – it had been a distraction, if nothing else – and when that was over, she'd driven with Clay to his old apartment, picked up the last of his stuff, thrown it in the back of her ageing Mazda and headed for her home on the fringes of Koroit.

The drive home had brought Vegas back to mind. Clay hadn't said anything about Vegas, but deliberately so, she could tell, and that was enough to make her mind race away from her again.

We spoke to Vegas only days ago. And now Vegas has been shot. Whoever killed him could be coming for us next. We might get shot. She tried to shut such thoughts from her brain, tried to reason with herself that there was no logic to them, but they wouldn't go away.

On the drive to Koroit, Clay had made idle chit-chat. He'd told her distracting facts about things they were passing along the way. Like how the stretch of highway from Illowa to Tower Hill was called the Mad Mile because it used to be the scene of illegal drag races and youths testing the speed limits of their cars back in the Sixties and Seventies. How the dunes at the end of Gormans Lane were said to hide the remains of the Mahogany Ship, a mythic Portuguese caravel that would rewrite Australian history if it was ever discovered. How Tower Hill was not classified as an extinct volcano, but rather a dormant one, which theoretically meant it could erupt at any moment, despite it being filled with water, bushland, koalas, and emus.

But Bec was only half listening, despite Clay's best efforts to entertain her and occupy her mind.

Clay had asked to stop at Koroit's lone supermarket and Bec had waited in the car for him. As she sat there she found herself eyeing everyone who walked past. What would a murderer look like? What did this Lerner character look like? Was it even him?

Clay returned with a couple of packets of smokes, a six-pack of Carlton Draught, and a couple of bottles of red wine. They drove on in silence until they reached Bec's house, which sat quite literally on the edge of town. On one side of the road was a long row of houses and beyond that, the entirety of Koroit. On Bec's side, there was her little former farmhouse, set back about four hundred metres from the road, and a bunch of paddocks, and that was it. Her home was an outlier, like a satellite orbiting a planet.

They'd unloaded Clay's stuff, which wasn't much – a swag, a pillow, a gym bag full of clothes, a plastic bag of toiletries, and a briefcase. She had no idea what was in the briefcase and didn't ask. Clay poured some wine for each of them and Bec threw together a stir fry while Clay commented on Bec's spartan set-up. She'd only been in the country for two months and the house was a combination of cheap thrift store furniture and a great deal of nothing. Whole rooms she had no need for remained empty. The only personal touches were the books she was starting to amass and pile up around the lounge room. Clay dumped his belongings in one of the empty rooms, rolling his swag out on the floor.

After dinner she took Clay out on to the back porch, which faced west. They watched the sunset, and finally, after her second glass of wine, he asked what was on her mind.

'Are we in danger?' she said.

Clay dragged on a freshly lit cigarette. 'I don't think so. For starters, no one would know we're out here. And secondly, why would anyone kill us?'

'Why would anyone kill anyone?'

'There are plenty of reasons to kill someone. But I'm pretty sure none of them relate to us.'

'Should we call the cops? Just in case?'

Clay laughed and for a split second Bec felt offended. 'And tell them what?' said Clay. 'That we were at a drug dealer's house one day and then he turned up dead and now we're scared?'

Bec didn't want to admit it, but her fears sounded childish when Clay enunciated them.

'And besides,' he continued, 'I don't know about you, but I wouldn't trust our call to be answered by an honest cop at the moment. The less potential contact I can have with Frank Anderson, the better I will feel.'

'Maybe we should call Eddie. I mean, just to be on the safe side.'

'Eddie's got enough to worry about just now.'

'I just thought, y'know, maybe he'd come and—'

'What? Get in the way of us being shot? I don't think he can help us, Bec. And besides, Eddie's likely on his way north right now. We got him transferred, if you recall.'

Bec turned to look at Clay in the fading light. She had so many questions on her mind right now. 'So who killed Vegas?'

He didn't seem perturbed by the question – his face showed that same blank look she'd come to understand as being Clay's thinking face. 'My best guess is Lerner,' he said. 'But it could just as easily have been a disgruntled client. Maybe a deal went bad. Who knows? Vegas was a drug dealer, let's not forget that.'

'Let's say it's this Lerner character; why would he do it?'

'Aside from the fact he's a violent meth-head who's probably already killed one other person?' Clay blew out some cigarette smoke, along with half a laugh. 'Jealousy, maybe? Paranoia? Maybe he thought Vegas spoke to the cops? Who knows? Most murders, as infrequent as they are around here, are either crimes of passion or random incidents with no major motive behind them.'

'So this was random?'

'Probably.'

'And Jacinta Porter?'

'Crime of passion. Lerner killed her in an ice rage because she left him or because she was an escort or some other bullshit reason.'

'And Kerry Collins?'

'Crime of passion or random incident… I'm not too sure about that one. Maybe the guy in the suit was a serial killer who hired her for a job on his boat and then he choked her and threw her overboard. Who knows? That one's still a mystery to me.'

Bec watched Clay's cloud of cigarette smoke catch the fading rays of the sun as it drifted away. 'So let's assume Lerner killed Jacinta Porter,' she said. 'And a serial killer killed Kerry Collins. Why would Frank Anderson cover up both of those murders?'

'That's the big money question.'

'Any guesses?'

'Anderson must be looking out for somebody. Or somebodies. That's the only possible outcome. But who? That I don't know. The fact that he's covering both murders up makes me suspect they're linked, but I can't see how. Same killer, maybe? Perhaps Lerner killed both girls.'

'But why would Anderson protect Lerner?'

'That's another good question. My best guess is Lerner is Anderson's son.'

Bec looked at Clay's face in the half-light, trying to discern whether he was joking or not.

'That's the wild card theory,' he said. 'Or maybe Lerner is the son of someone who is blackmailing Anderson. To be honest, I don't have a clue.'

Clay reached forward and dropped his cigarette butt into an empty Carlton Draught bottle. 'I think I left a couple of packs of smokes in your car,' he said, as he stood up.

'Car's unlocked,' she said, and watched as he walked along the verandah and disappeared around the side of the house.

She turned her gaze back to the darkening sky. Clay was right – why would anyone come after them? She realised being so close to all this – murders, drug dealers, prostitutes – had gotten her increasingly wound up. She'd come to Australia with a particular mindset. She wanted a quiet, normal, Western life. No more bustling Asian and subcontinental cities, no more ashrams or remote shacks on distant beaches. She had wanted something like where she had grown up, but which wasn't where she had grown up. She wanted no fear, whether it be from criminals or from a domineering mother.

Bec shook the thought out of her head. Even thousands of miles from her mother, the influence lingered. Bec had come to Australia, and not Ireland, to find normality because she couldn't stand to be in the same country as her mother. And her mother symbolised Bec not being in control and it meant living with a kind of nagging fear at the back of her mind.

That is what these murders have brought up in me, she thought, not just fear, but a feeling of being out of control. She detested the fact that someone with power and influence could whisk away a man she was seeing. She hated that someone could turn up at her friend's house and beat him for doing his job. She abhorred the idea that someone could kill someone she had just met.

It all sounded so silly in her head now. The idea that she could control anything was ludicrous, whether it be in a farmhouse in Koroit or the crazed rush of Bangkok. Bec laughed out loud, a short sharp sound that burst the night air and its buzz of crickets. Did I even have anything to fear in the first place?

Obviously Clay getting beaten up was a serious matter, and Eddie getting transferred was worrying, but earlier in the day Bec had feared for her life. Maybe she'd gotten a bit too wound up without really thinking things through.

That was when she heard the gunshot rip through the night air.

Chapter 37

You know you're in the country when you can leave your car unlocked outside your house at night, thought Clay, as he strolled toward Bec's beat-up red Mazda.

Beyond the car the lights of Koroit shone. The nearest houses showed warm yellow glows ringing dark curtains – they looked inviting, but quiet. Clay realised there was very little noise. The distant murmur of traffic on the main road, maybe the hum of cars from further away on the highway, even the low roll of the surf less than ten kilometres away, but beyond that there was little but crickets and the occasional dog barking somewhere in town.

Then he heard something else and turned to look at Bec's house. The front porch light above the door was on and Clay could see a figure standing a few paces back from the entrance step. Whoever the person was hadn't seen Clay come around the side of the house, but Clay couldn't make out who it was due to the angle of the light. It appeared to be a male, by the size and shape of the figure, standing motionless. Clay wasn't sure why it was, instinct maybe, but something seemed off about the situation.

Clay was next to the car, but there was nothing between him and the dark figure. Keeping his eyes on the silhouetted man, he reached into his pocket and pulled out his phone to call Bec and alert her. It made a beep that seemed louder than any beep his phone had ever made before as it lit up. Clay glanced at the illuminated screen and swore to himself. No reception. Typical. Not even twenty kilometres from Warrnambool and may as well be in the middle of the outback.

Clay looked back at the distant shape he had down as a male and then it turned, slowly revealing a quivering outstretched hand holding the unmistakable outline of a handgun. For a second, Clay's heart dropped into his guts and he took a sharp intake of breath. He thought of Bec, sitting on the far side of the house, oblivious to what was happening and to what could potentially happen. I need to get this guy away from the house, thought Clay.

The shape was slowly coming toward him, as if uncertain, not quite stumbling but shambling in a slow, ragged gait. Clay tapped his pockets for something resembling a weapon but came up with nothing. He didn't know what he was hoping to find; a lighter, perhaps? Maybe a pen or pencil? The futility of his actions dawned on him. He was being stupid. He steeled himself, willed his breathing to calm down again, and decided his only hope was the direct approach.

'You alright there, mate?' he said in his most convivial, non-threatening voice.

The figure halted, stopped moving. Clay still couldn't see any facial features, but he was starting to make out dishevelled hair, sticking up in short clumps, and baggy unkempt clothes that looked like they hadn't been changed in days.

Clay tried again, this time risking a step forward to lure the figure's attention away from the house and Bec. 'You OK, fella? You wanna hand with something?'

'Stop moving.' The voice was a tired bark, flat and low.

Clay complied and raised his hands above his head in a surrender gesture. 'I think you might be a bit lost there, mate.'

'Are you Clayton Moloney?' The voice sounded detached, drained of emotion; there was little intonation in the words, which were dragged from deep inside an exhausted frame.

Clay's gut knotted up at the mention of his own name. His eyes were adjusting enough to make out the exact shape of the gun; it was certainly real, and pointed straight at him. His mind flicked through the possible responses. Do I say 'yes'? he thought. Do I say 'no'? Do I say 'who's asking?'

There was no instruction manual to consult, no real life reference he might utilise. All Clay's images of men with guns came from film; he realised at once how unrelated to reality they all were. For reasons unknown to himself, the best he could fathom was misplaced gallantry, so he responded in the affirmative. 'Yeah, I'm Clayton Moloney.'

There was a pause from the gunman.

'What do you want, mate?' asked Clay. 'I haven't got any money or anything.'

'Frank Anderson sent me to kill you.'

Clay's head flipped, he felt dizzy, like he was recovering from a fainting spell. He was acutely aware of an incredible silence around him, like the crickets had stopped their chirping to listen in on the conversation. A dozen thoughts ran through Clay's mind all at once. Oddly, the one clear idea he could grab hold of was the fact that his life wasn't flashing before his eyes, which made him think either he wasn't about to die or that the notion was a myth.

The feeling of vertigo passed, but Clay remained in a kind of stasis, waiting to see what would happen next. The sound of crickets returned. A dog howled off in the distance. Clay's heart kept up its heavy pounding. After what felt like a full minute, the gunman spoke again. 'But I'm not going to.'

Clay realised he had been holding his breath, and for the first time in a short while, he exhaled. 'I'm glad to hear that,' he managed.

'Not if you do what I say.'

'OK.'

'We're going for a drive.'

There was a blur of movement and the gunman grabbed Clay by the arm and dragged him past Bec's Mazda. Clay could smell sweat and body odour and estimated the man hadn't showered in at least a couple of days.

The gunman stopped suddenly, as if a thought had just reached him. He turned, swinging Clay out of the way without letting go of him, and pointed the gun at the red car. There was a loud crack that echoed through the empty night and the sound of air rushing from one of Bec's tyres. Satisfied, the gunman wheeled around again, heading down the long gravel driveway, pulling Clay along with him.

Clay's ears rang from the handgun's blast as he stumbled down the track. He felt like he was in a dream, but urged himself to get a grip.

The man dragged Clay off the driveway and into the knee-length grass before letting go of his arm and shoving him away. 'Get in,' said the man, and Clay noticed for the first time a dark car not more than twenty metres away. He looked back and saw the gun still pointed at him. It flicked in the direction of the car. 'You drive,' said the flat voice.

The gunman climbed into the passenger seat, the gun trained on Clay the whole time. Clay noticed a bad smell in the car. A glance in the back seat seemed to indicate someone had been living in there, amongst the Maccas wrappers and take-away cartons.

'Start it. Drive.' Clay was more than close enough to make out the face now. The man hadn't shaved, or spent much time outdoors in a while, his skin was so pale it almost glowed in the dark interior of the car. Only the wild black hair, the beginnings of a beard, and the dark sunken pits of his eyes detracted from the paleness.

Clay reached forward and found the keys in the ignition. The starter motor failed the first time and for a second he thought he'd received a reprieve. The gun-toting passenger said nothing and Clay tried again. This time the engine roared to life. Clay turned on the headlights, but in his peripheral vision he could see the gun being shaken at him. 'Lights off,' said the gunman.

Clay followed the instruction and pulled slowly onto the driveway, hearing the wheels crunch the gravel as he rolled at low speed back toward the road. 'Where are we going, mate?' he asked, desperate to keep his tone light and informal. This guy might not want to kill me at present, but it's still a possibility, thought Clay. Best to keep him on side.

'Port Fairy. We're going to see a man. I thought you might know where to find him.'

The longer sentences gave Clay a better example of the man's voice and a better insight into his state of mind. The tone was weary and flat, yet there was still a racing edge to his delivery. This guy's tired and probably coming off a long bender, thought Clay. If that's the case, he's also likely to be propping himself up with something – ice or speed or maybe just caffeine.

Right on cue, the man reached forward to the glovebox and opened it. The light inside came on and illuminated glassy bloodshot eyes, ringed with fatigue lines. Switching the gun to his left hand but keeping it pointed at Clay, the man pulled a small sandwich bag of white powder out of the compartment. He opened the seal, licked a finger, plunged it into the powder, and then rubbed the drug on his gums.

Clay was relieved. The gunman was powering himself with speed, not ice. Crystal meth would have made him erratic and liable to do anything, increasing the danger level by a long way. Speed was going to keep him awake and focused, probably talkative, too, but less likely to do something totally unexpected or unnecessarily violent.

As the gunman sealed the bag, Clay was struck by an idea. 'May I?' he asked. He licked his finger and pointed at the bag.

Clay kept his eyes on the road – they were about to reach the end of the driveway and turn onto the asphalt – but he could feel the gunman glaring at him, trying to figure out what he was playing at. With careful movements, using both hands, the gunman opened the bag again and cradled it over toward Clay. It meant the gun was pointed straight up into Clay's face and from the way the man was holding the bag, Clay guessed he was scared of Clay tipping the contents all over the place as a form of distraction.

But Clay held to his plan – he simply dipped his finger into the bag and rubbed what stuck to his finger onto his gums.

'Thanks, man,' he said, pulling the car onto the main road. 'I needed that. Probably not as much as you, but I definitely needed it.'

Clay snuck a look at the gunman's puzzled expression as the bag of speed was tucked back into the glovebox. The taste of the powder was bitter and chemical, and it wouldn't start kicking in for a good twenty minutes or half an hour. It would take less than that to get to Port Fairy.

'You seem pretty relaxed for someone who has a gun pointed at them.'

Clay smiled. Maybe it had worked. The ultimate ice-breaker, he thought – do drugs with someone. It immediately made them equals and defused the situation. And it was the best ploy Clay could think of to get the gunman talking.

'You've already told me you're not going to kill me,' said Clay. 'Although I'm curious to know what old Frank Anderson has against me. By the way, I'm turning the headlights on so we don't get pulled over.'

The gunman nodded and Clay flicked the switch on the end of the indicators. The road ahead and outskirts of Koroit were illuminated. 'Frank said you were snooping around Vegas' place, asking questions about me.'

Lerner. Clay felt almost certain this was him.

'Man, I've known Vegas for years. And I didn't "snoop around", I went to his house to buy weed,' Clay lied.

'Frank said you're a journalist. That you're gonna pin Jacinta's murder on me and print it in the paper. Even though I didn't do nothing.' The tone and volume of his voice was rising.

Clay slowed and stopped at an intersection. 'Frank Anderson is a liar,' he said calmly, keeping a lightness in his voice. 'I can't just print accusations like that in the paper without proof. That would mean you could sue me and make a bunch of money. Why would I do that? Why would I give you free money?'

The car pulled through the crossroads at a gentle pace. There was very little traffic around, but Clay was in no hurry to get to Port Fairy, not while he had Lerner talking.

'I didn't kill Jacinta,' said Lerner. Clay's explanation seemed to have calmed him a little. 'And I didn't mean to kill Vegas.'

Whoa, thought Clay. A dozen questions flooded his brain, but he went with the one most likely to keep Lerner talking. 'What happened?'

'He went for the gun,' said Lerner, the tiredness creeping back into his voice. 'I was a bit on edge, it just went off. I didn't mean it. I was pretty high on ice at the time. I wanted to just chill out with Vegas, ya know? Smoke a bowl and come down. Get my head straight. I had the gun. Frank gave it to me. But… I dunno. I wasn't thinking straight. Frank had put ideas in my head. Ideas about you. He told me you were talking to Vegas. I didn't mean to shoot Vegas. I told Frank that. Then Frank told me where to find you. He told me to go after you, not Fullerton.'

'Wait. *What*? Fullerton? Lachlan Fullerton?'

'The guy we're going to see in Port Fairy. He's the one who had Jacinta killed. I know it. No matter what Frank tried to tell me, no matter how much bullshit he fed me, I know it was Fullerton and his dudes. The bastard killed Jazzy.'

The immensity of that comment made Clay's heart stall and he found himself holding his breath again. Here were the answers to many of the questions that had been driving him crazy over the past couple of months. 'How do you know that?' he said. Clay wished he had his notepad, or a voice recorder. His phone was in his pocket, but he couldn't do anything with it without being noticed and potentially shot.

'Jacinta was getting money off Fullerton to keep her mouth shut. She was seeing him a couple of times a week and getting cash off him. Screwing him, too. But she told me she kept asking him for more and more money. I told her she was gonna get in trouble. She said she knew too much, he couldn't touch her. Then one night she went to see him at Thunder Point. I drove up there and she was by herself, so I went away and came back later. There were two guys driving off in a real posh car and her car was in flames. They were Fullerton's guys. She'd told me about them. They were usually around whenever she met up with him. A bald one, and a guy with slick black hair. Tough looking bastards.'

'What did she have on Fullerton? Some kind of dirt?'

Lerner had lowered the gun, lost in his memory. 'You could call it that... she saw someone get killed and thrown off his boat.'

Clay almost drove off the road. He opened and closed his mouth a couple of times but no words came out. He tried again. 'Kerry Collins.'

'She was in all the news and stuff.'

'What happened? What did Jacinta see?'

Clay could feel Lerner sizing him up all over again. He'd come off too keen, and now Lerner was suspicious.

'Tell me, Lerner,' he said.

'How do you know my name?'

'Don't worry about that. Just tell me what Jacinta saw or I'll pull over and I won't take you to Fullerton.'

'I've got the gun, ya smart-arse.'

'Lerner, we both know you're not going to shoot me. You would have done that already. You didn't mean to kill Vegas. You're not that kind of guy.' Clay was taking a serious punt on that last bit, but he was desperate. The last piece of the puzzle that had been plaguing him, that had been keeping him up at nights, was in the passenger seat beside him.

'You gonna put this in the paper?'

'I won't lie to you, mate – it's more than likely. But I need to know. There's some big, powerful people involved here, and with your help, I can bring them down. But you've gotta tell me what you know.'

Clay had turned the car down a side road and was passing an old church and hall. They were about ten minutes from Port Fairy and Clay had no idea what would happen when they got there, but he didn't care about that just yet. He needed to know what Lerner knew.

Lerner pulled a packet of cigarettes out of his pocket and removed two smokes. He lit them both and handed one to Clay, who took it gratefully. Lerner dragged on the other Peter Jackson and wound the window down a smidge with his gun hand. He nodded finally and let a plume of smoke flow out his mouth and out the gap in the window. 'So Jacinta gets this job on a boat,' he said. 'Supposed to service some real high-flying client. One of Fullerton's mates. Fullerton hired her, but she was gonna do this other guy. She was some kind of deal sweetener, she told me. Anyway, there's this waitress on board, too, real young bird, and Fullerton takes the boat out into the Lady Bay, and it's nice and calm and everything's cool. The waitress serves them drinks and nibbles, Jacinta has a few drinks with them and whatever. Then this client, Fullerton's mate, gets a bit grabby with the waitress girl. He can't even be bothered with Jacinta, he just starts going the grope on this teenage chick. The girl fights back. Jacinta walks in on all this in the little room on the boat. The cabin, or whatever you call it. And then as this girl sees Jacinta come into the room, she slips out of the guy's arms, but she falls over and whack! She hits her head on the edge of a rail or something. Blood everywhere. Jacinta screams her tits off.'

Lerner seemed to be relishing telling this part of the story, and Clay suspected he really was 'that kind of guy'. 'So this Fullerton comes in and the girl's dead. Died right there and then. So he drives the boat out to sea a bit further and they throw her overboard and clean up the blood. Jacinta's freakin' out. She's scared they're gonna throw her overboard, too. But these guys are chickenshit, they won't get their hands dirty like that. So they do a deal with Jacinta. Fullerton says he'll look after her if she looks after him. If she says nothing, he'll pay her. Weekly visits, good money. Jacinta's just stoked not to get killed at that point. But when they get back to land and time goes by, she starts pushing her luck. Couple of times a week she catches up with this Fullerton. She screws him, she gets paid big money. But she starts gettin' greedy and starts askin' for more money. So he gets these two dudes to take her out. Bald guy and a dark-haired fella. I got a real good look at them as they were driving out of Thunder Point. They were in a hurry, but I saw 'em.'

Clay dragged on his cigarette feverishly, as his brain finally connected the last dot. 'The client on the boat that was groping the waitress girl – he was a politician, wasn't he?'

'Yeah, yeah, that's it. What was his name? I know it...'

'Wayne Swanson.'

'Yeah, that's the one,' said Lerner. 'That's the guy, bloody mongrel.'

Clay knew his guess was right even before Lerner confirmed it, but he was still astounded. He felt a wild mixture of absolute calm and utter excitement, like his mind was at one with the universe because everything was in its proper place, but his gut was still churning over.

'Swanson kills Kerry Collins,' said Clay. 'Swanson gets Fullerton to take care of Jacinta Porter and in return gives him the airport deal. Fullerton gets sick of looking after Jacinta and gets his goons, most likely the ones that beat me up, to take her out. Meanwhile Fullerton or Swanson or both get Frank Anderson to sweep the whole thing under the carpet, as they know full well it was possible to trace it all back to them. Probably paid Anderson off, or promised him something, maybe even had something over him.'

Clay saw Lerner was eyeing him in a peculiar way, and Clay realised he probably seemed like he was talking to himself. 'Meanwhile, I'm snooping around,' Clay continued and threw a glance Lerner's way. 'You're snooping around. We're both asking questions. Anderson figures he can take out two birds with one stone and sets you onto me. He was setting you up, Lerner. He gave you that gun to set you up. It's probably the gun that killed Jacinta.'

'*What?* She was burnt to death.'

'No, mate. She was shot. I saw the autopsy report. The burn job was an attempt to cover the evidence.'

Lerner looked at the pistol, as if suddenly remembering he had it. He raised it in a half-hearted way then lowered it again. The eerie near-silence of driving in the country at night enveloped them as Clay drove on, telling himself that everything made sense. Could the weeks of confusion really be over?

He reached the highway and turned right towards Port Fairy. As he stared at the road ahead he realised the night still had a long time till the sand ran out. Clay took his eyes off the road to assess the look on Lerner's face. His passenger's expression was one of stony determination. Lerner's eyes blazed and when he wasn't sucking hard on his cigarette, he was grinding his teeth. He was still fending off sleep by the looks of it, too, and Clay was worried all over again.

'You can't kill Fullerton,' he said.

'Why not?' Lerner didn't take his eyes off the road. The gun was now cradled in one hand in his lap.

'You'll go to jail.'

'I killed Vegas, I'm going to jail anyways. I wanna take that bastard that killed Jazzy down as I go, though.'

Clay shook his head and started to let the car slow. They were heading through the township of Killarney. There was a hotel up ahead he could pull into. 'I can't be part of this. I can't take you to Fullerton's house so you can kill him.'

Lerner took the gun in his right hand and pressed the muzzle against the side of Clay's head. The steel was surprisingly warm.

'I've been thinking,' said Lerner. 'It doesn't really matter if I kill you. Like I said, I'm going to jail anyways. And I'm sure I could find Fullerton's house one way or another with this.' He waggled the gun before putting it back to Clay's temple. 'But, y'know, I'm kinda hoping you will be there to watch it all go down and write it up in the newspaper. Big headlines about my big revenge. How I got my revenge for Jazzy. How I was the big hero who killed the scumbag. So here's your choice – keep driving and write the biggest story of your life, or stop driving and I'll shoot you in the head and leave you in a ditch on the side of the road.'

Chapter 38

'Port Fairy – world's most liveable community' said the road sign as they reached the fringe of town. Not tonight, it won't be, thought Clay, as he let Lerner's car decelerate.

Lerner still had the gun pointed at him and Clay could tell the speed was starting to affect them both. Clay felt energised and upbeat in spite of the mortal danger, and his mind was on high alert, playing scenarios and ideas out in his head, while Lerner was letting his mouth run. It was no longer stuff Clay cared about, though. Lerner was talking about how he hadn't slept for three days and the copious amount of drugs he'd been taking over that period of time.

'But it was all leading up to now,' Lerner said, still rambling. 'I was just working up my courage and getting my head straight so I could do this. So I could get my plan together and shoot that evil bastard right in his smug face.'

They were only a couple of minutes from Fullerton's house, maybe less. Clay's furtive plotting had come to nothing. He'd considered driving to the Port Fairy police station, but it was about 9 p.m. and no one would be there. Plus, he suspected Lerner would know where the cop shop was and figure out what Clay was trying to do.

Plan B was to drive the car into the Moyne River on the way to Fullerton's mansion and attempt to get away in the confusion as he and Lerner tried to swim to shore, but Clay guessed Lerner would probably shoot him before they even hit the water.

Plan C was to slow the car enough for Clay to dive out, but he figured that would end badly – it was something that would likely get you killed, even at low speeds. And once he was out of the car: then what?

Plan D was to stop at the wrong house and hope that

someone would call the cops in the ensuing mix-up. But Clay realised this would put innocent bystanders in danger, which wasn't a prospect he was prepared to consider.

All these options and arguments ran through Clay's mind at a rapid pace, fuelled by the amphetamines in his system, but he realised he was one step from checkmate. His only course of action was to do as Lerner said and hope for a miracle. Maybe Fullerton or his wife would get an opportunity to call the cops. Maybe Lerner would have a change of heart. Maybe Clay would get an opportunity to disarm him. Maybe Clay could still talk him out of this... except he had no idea what to say.

The Moyne River approached and Clay followed it in Lerner's car, the expensive houses overlooking East Beach on their left, the dark waters of the Moyne to their right. The time for brilliant plans was over. Clay slowed the car and pulled to the side of the road in front of Fullerton's house. There were lights on. In fact, the house was lit up like a fairground. As he stepped out of the car, Clay could hear faint music coming from the mansion and the murmuring of jovial voices on the breeze. Christ, not a party, he thought.

The night was warm but the town was quiet, not surprising for a Wednesday night in Port Fairy. None of the other houses were as brightly illuminated. Clay gulped down the stomach acid that was rising in his oesophagus. Apparently this was the place to be.

He and Lerner stood on either side of the car. 'Which one is it?' asked Lerner.

Clay pointed. 'The big one with all the lights on. Sounds like they're having a party.'

'Move it,' said Lerner, gesturing towards the house with the gun. He didn't seem to register Clay's comment.

'I said, it sounds like they're having a party,' he repeated.

'I heard ya. And I don't care.'

'It's going to be full of witnesses, Lerner. Innocent bystanders.'

'Shut up, Moloney. Get moving.'

Clay steeled himself and began walking towards Fullerton's home. The driveway sloped upwards away from the road to the top of what was once a sand dune. Clay had a vague idea of the layout of the house from his previous visit. There was a path that ran up beside the garage and led to the main entrance. As he got closer, his worst fears were realised. There was indeed some kind of gathering happening. It sounded like it was going on near the deck at the ocean side of the house. A set of wooden stairs, further on past the front door, appeared to lead up to the deck.

They reached the front door and Lerner poked Clay in the back with the gun. 'Up the stairs.' His voice was now a menacing whisper.

'Are you sure you wanna—'

'Up the stairs.' The hard metal of the gun was once again pushed in his kidneys.

One begrudging step after another, Clay ascended the stairs. He could hear Lerner's footsteps right behind him.

At the top of the stairs, the party came to life before his eyes. It wasn't a big gathering, only about a dozen people. Two women were dancing in bare feet to music piping through expensive speakers attached to the corners of the roof over the deck, while the rest of the people sat in two groups, one around a large table covered in empty and half-empty alcohol bottles, the other on chairs facing out across East Beach and the ocean beyond. Off in the distance, Warrnambool twinkled like a faraway constellation.

At first no one noticed Clay entering the deck from out of the darkness. The dancers were too busy enjoying Bowie's 'Golden Years', the group at the table were deep in conversation, and the other group had their backs to him. Clay took a step forward and still no one noticed him. He felt the prod in his back again and took another step across the wooden floor, this time raising his hands in a 'don't shoot' gesture. That movement caught in the periphery of the party guests' vision and one by one they turned to look at him.

Lerner moved out from behind him and to his side, gun pointed at Clay's head now. 'Put your arms down, you idiot,' said Lerner, and Clay obliged.

One of the two dancing women turned off the music, and now the people facing the ocean looked around to see what was going on. Lerner had everyone's attention as silence descended on the party.

Clay scanned the deck and spotted Fullerton. He was seated at the table next to his wife. Next to them was a Moyne Shire councillor and his wife. Also at the table was a lawyer Clay vaguely knew from his time as a court reporter, and a Warrnambool City Council executive. He didn't recognise the two women dancing, and he couldn't quite make out who was sitting overlooking the ocean, except for one of them – the Right Honourable Member for Warrnambool, Wayne Swanson.

Swanson was the first to stand. He wobbled his way free of his chair and took a couple of steps toward the table. Obviously drunk, Swanson looked paler than ever. 'Moloney,' he called in a buoyant manner, before stopping as he noticed Lerner's presence and the gun. 'What's going on here?'

'Who are you?' growled Lerner. His voice had taken on an edge and Clay realised Lerner was muttering to himself. He's psyching himself up, Clay thought. Holy shit, he's going to go through with this.

'I'm MP Wayne Swanson, member for Warrnambool,' said Swanson, attempting to square his shoulders. 'Who the hell are you?'

'Where's Fullerton?' said Lerner, ignoring Swanson.

Fullerton stood up from the table, pushing his chair back; it made a jarring sound as it slid across the wooden deck. 'I'm Lachlan Fullerton. What do you want? What's going on here, Moloney?'

'Don't talk to him, talk to me!' Lerner wasn't trying to disguise his rage any more. Seeing Fullerton had brought it out for all to see. Lerner shoved Clay aside, causing Clay's foot to catch on the decking. He dropped to the floor and scuttled out of the way, towards the two women who had been dancing. They were cowering in a corner of the deck that was not far enough away from Lerner for their liking. Clay rose and backed up to them. He noticed they were standing in front of a glass sliding door.

Lerner's attention was on Fullerton and Swanson, who stood close to each other. The table was between them and Lerner.

Clay placed his hands flat against the glass door and started to slide it open, trying to make as little noise as possible. Inch by inch it started to move. Lerner hadn't noticed – he was too focused on his prey.

'You guys have been very bad,' said Lerner. He pointed the gun, first at Fullerton, then at Swanson. 'You've been doing some very bad things. You killed Jazzy.'

'I'm sure I don't know what you're talking about,' said Fullerton.

'Don't lie!' yelled Lerner, moving the muzzle back in Fullerton's direction. 'You had her killed. You got your guys to shoot her in the head and then set her car on fire.'

'I think you need help, my friend,' said Fullerton.

Clay had the glass door open enough for a person to fit through. Lerner didn't appear to notice. Clay half turned his face to the two women next to him. They were pale, with panicked expressions beneath their heavily made up faces. Clay dropped his voice to a breathy whisper that was almost inaudible. 'Go in. Quietly. Call the cops.'

The two women slowly stepped through the door and padded on bare feet into the house. They were outside Lerner's line of vision, but Clay could see the gunman was building into a rage and had only Fullerton and Swanson in his sights.

'No, you need help,' said Lerner. 'You both need help.' The gun barrel swung to Swanson. 'You killed a girl. You were trying to screw her. Then you threw her into the ocean.' He moved the pistol back to Fullerton. 'And you tried to cover it up. You tried to pay off my Jacinta, and then you had her killed. Because she saw it all.'

Everyone had been staring at Lerner, transfixed, but now they were sliding glances in Fullerton and Swanson's direction. Clay could see the confusion in their eyes. Their nice evening had been shattered in horrific fashion.

'I've got no idea what you're talking about,' said Fullerton, his expression unmoved. But Swanson had gone a diminishing shade of grey and he looked like he was about to throw up.

'Yeah, you do,' said Lerner, taking a couple of steps forward. His hands were a little shaky but he looked in control. 'You know exactly what I'm talking about. Two women are dead because of you two greedy bastards.'

There was a sluicing sound from Swanson as he emptied the contents of his stomach all over the decking. Clay looked away, but from the sounds of it, Swanson had enjoyed a liquid dinner. The politician crumpled to his knees, panting and retching.

Fullerton appeared overjoyed for the distraction and turned to help Swanson. 'Someone get him a glass of water,' said Fullerton, and one of the guests obliged. Fullerton crouched down next to Swanson, who accepted the glass with shaking hands. Everyone in the room was watching him now.

Clay realised this might be the opportunity he was looking for. He could disarm Lerner if he could take him to the ground. Clay took a careful step forward, then another. He was still a good ten steps from Lerner, but before he could move any further, Lerner turned to him, gun aimed right at his chest.

'Get him up, get him on his feet,' said Lerner.

'I'm not helping you, Lerner,' said Clay.

'Do it.'

'You don't have to do this. Let the cops handle this.'

Lerner laughed. It was a disturbing, haunting sound devoid of humour. 'You mean the same cops these two have been paying off? The same cops who gave me this gun and sent me after you?' Lerner turned back to Swanson and Fullerton. 'You two think you run this town, don't ya? You two think you can do whatever you like to whoever you like, don't ya? Well, this guy's got the right idea – you make me sick.'

Fullerton stood back up. 'We do run this town and when the police get here, we're going to see to it that you're put away for a very long time.'

A hand reached out and grabbed Fullerton's arm. It was his wife, terrified. Her eyes pleaded and Clay read the look: please, don't antagonise him.

Lerner noticed her as well. He moved around the table toward her. 'Is this your wife?' he asked, a hint of glee edging into his tone. 'Maybe I should do to her what you did to Jazzy.' Lerner looked at the terrified woman. 'Of course, I wouldn't bother paying her.'

He was right next to her now. Fullerton was on the other side of her, but Lerner's gun was trained right on him. Lerner looked Fullerton's wife in the eye. 'Did you know he was bangin' hookers, love? Did you know he was doing my missus 'til he decided it was cheaper just to have her killed?'

Fullerton's wife burst into tears, her body racked by sobs. Her husband moved closer to her. 'Leave her out of this, you animal,' he sneered.

'You don't get to tell me what to do, mate. I'm the one with the gun.' Lerner moved back around the table and came to a standstill facing Fullerton and Swanson. A large pool of liquid lay between them, and Swanson was still on his knees, panting and swaying. 'Get up,' said Lerner.

Swanson shook his head and retched again, then started to gulp air.

'Get up!'

Clay heard a distant sound, like a car door closing. It had been a couple of minutes since the women had gone inside. He hoped a cop car was in Port Fairy when they'd called the police. Please let the police be here, he thought.

'Get up!' Lerner's rage was back in full flight.

Swanson shook his head again and started to sob.

Lerner raised the gun to the roof and fired a shot. The noise was deafening and shocking, like an overhead explosion, and Clay was struck by a premonition. He's really going to do it, he thought. Up until that point it had seemed surreal, as if it were impossible for Lerner to shoot Fullerton and Swanson, as if the universe wouldn't allow these two important men to be wiped out by a vengeful drug fiend. But the frightening sound of the gun going off sliced through all doubt. Clay knew Lerner wanted to kill these two men, but now he knew Lerner was actually going to kill these two men.

'Get up!'

Swanson rose to his feet with great effort. He was crying, spools of his own sick and tears running down his face. He had wine-red vomit on his shirt. The member for Warrnambool had been reduced to a physical, trembling mess.

Clay turned away and heard the sound of salvation – booted feet racing up the wooden steps. The police were here. Rescue had arrived, they could still be saved. Clay looked back to Swanson, he was spluttering, almost in convulsions, as he tried to form the words to reason with Lerner. But Lerner had heard the sound of footsteps drawing closer, too. The gunman's face registered shock as he realised what was happening, and how his time as tormentor had run out. The first shot sent screams into the night air as Swanson dropped back to the deck, trailed by an arc of his own blood. It took a further two shots to fell Fullerton, his wife throwing herself on top of his lifeless form as Lerner turned to face the sprinting cops. With their guns drawn, the cops didn't wait for Lerner to fire again; their shots were precise, clinical. Lerner went over on the deck and was motionless.

Epilogue

'I feel like I haven't seen you for a week,' said Bec, as she joined Clay's table in the smoker's lounge at the Hotel Warrnambool. Her friend looked tired, but healthier than she'd seen for a while, and he flashed her a wide smile when she sat opposite him.

'It's been a hell of a week,' he said, between sips of a pint of beer and drags on his Peter Stuyvesant.

It had only been four days since the shooting, but it had felt like an eternity to Bec. On the night Lerner had killed Lachlan Fullerton and Wayne Swanson, Bec had spent a couple of hours in abject panic. After hearing the shot that had punctured her tyre, she'd raced around to the front of the house to find no sign of Clay, and see a strange car driving away. She'd called the police and sat on her verandah, nerves mangled, praying for answers.

'A hell of a week might be an understatement,' she said. 'You're a celebrity.'

'For now. That won't last, thank Christ.'

As a journalist who was witness to the murder of a federal politician and a prominent businessman, Bec was aware that Clay had spent most of the past four days in one of three places – the Warrnambool police station; the office, churning out stories about what had happened; and in front of cameras and microphones, as the story went national.

'You haven't been enjoying the limelight?'

'Maybe a little.' He grinned. 'It's gotten Tudor off my back, if nothing else.'

'Your stories – I've read every one of them. They've been amazing.' Clay's account of last Wednesday night, or some variation of it, had run in every paper around the country.

'Thanks,' he said.

He'd also written a huge amount of follow-up copy after the

incident. There were stories with grieving family members, from Kerry Collins' parents to Lachlan Fullerton's relatives. There was a colourful but disturbing profile on Lerner. There was the story about the airport deal being torn up as more details on Fullerton and Swanson's corruption came to light. When Clay hadn't been at the police station or giving an interview, he'd been sitting in a quiet room at the office working on articles and interviews, rarely sleeping. Bec had waved to him while walking past a few times, but that had been the limit of their interaction over the past few days.

'What's going to happen to Frank Anderson?' she asked.

While Clay had been buried in his office, Bec had overheard discussions between the editor and deputy editor about the resultant stories Clay was churning out. Usually they were ecstatic with what they read, but Clay's unexpurgated details about Frank Anderson's involvement in the killings had given them conniptions. Accusations of cover-ups and providing a killer with a gun were pretty big rocks to throw at a senior police officer. The lawyers had been called in, but Clay had stood by his story and in the end they'd sided with what Clay wrote, fingers crossed that it was one hundred per cent true.

'Last I heard, he was dodging some stuff, pleading ineptitude on other parts,' said Clay. 'He's claiming he didn't cover anything up, that he was just incompetent. My interviews with a few of his fellow officers are suggesting that's not the whole truth, but as much as they're trying to throw him under the bus, the fat bastard will probably escape with a demotion.'

Bec could hear the bitterness in Clay's voice. It was the only part of the story that hadn't wrapped up neatly for him and she knew the personal animosity between the reporter and the policeman would only grow. There was unfinished business there, despite Clay's best efforts to take Anderson down.

'And what are you going to do now?'

Clay blew a long plume of smoke into the air. 'I'm going to take a few days off; I think I've earnt them. Tudor's letting me have Monday and Tuesday off.'

'Your stuff's still at my house.'

'Yeah, sorry about that. Never did get to spend that night on your couch, did I?'

Bec smiled. 'Where have you been sleeping?'

'Tudor put me up at the motel next to the office. I think his conscience kicked in. Either that, or he didn't want anyone finding out that his star journalist was homeless.'

'You're still welcome to crash at my place.'

Clay gave her a quizzical look. 'You know, I half expected you to hand in your resignation and skip town after everything that happened,' he said. 'I wouldn't have blamed ya.'

'I'm not going anywhere,' she said, with a tiny hint of defiance in her voice. 'I kinda like it here now things have quietened down a bit.'

'Well, thanks for the offer, but I might see how long Tudor's largesse lasts for now. Having my room cleaned for me every day ain't a bad thing. In the meantime, I've got a lead on a couple of apartments that... oh, crap.'

Clay's train of thought had been derailed by something in his line of sight and Bec spun around in her chair to see what it was. It was Clay's face, larger than life, on one of the big screen TVs looking down over the smoker's lounge. He'd been a fixture of news broadcasts and current affairs programmes for the last few days. She let out a laugh.

'You look alright on television,' she teased.

'Ha. They must have got my good side.'

'Actually, you're looking better than I've seen for a while.'

Her compliment appeared to catch Clay off guard and he looked embarrassed for a second. 'I'm sleeping better,' he said. 'The bad dreams have stopped. At the risk of sounding like a nutcase, I feel like Kerry Collins is satisfied and is leaving me alone.'

Bec met his gaze and something like an unspoken thought passed between them; after all that had happened there was no escaping the hurt Kerry Collins' death had caused. Clay took a sip of his beer and his usual mask of bravado slipped back into place. 'Now if only the news crews would leave me alone,' he said, frowning at the TV.

Bec looked around the lounge to see if anyone was paying attention to the screens or if they had noticed Clay was there. No one so much as looked at him. In this setting, with his cigarette and his pint, he was anonymous, despite being one of the week's biggest newsmakers.

Then Bec spied the young girl; she seemed barely old enough to be in a pub. She was standing near the door to the lounge with a backpack over one shoulder, long dark hair down to her shoulders, and dressed in a T-shirt and jeans that highlighted her slim physique. She was looking up at the screen and across to Clay, then back up to the screen. Bec turned to Clay but he hadn't noticed the girl, and when Bec looked back at her she was making her way towards them.

'Hi,' said the girl as she stopped at their table.

Clay stubbed out his cigarette and gave her a polite smile. 'Hi.'

'That's you, isn't it? On the TV.'

'Yeah, that's me.'

'Clayton Moloney?'

'Yeah. And you are?'

The girl ignored the question or didn't notice it, too lost in her own thoughts, like she had rehearsed what she was going to say. 'You've been on the news for the last few days. You saw those people get shot.'

Bec noticed it before Clay did. There was something in the way she spoke, her mannerisms, a look in her eyes. Oh, my God, she thought, her gaze darting between Clay and the girl.

'Yeah, I saw them get shot. It wasn't pretty.' Clay looked at the girl as if trying to figure something out. 'Do I know you?'

'No,' she said quietly. 'I guess you don't.' She took a deep breath and forced a nervous-looking smile. 'I'm, *well*, I think… I'm your daughter.'